The Friendship of Scholars

By Rosie Nee

Clachan
Publishing

The Friendship of Scholars
By Rosie Nee

Clachan Publishing
26 Rathlin Road, Ballycastle,
Glens of Antrim, BT54 6AQ
Email: clachanpublishing@outlook.com
Website: http://clachanpublishing-com.
ISBN: 978-1-909906-60-0
Copyright © Rosie Nee

About the Author

Rosie Nee was born in Birmingham and returned with her family to Renvyle in Connemara in 1964. An old way of life was passing among the people, where the seen world existed side by side with the unseen. Self-sufficiency was the norm and old people still identified the route taken into the Renvyle peninsula by Cromwell's soldiers.

She was educated in Tully National School and Kylemore Abbey School. She furthered her education at the National University of Ireland, Galway from 1975 to 1979, where she obtained a BA in History and English and a Higher Diploma in Education. In 1989 she obtained an MA in Anglo-Irish Literature and Drama from University College, Dublin, and a Diploma in Primary Education from Hibernia College in 2006.

She has worked as both a primary and secondary school teacher and as a library assistant, as well as an English teacher in north Africa and Dublin, with intermittent periods of being a homemaker.

In 1993 she moved from Dublin to County Roscommon with her late husband Mícheál Ó Ceallaigh, where she lives near Elphin and is now retired. She has a grown up family, Anastasia and Dima, Anastasia's partner Jason and grandson Ruairí.

The Friendship of Scholars is her first book.

I ndíl chuimhne Mhíceál Ó Cheallaigh
agus d'ár gclainne uile Anastasia, Dima, Jason agus Ruairí.

What we would not give for the merest hint by Mac Fhirbhisigh of what conditions were like in the stricken city while he was penning his list of Irish kings!

The Celebrated Antiquary Dubhaltach Mac Fhirbhisigh'.
Nollaig Ó Muraíle, 2002.

Acknowledgements

The Friendship of Scholars is a fictional story about Roderic O'Flaherty, an tOllamh Dubhaltach Óg Mac Fhirbhisigh, Archdeacon John Lynch, and their contemporaries. The characters in this work bear no resemblance to living people. It is an imagining of real historical figures, their thoughts, words, feelings, relationships and actions, based on the historical sources of the period as well as more modern references as indicated in the bibliography.

The title is a quotation from the work of Mary Donovan O'Sullivan's *Old Galway*. I am grateful to the librarians and staff of the National Library, National University of Ireland, Galway, University College, Dublin, Trinity College Dublin, the National Archives and the Genealogical Office for their kind assistance to me with this work during the years 1989 and 1990. I am also indebted to the works of James Hardiman. I am especially and above all greatly indebted to the publications and works of an tOllamh Nollaig Ó Muiríle National University of Ireland, Galway. Professor Ó Muiríle has written Dubhaltach's biography, a wonderful, unforgettable, poignant and scholarly inspiration. He has also brought Dubhaltach's *Great Book of Genealogies* into print finally in our day.

And finally, I am hugely grateful to Seán O'Halloran of Clachan Publishing for his wonderful support, advice and endless patience in editing and publishing this story.

Contents

Glossary of Irish Words, Names, Places and Non-Current Terminology

a bhean	woman.
a dhuine uasail	gentleman.
a fhear óg mo chroí	young man of my heart.
a fhearín	little man.
a mhacín	little son.
a mhaicín shéimh	gentle little son; *a mhac*, son.
a Ruaidhrí mo chroí	Rory, my heart.
a rún	my heart's beloved.
a stóirín	little dear (the vocative case '*a*' is always used in addressing a person or object, 'o little dear') *a stór*, dear.
aftergrass	The grass that grows in a field after the first crop of hay or among the stubble after oats, rye etc are harvested.
amadán	a fool.
amanuensis	(Lat.) an assistant working on manuscripts.
Amergin	a son of Míl, who was the druid and poet of the Milesians.
bacach	a lame person.
báid mhóra	large boats with sails, such as hookers.
bán	bare land, meadow.
booley house	a temporary dwelling for transhumance livestock when moved for grazing.
cailleach bed	the bed for an old woman in an annex beside the fire, called the outshot.
Caol Sáile Ruadh	(Lit. 'Narrow Red Salt Water') Killary Fjord in north Connemara.
Ceann a' Bhaile	the Head of the Wall.
Cessair	The woman who led the first invasion of Ireland.
cladach	the shore.
Cormac's Glossary	(*Sanas Cormaic*) Contained within the *Leabhar Breac*
creacht	a foray, raid.
currach	a boat made from hides.
Daideó	Grandad.
Dalriadans	from *Dál Riada*. The Irish kingdom stretching from County Antrim to the Hebrides and Argyll in Scotland from the 5th to the 9th centuries AD.
dubh 'gus páipeár	paper and ink
dúirling	a stony beach.

Éamonn *na Maor* O'Flaherty	Éamonn *of the Stewards* O'Flaherty.
factor	an agent, middleman.
fenechus	the body of Irish law as a whole, 'relating to the *feine*',ie, the free classes of Irish society; Brehon Law.
Fir Bholg	the descendants of the People of Nemid
Foras Feasa ar Éirinn	*Foundation of Knowledge of Ireland,* the work by Geoffrey Keating (1644 - 1750).
Formorians	the opponents of the *Tuatha de Danann.*
'Fuil an Rí'	'the Blood of the King,' a relic of the executed king Charles I.
gabhál	an armful.
Gael agus SeanGall	the Irish and the Old English.
gan talamh ná trá	(Lit. *'with neither land nor strand'*) One possessing neither land nor shore rights.
gasúr	boy.
gawk	an awkward, shy person.
gearrán	gelding, nag.
Giraldus Cambrensis	(Lat.) Gerald de Barry of Wales, (c1146 – c1223) author of *Topographia Hibernica* and *Expugnatio Hibernica.*
gleoiteog	a smaller type of sailed boat.
gom	a foolish person.
haggard	a small, enclosed area at the back of a farmhouse.
Heber and Herimon	sons of Míl.
Iar Connacht	West Connacht. This refers to the territory of south Connemara today, from Loch Corrib to the sea, lying south of the Twelve Bens.
lacuna	(Lat.) a blank space, missing part
laidín	little lad.
Laws of Fithil	The decisions of Fithil, who was the judge (*'Ard-breitheamh'*) at the court of Cormac Mac Airt.
Leabhair Uí Mháine	The Book of Hy-Many, also called the Book of the O'Kellys. The *Uí Mháine* were the descendants of *Máine Mór,* a large dynasty of kings in Counties Galway, Roscommon and Clare.
Loch a' tSáile	*(*Lit. *'Lake of Brine')* Loch Atalia. A salt lake on the east side of Galway city.
mac tíre	(Lit. *'son of the country'*) a wolf.
mantach	a toothless person.
marbhfháisc oraibh!	(Lit. *'may the death bindings be on ye!'*) bad luck to you!
Míl	*Míl Easpáine,* the ancestor of the sons of Míl, who came to Ireland from the Iberian Peninsula.

Milesians	*gairthear Mílidh Easpáinne,* the descendants of the sons of Míl.
Morogh Mac Morogh	Morogh son of Morogh son of Daniel *of the Wars* Mac Dónal *an Chogaidh*
Morogh *na dTuadh* O'Flaherty	Morogh *of the Battle Axes* O'Flaherty i.e., of the Gallowglass mercenaries hired from Scotland who fought with long-handled battle axes.
Morogh *na Mart* O'Flaherty	Morogh of *the Cattle* O'Flaherty.
Nephin	a mountain west of Loch Conn in County Mayo.
óinseach	a foolish woman, fool.
ollamh	professor.
on the *seachrán*	*('ar seachrán'),* drunk, to lose one's way, to be astray.
outshot	The small extension near the fire, usually to contain a bed, once common in houses in the north-west of Ireland.
poitín	home-distilled whiskey.
polyhistor	(Gr.) a person learned in many subjects.
púcan	a traditional Connemara boat with sails.
ratio studiorum	(Lat.) The Jesuit curriculum in 17th Century European schools.
riabhach days	the cold, windy days at the end of March and beginning of April
scian	a knife.
Sea of Moyle	*Sruth na Maoile.* The North Channel between County Antrim and the Mull of Kintyre.
seafóideach	nonsensical, silly.
seanchas	the collection of ancient Irish law, history, tradition and genealogy, *An Senchus Mór.*
shambles	a place where animals were slaughtered.
súgán	a rope made from straw.
Tadhg an tSléibhte	'Tadhg of the Mountains.' The nickname of Brother Mícheál O'Cléirigh, whose name was Tadhg. He travelled the country while working on *The Annals of the Four Masters,* compiled between 1632 and 1636.
thar clár	(Lit. 'over a board)' the term used to describe a corpse being waked in a house.
the *Beanna Beola*	(Lit. *Peaks of Beola.* Beola was a leader of the Fir Bholg.) The Twelve Bens mountain range in Connemara.
the college in Louvain	The Irish Franciscan college established in The Low Countries in 1617 to further Irish and religious studies.
the good people	the fairies, the people of the dead.
the Leabhar Balbh	the Dumb Book of Mac Fhirbhisigh.

the Leabhar Breac	the Speckled Book. It is also called the Great Book of Dún Doighre (Duniry in County Galway.)
the Leabhar Buí	the Yellow Book of Lecan, i.e. of Mac Fhirbhisigh.
the unprecedented bad weather	the mini-ice age of the seventeenth century.
Tholsel	a town administrative building.
Tír Amhlaidh	Amhlaidh's country. Amhlaidh was Fiachra's son. This is an Irish territory ('*tuath*') stretching from north-east Mayo as far as the Sligo coast.
trá	a sandy beach, strand.
traithníní	straws, feathers.
Tuatha de Danann	the people of the goddess Danu.
tuatha	the people, tribes of a territory (*tuath*).
Uí Briúin of Maigh Seóla of the line of Eochaidh Muighmheadhoin	The *Uí Briúin* were a Connacht dynasty of kings descended from Brión son of Eochaidh Mugmedon, father to Niall of the Nine Hostages. The O'Flaherty kings descended from the Uí Briúin Seóla whose territory extended originally on the east shore of Loch Corrib in County Galway.
Uí Fhiachra Eachtgha	the territory of Fiachra's descendants along the Sliabh Aughty mountains in Counties Galway and Clare.
Uí Fhiachrach Aidhne	the territory of south County Galway where the diocese of Kilmacduagh is today. The Uí Fhiachrach were the descendants of Fiachra, the rulers of Connacht.
Uí Fhiachrach Mhuidhe	the territory of Fiachra's descendants around the river Moy in Counties Mayo and Sligo.
Úir Mhúmhan	East Munster.
uisce beatha	(Lit '*water of life*') whiskey.

The Rising of 1641

uaidhrí O'Flaherty and young men sitting beside him toiled at their books, while monitored by older tutors under the master. They shifted uncomfortably in the dark room, longing for the shutting of the master's book to release them from their exhaustion.

He felt alone in the town. His mother, Elizabeth Darcy, had left the plagues of the town behind on her marriage and went to live in Moycullen in his father's stone house. It was a different world. Boats on Loch Corrib came in and out nearby, ferrying country people with their loads of turf, sacks of oatmeal, butter, eggs, firewood and sheep for the town market. Fair days on the street of the village assembled crowds for three days selling stock, fowl and wattles. The travelling families of the roads made their camps in the same sheltered hollows beyond the houses from year to year, bringing their music and stories. Strangers speaking in indecipherable accents came from God only knew where with their tricks, booths and outlandish tales.

His father, Aedh, presided on the bench with the constable, sheriff and bailiff in the courthouse beside the inn house.

'We are the appointed magistrates of the law in our own realm, *a Ruaidhrí mo chroí,*' his father said to him when he was a child sitting on his knee. 'And one day you will be at the bench too.'

He died leaving Ruaidhrí a ward of the crown before the boy knew his father, so these words were handed down to him as a little barefoot boy on the flags of the hearth. To prepare him for this, strange priests in heavy cloaks came from the wardenship to hear him recite Latin and Greek.

'Send the lad to the school in town and make a respected gentleman of him,' his mother's relatives advised the grieving widow. They came up the lake in their boats to attend the funeral.

To add to this loss, Ruaidhrí's mother, who had remarried to John Bermingham, his new stepfather, died shortly after.

He found himself in town soon after this, lodging with his mother's cousin, John Fitz Richard Darcy, a prosperous leather merchant in Cross Street. The world he had entered was perplexing. He was one of the O'Flahertys, Gaelic Lords of Connacht, and was heir to the O'Flaherty Moycullen estates. His mother, Elizabeth

Darcy, was the daughter of Martin Darcy, freeman and councillor from a wealthy Galway merchant family and one of the prominent families. Though the mutual antagonism between the two groups was subsiding, especially among the leading families, there remained a legacy of mistrust and suspicion.

The conservative, prosperous, Catholic town's people of Galway, later known as The Tribes, were descendants of an old Anglo-Norman colony established the time of the Norman invasion under the de Burgh knights who had conquered and fortified much of Connacht. The most prominent of these were the de Burghs, later called de Burgos or Burkes, led by the Earl of Clanricarde. However, the entrepreneurial townspeople were less interested in land than trade, and gradually obtained independent trading charters and wrested control of the port and its wealth from the de Burgos and the Hibernicised Irish-speaking Norman landowners who had settled in the countryside. But they were constantly reminded of the threat posed by Burke castles and strongholds which dotted the feudalised landscape of east Galway and Mayo. Indeed, Ruaidhrí's stepfather, John Bermingham, was of a Hibernicised Irish-speaking Norman landowning family, resident in Turloghvaughan castle near Tuam and known as barons of Athenry. The young scholar grew increasingly aware of many strands and identities pulling at both the city and himself as he made his way to his clandestine school.

The city dwellers, who in time called themselves Old English, rose in power and wealth through trade and rents and came to govern the walled city, yet they lived in constant fear. The threat of attack from the O'Flahertys and the O'Hallorans to their west remained real over the centuries. These were the same Gaelic lordships that had been driven into Iar Connacht by the all-conquering Norman de Burghs who ravaged the province for generations. These were Ruaidhrí's ancestors, and he was being sent to school to prepare him to be the chief among them.

However, there was another threat. Gradually the Old English saw new English Protestant arrivals being planted by the new men who were obtaining Irish land for themselves and who were powerful in the cities and towns of Leinster and Munster. In Connacht Protestant families like the Cootes acquired land, fortifications and political power in the Irish Parliament. The older Sir Charles Coote was killed in County Meath by the risen Irish and Old English after the Rising began. His son, also called Sir Charles Coote, led the Parliamentarian army in Connacht with a vengeance after that.

Such was the world Ruaidhrí was entering. Dressed in cloak and boots like John Fitz Richard Darcy's three sons, Dominic, Ambrose and Robert, he went along with them, books under his arm, to follow at their appointed time into a cellar entrance off a lane so narrow the walls nearly touched. At certain times boys slipped down this lane and disappeared in the dawn, each concealing his books as he hurried. A ladder led down into the darkness of a cellar from which a pungent-smelling room could be entered behind a wine shop. The Lynches were waiting for them seated at their table beside a blazing turf fire as the students silently sat on the floor and took out their books.

His religion was under threat since the Tudors ascended to the throne of England and receiving a Catholic education was still a dangerous business. But the prospect of change was in the air after the arrival of the first Stuart king, James I, and his son, Charles I.

He was going on fourteen years of age when the English garrison guarding the city for the king was busily admitting reinforcements since disturbances had broken out. One day more new soldiers arrived in the harbour in force. It soon emerged they were Puritans for the Parliament side in the civil war raging in England to overthrow the Stuarts. The inhabitants stopped in their tracks open-mouthed at dawn when they beheld the unbelievable sight of Parliament's flag flying up on the fort above the sea. When had the garrison gone over to the Parliament? It must have been the night before! How could it no longer function in the name of the king? And how could far off English disturbances reach all the way to their town on the western Atlantic coast like this?

Where did this leave the loyal freemen of Galway?

The masters prevented the students rushing outside their hidden schoolroom to find out if it was true. Men scrambling onto the roof of the house opposite could see this flag fluttering against the sky on the height and shouted the news across to the priests listening in consternation, heads out the upstairs windows.

'Rogues and traitors! You will have a new king!' The new English soldiers were yelling in anger across at the townsmen as they climbed up onto their walls in great shock.

The wealthy Galway city merchants had begun investing in land all over Connacht and as landowners they felt new vulnerabilities. England's Lord Deputy in Ireland had years before used illegal procedures to query land rights and many people had been affected by this. Lands were seized and planted with English. It was in the long-term interests of Protestantism to weaken these landowning patrons of the Catholic clergy. The biggest Galway landowner and royalist was the Earl of Clanricarde and even this prominent man had lost some land.

The complexities of the war years brought in a new powerful faction, the Parliamentarians who followed the new Puritanism. It also brought to the fore a new Scottish army, the Covananters, led by Monro and Hamilton.

As the population of these newcomers increased, thus strengthening the new English elite, the Old English Catholics, such as the Earl of Clanricarde and the freemen of Galway, were finding themselves left out in the cold on religious grounds along with the native Gaelic Irish. The unhappy relationship into which these factions were forced to protect their common faith, was only going to be fraught.

The Old English saw the Irish as beneath them in every way, dreading the possibility that the new English would soon see *them* as 'native Papists.' The freemen did their best to keep a distance between themselves and the Gaelic Irish. The Earl of Clanricarde and the merchants, wary of the de Burgos for generations, felt the new Earl of Clanricarde, Ulick Burke, born and bred in England and married to an English wife – was a man very different from his father.

The most important leader of the Old English faction in Ireland was James Butler, Duke of Ormond, another English-born and educated nobleman, who had accepted Protestantism. Ormond and his many family connections were the most prominent of the old nobility of Leinster and Munster. Some of these also accepted the new religion to hold on to their land.

The Catholic clergy of Ireland organised a meeting of prominent Catholics to defend the king's rights and their own rights against the new Puritan threat. They chose Robert Shee's house in Kilkenny city for the venue. The formation of the Confederation of Kilkenny was the result of this assembly gathered in Shee's large, beautiful, Elizabethan house on the Parade. It was in effect an alliance between the Irish and Old English. The assembly undertook the governing of Ireland's territory outside Ormond's control. O'Neill was appointed general of the Ulster army and Preston general of the Leinster army under the Confederation. A Supreme Council was elected to oversee the business of the Confederates. Galway's lawyer and politician, Patrick Darcy defined the Confederation's aim in his 'Argument', that it was the king's prerogative to make the laws. Seeds of jealousy and distrust between the two factions were however buried deep throughout the country.

The war, as it dragged on, involved various military commands operating under the Supreme Council of the Confederates: the native Irish armies, mainly Catholic and the Old English Catholic armies. These campaigned and skirmished for years against both the Parliamentarian's and Scots' garrisons and armies in the field, sometimes with each other and sometimes against each other.

Shortly after the garrison in the Galway fort went over to the Puritan side, Ruaidhrí's schooling was thrown into disarray by a hysterical young lad attempting to recruit the students. This was when war became a reality for the children. The boy's eyes were like water when the sun shines on it and spittle ran down from his mouth. He had been absent for days and reappeared in the room looking terror-stricken. Bloodstains tarnished the front of his coat. Some who saw him drew back in horror, blessing themselves, while others pushed forward, shouting for him.

'Lads! Follow me out to assemble at the Cross!' the boy was calling. 'Quick, quick, take up arms for the king against his enemies!' He threw back his arm to reveal the ancient pistol concealed in his belt.

John Lynch and the prefects arrived in a run from the adjoining room. Lynch was well in the lead, a fit and strong forty-year-old man who could run as fast as any lad in the school. Their books of

Phaedrus still in their hands, they were nearly felled by the charge of heated boys rushing out the door.

'Why are you raising an armed commotion in this house, Nicholas French?' John Lynch asked, not shouting but almost kindly.

'My brother has taken up arms with Dominic Kirwan at the marketplace, master!' cried the boy, halting because Lynch stood firmly in his way.

'Which brother is this?'

'Walter Óg, master.'

On a wordless command, the servant dragged Nicholas outside, along the lane to the street. A group of men watching from neighbouring doors followed, pistols in hand, to beat him with fist and boot the length of town, pinning his arms to his sides and taking his weapon forcibly from him. Ruaidhrí watched terrified from the upstairs of their fellow student Patrick Bodkin's house, a crowd of students leaning out of every window.

People were dividing, taking sides. Those living near the school, wealthy merchants and freemen, were suddenly greatly strengthened by armed youths coming out of nowhere to join in facing down Kirwan, who occupied the centre of town. They were a strong student faction, sons of freemen allied to Sir Richard Blake's men, who were also under arms. Sir Richard, the foremost of the freemen, was determined to maintain peace and the new status quo - stay in favour with the new Puritan party and protect his property and standing.

This was the first time Ruaidhrí had seen soldiers marching with pistols and swords inside the walls. They clashed head-on with the risen followers of Dominic Kirwan - apprentices, servants, day labourers and the poor of the suburbs. All were running from the marketplace with Dominic. All filled with religious fervour, shouting for faith, king and country.

Suddenly the spectators saw a yelling priest carrying a cross emerge into the street. He was followed by armed students and seminarians with a large party of priests and friars close behind them praying aloud. As they drew nearer, the reddened, agitated face of Walter Lynch, warden of St Nicholas's Church, could be made out as he ordered the armed men into the fray to join Kirwan's faction. They engaged with the freemen in wild shooting, swerving past two fallen young men who lay sprawled in pools of blood in the street.

The clergy of the city under Walter Lynch had risen up to defend the Catholic faith with Dominic Kirwan and his men. Walter was about to experience the greatest crisis of his life as his spiritual loyalties to the faith of his flock collided disastrously with his temporal loyalties to the elite of worldly townsmen to which he belonged. He was not the only member of the town's ruling class torn between alliance with the dreaded native Irish, thus being tainted with involvement in rebellion - or the alternative, which was subjugation of their faith under a new, hostile, heretical order of the English Puritans.

Sir Richard Blake arrived, stern-faced, soon after midday accompanying the angry, well-armed Ulick Burke, the Earl of Clanricarde and his militia. Once they had occupied the streets, they drove the belligerents indoors or out the gates, regardless of what side they were on, and arrested anyone who resisted. Sir Richard, the city council and the freemen met with the Earl in the Tholsel that evening to clarify their position after such a shocking, unprecedented day. All were agreed that the city would have to suppress riotous behaviour. They would, moreover, support other Old English nobility against the new threat from the Irish leaders which had appeared since the English civil war erupted.

A change, sharp and sudden like an onshore wind in spring, was blowing through their lives.

As killings continued in town and county, the school masters in alarm released the students and closed the school. The Puritans, heavily armed and strengthened, were nevertheless successfully shut out from the city by armed men united under Kirwan in a mighty assault, throwing closed the gates in their faces. In retaliation, the Puritans began a terrifying, revengeful campaign burning and slaughtering in the defenceless suburbs and the rural townlands.

Word was brought that colonel Éamonn Mac Morogh na Maor O'Flaherty along with his cousins Morogh na Mart and Morogh na dTuath were already marching at the head of a large force from Iar Connacht on route to Galway city. Ruaidhrí's people had arisen.

Children of Loch Corrib

Ruaidhrí embraced reading from childhood in Moycullen with a passion he was unaware he possessed until Sean Chaití Éamonn, the vigorous, cantankerous, elderly relative in charge of the house informed him.

'You're like your grandfather Ruaidhrí Mór, do you know, who was reared in England and married Kirwan's daughter when he returned, almost joining the gentry of the town when he became too big in himself. He became more like them than us and the pen came easier to his hand than the sword. He left off the struggle against the Gall when the old queen made his father the head of his name. Little good that did him when his enemies came to his door. All it did was cause bad blood with the friends beside the sea.'

In the cooking house out the back among nettles, briars, midden and ash heaps, the woman stirring the pot nodded in the direction of the wall where Ruaidhrí reclined, reading a book. The other lads of the place were throwing javelins, cursing each other energetically and practising sword fights on the grassy slopes in the field.

'Do you think that *gasúr* is sickening for something, his head in a book and not a word out of him?'

'Sure, that's handed down in him, *a bhean,*' Sean Chaití Éamonn retorted succinctly without looking up from her rapid carding.

'Well, do you know who he reminds me of? Macdara Mháire Thadhg, never right in the head from the day he was born, going about the roads talking to himself, wandering the house full of grand talk and not a spark of sense behind it.' The woman at the fire continued, eying the reclining figure on the wall, moving coals vigorously with the poker under the steaming pot.

'This lad's a different case from Macdara,' Sean Chaití Eamonn replied. 'Books have his head turned like his grandfather.'

Ruaidhrí Mór was the grandfather he was called after. His father, Aedh, who married Darcy's daughter from the town, died when he was an infant. His mother Elizabeth remarried an aristocrat, of one of the Berminghams. She died young too, leaving her four daughters with the stepfather to raise them, while he, as the son and heir, was made ward of the crown.

When he was old enough to ride in the saddle without falling off, and row the boat on Loch Corrib, Ruaidhrí visited Morogh na dTuadh O'Flaherty's house. Morogh's oldest daughter, Máire, a precocious child, developed the habit of following him around the house and the gardens, perhaps because she had heard they were already matched. Maybe it was due to his difference. He was more approachable than the rough young warriors of her family who longed for battle and weapons, who would engage with nothing else and only converse coarsely with older men. As the daughter of the house, Máire was above the other girls in social station and kept aloof from them on the instructions of her mother, Síle Burke. She knew they called her proud and 'big feeling' behind her back. She lilted a wordless song to herself as she played with dogs and cats around the place, made daisy chains with the small children, observed birds' nests in mossy banks, all the time keeping an eye on Ruaidhrí as he occupied himself in solitary activities. She watched him at the table in the evenings, noting the restrained way he took his food, quieter even than the priest of the house.

One fine summer day, Máire waited for him by the lake when he returned from a solitary expedition he had taken up the hill.

'Were you rounding up sheep?' she enquired - the first time she addressed him away from the joking and shouting of the young people outside the house.

'They were bringing down ewes today, but I enjoy viewing the countryside around me,' he replied, barely glancing at her as he carefully followed the movements of women pulling fishing lines from boats while their husbands rowed.

She wanted to know what was to be seen up on the heights, eager for dark news of strange travellers, ragged recluses from hidden valleys or sinister people from the otherworld.

'I saw Loch Corrib and the Burke country beyond in the east, and in the west our country to the mountains and as far as the sea,' was his reply, speaking over his shoulder as if he did not care. She said nothing, so he glanced at her again to see if she was mocking his simplicity. Pity and love stirred in her before his sensitivity and watchfulness – his weakness before the world, as if he were a woman or servant, instead of the heir to the place. There was a nature in him she had not seen before in anyone.

'I saw the sea on the pilgrimage to Mám Éan last year,' she said encouragingly, her face serious and tanned in the sunshine. 'It's beautiful and shining between here and the islands.'

He in turn was looking closely at her for the first time. It was clear her words struck him as he stood silent and wary.

'It is beautiful,' he replied eventually, 'and from up beyond I saw all Gnómór and Gnóbeag and boats going in and out to Aran.'

'Did you see the mound on top of the hill where the good people are living?' the words burst out from her in thrilled anticipation.

'I did,' was all he said, and they blessed themselves against the dead who lived under the earth, petrifying passers-by when they travelled the roads on their unearthly business or, God forbid, came into your house.

They turned to stroll together back to the threshold of the house as something new and nameless settled between them.

She heard news the following year that he had gone away to the priests' school in the town. She pictured the wonders of the world he was learning and how he would savour this knowledge, strange words inserting themselves into his beautiful, effortless speech. However, as she busied herself in the fragrant grazing and hay fields and in the woods, she mainly forgot about him in time. She ran after the black herds at milking time down on the lakeshore when they wandered to drink knee-deep in the evening, swishing with wet tails at horse flies crawling on their backs.

'There's war beyond in England,' an older cousin from the village who worked for Máire's father announced. The household were binding sheaves of oats in the sunshine. She looked across the gleaming surface of the lake, the countryside on the far shore shimmering in the distance. England was many days away by sea.

'Why is there war?' asked one of the children. They all stopped stooking oats to listen.

'The heretics are fighting the holy church of Rome,' replied the older lad, holding the sheaf between his knees while a child bound it with the *súgán*. He tossed it to the women who seized it and flattened it against the stook they were building before he swaggered off, straight backed, long hair blowing on his broad shoulders. No one knew what heretics were until the priest preached against them in his sermon one Sunday calling them the agents of the devil. Máire learned what heretics were as she sat squeezed in the front seat between her siblings, mother and father in the church.

'The archbishop is calling for a rising of the faithful against these enemies of the church', the priest proclaimed in terrible tones at the mass. 'Eoghan Ruaidh O'Neill is home from Spain and in the field against our enemies with the Irish and the Old English. Now all Catholics are obliged to rise up in war against the evil heretics of the English Parliament who are opposing the king and church, who would suppress the very worship of the faith Patrick brought us.

'We are obliged to arm and prepare to fight and die for the one true faith,' shouted the priest, an old man, red faced and agitated.

Her father Morogh na dTuath was whispering, 'Yes! In the name of God!'. his eyes burning when they walked home together. She glanced at her mother and her heart stopped on seeing the anguish on her face. No one said anything as they walked in groups through the street of the houses. Even the dogs were silent and the birds in the trees nowhere to be heard, the strangest silence after mass she had ever experienced.

Life beside the lake was never the same after that day. Her father sent two of her uncles travelling by boat from Ros a' Mhíl north to the relations on the coast, asking the friends to answer the call of the church. The territories of the senior houses were situated between the Beanna Beola and the sea and islands, the ancient division of the descendants of Conmac of the sea — Conmac na Mara — one of the three sons of Meabhdh and Fergus. Her cousin, Morogh na Mart O'Flaherty, in the castle of Bunowen was the most powerful of their clan in land, cattle, men, fishing craft and long boats for trading.

Éamonn na Maor O'Flaherty of Rinn Mhíl was chieftain of their name under Irish law. Éamonn's fine house was built a few miles along the coast from their castle destroyed in earlier conflicts. Around the point from the ruined castle a stone fort had been built long before on the peninsula's cliffs by the dark, wiry Fir Bholg who lived there by hunting, foraging, trading stone heads and flints and defending the sea routes from seaborne or inland attack. Over the years the warrior sons of Míl arrived in Ireland from Spain bringing livestock, farming tools and finally iron weapons. They took Tara from the Tuatha de Danann, established themselves as masters of all Ireland and then these western peninsulas were renamed after them.

Morogh na dTuath's word spread that day through the townlands. The news was carried swiftly to old people minding children from the fire. The elderly women started the wailing they heard from their grandmothers nearly two generations before. That was the time English soldiers came in by sea to attack them during the wars of O'Neill and O'Donnell. Well-off young men of the big house who were enjoying themselves hawking on the hill, returned home to a scene of consternation that evening.

Sometime later, a large group of tall, strong, well-dressed, sea-weathered men dismounted outside Morogh na dTuath's door beside Loch Corrib. Their arrival sent a shiver of apprehension and foreboding throughout the place, halting work in the fields, bringing people onto the street to discuss the inevitable course events were taking.

Inside the big house a feast was laid on the table in the afternoon and the room filled with people laughing, eating and drinking. No one slept when night fell, and the fire was built up with sods. Its flickering light illuminated faces of the men, women and children and the priests beside the hearth. The dogs lying under the table shuffled on the rushes and the drink was poured liberally into cups as the atmosphere changed. It was time for the man of the house to broach the subject weighing on everyone's mind - the war.

Máire awoke in her bed at the end of the house when voices were raised in the early hours. She heard her father shouting, 'If Clanricarde is to lead us by the Grace of God to fight for faith and king, then I have my personal score to settle with that fellow first, Morogh mac Morogh mac Dónal an Chogaidh, whatever you say!'

Her mother was a Burke herself and kept silent in the face of these new developments. Everyone was assessing how they could gain from the new war.

A chorus of shouts were drowned out by the voice of Morogh na Mart, 'We have no choice except to stand with the Old English or be destroyed by the new ones!'

Men were coming and going at the house after that, storing muskets under the roof. The blacksmith ordered his sons to work day and night forging iron, casting weapons, tending the fire.

Broadswords, bucklers, half pikes and javelins piled up in the cow house behind the forge, where one of the men slept at night to guard the stores.

On a moonless night Máire's father and the men silently and stealthily surrounded the castle of Aughnanure, almost unapproachable on its river island on the lakeshore. They attacked and routed the garrison of the Clanricarde Burkes who were guarding it. Thus, an ancient score was swiftly settled when Morogh na dTuath repossessed the seat of his ancestors and Ulick Burke lost his only foothold in Iar Connacht.

A large army assembled near the village after dawn, appearing through the mists from the passes, ensigns and old flags carried high, Éamonn na Maor riding at their head, colonel of his people. A white-robed priest rode at his side carrying the cross of Christ, followed by the black-robed priest of the house. Troopers with muskets, broadswords and shields came behind, their mantles flowing from their shoulders, followed by their javelin boys. Hundreds of wild-haired infantrymen of pike and javelin in home-spun jackets marched in the rear, followed by the people driving cattle and sheep. They made camps outside the village where strange women and children guarded livestock and set up cooking fires. Factors erected booths to sell ale and food. The smoke of their campfires hung low over the houses that night and the laughter and singing of the women disturbed Máire's sleep.

When they departed, her father, the priest and the men marched with them, an army nearly two thousand strong, down the road to Galway city. She huddled by the road with the inhabitants of the place, keening and praying until the moving mass was out of sight.

The Taking of the Fort

Eamonn na Maor's army reached the fort of St Augustine with the purpose of joining the townsmen in the field. United they besieged it and at the same time a detachment went out to the Aran Islands and routed the other English garrison there. The army campfires on the fields beyond the suburbs lit up the night, smoke carrying across the city walls and wafting along the streets of the traumatised town people as they prayed on their knees inside their locked front doors.

One morning, John Fitz Richard Darcy, the cousin with whom Ruaidhrí lodged, rushed home to Cross Street from the Tholsel to lock his house and business, shouting up the stairs, down the kitchen and out the back quarters to assemble his family, tenants, servants and Ruaidhrí in the quiet, sunlit parlour. His face was strangely reddened and haggard, hair in disarray, his always calm eyes tormented with the unprecedented stress of the changes coming down on their lives.

'It's here the lot of you will stay,' Cousin Darcy shouted, glaring at his young sons, swinging his keys aloft.

'You are forbidden to leave this house without my permission, or I will have you beaten and sent out of town.'

Everyone looked accusingly at Dominic Fitz John, the handsome, oldest Darcy boy, student at the school, whose misbehaviour in following older lads out on the streets had resulted in this set-back.

'Now we're missing it all,' the boys whispered angrily in their room that night while Ruaidhrí kept his face to the wall.

'And everyone else is out in the port with Dominic Kirwan. Father has all the shutters locked too. And he's after taking the back door keys off Ulick Fitz James.'

This was the most shocking of all, their elderly kinsman Ulick had been their father's factor and right-hand man for half a century. What possible mischief could an old fellow like that get up to?

They nudged Ruaidhrí's prone shape in the bed beside them.

'Your crowd from the bogs are here under arms too. Did you not hear the news yet? Don't you want to join them?'

He did not say anything.

14

After whispered consultation, they shook his shoulder. 'Here, bookworm, can't you let on to father tomorrow the priests want you for pressing instruction in something or other and he might allow *you* out, seeing as books are all you ever want? You could take the keys from his room when you're passing his door and leave them for us in the privy. What do you say?'

Ruaidhrí muttered something.

'What did you say?'

'I'm a guest here, I cannot do that'.

'What? Ahh, what would one expect from the likes of you, you priest's boy!'

Outside in the port a boat from France, the *Elizabeth and Francis* under the English captain Clarke had come in on the tide with a load of salt, and this had set the town upside down. The boat was surprised and boarded by the fearless hothead leading the city uprising, Dominic Kirwan, factor to the merchant Stephen Lynch who was on board with his cargo. Kirwan and his followers, intent on other business, surrounded the vessel in their boats and took it at gunpoint. The master's mate attempted to lead resistance and was shot dead and several of the crew were gravely wounded. The boat was known to be secretly carrying ordinance, ammunition and powder for the English garrison, brought in by Thomas Lynch the boat's owner and Gregory Browne.

A crowd from town rowed out in a flotilla of boats a few hours later to board the captured vessel in triumph. The seized munitions were brought ashore and paraded up Quay Street and through the town. The noise of the celebrations reached even through the locked windows of Cousin Darcy's in Cross Street, to the consternation of the grounded Darcy lads. It reached the ears of the censured serving men sitting tight-faced on the kitchen floor. The harassed women, finding these fellows sprawling under their feet as they tried to cook supper, joked and jibed at them. The men started up a commotion of disappointment when they heard the cheering in the streets, until the women threatened to send for the master.

Two years after the Rising had broken out up the country, the Connacht Confederate army was formed under the command of John Burke of Mayo. He was a continental war veteran and a relative of that other Burke, the powerful, wealthy Ulick Burke Earl of

Clanricarde, Connacht's most prominent family. When colonel John Burke arrived in Galway to join the Rising, the haughty earl did not admit he even knew his rebellious relative, and no one dared mention John's name in the noble house of de Burgo after that.

Next day when Kirwan's followers and the apprentices joined John Burke, Ulick Burke decided that he would get rid of this old fellow who thought he could arrive in Galway at will to create chaos. From then on, Ulick did everything he could to curb the new Connacht army and expand his own force.

The colonel was back from exile in the Irish Regiment along with others of his generation. John Burke was an old soldier with long experience of the wars in Flanders and Spain, a veteran of many sieges over forty years, like Eoghan Ruaidh O'Neill himself. He was rapidly turning out to be quite a magnet for the idealistic youth straining to prove themselves against the cautious older generation of the city. He and another well-known veteran in his sixties, Thomas Preston, were inspired by the idealism and patriotism inculcated from their experiences. They were eager to carve out a future for themselves once again in their homeland, abhorring the conservatism, self-interest and compromise of their relatives who had been fortunate enough to survive confiscations, inherit wealth and therefore remain at home in comfort.

The latter only desired to safeguard what they possessed, appalled by the return of the penniless, dashing, foreign Irish Regiment men - loose cannons intent on shaking up life at home and bringing everyone down with them.

Fearful on the news that English Parliamentary forces had marched from inland to attack the city in support of those soldiers still active in the area under Willoughby, Ruaidhrí's cousin, John Fitz Richard Darcy, instructed the household at dawn to make ready to get out of Galway.

Then without allowing them time to find their clothes or assemble their bags, he ordered them all out on the street and locked the doors of his house. Bridget, his wife, and his daughters, along with his sulking boys and horrified servants, stared at him in terror, shaking in the driving rain.

'Where are we going, father?'

'Out to shelter with my brother Andrew in Tuam. There have been threats made to some of our families, they're promising now to burn this whole town in reprisal while we are asleep in our beds.'

Silently they followed the manservant in a ragged run towards the gate, joined by neighbours running through the streets, alarmed by the intermittent sound of shooting towards the eastern side.

Ruaidhrí felt his relative's hand on his arm.

'I'm sending you home to your own people, you'll be safe out there, *a mhaicín shéimh* and may God protect you.'

And kissing Ruaidhrí, he bundled him into the first transport leaving west, wordlessly flinging coins into the driver's lap before rushing for his horse at the Abbey gate to follow his family already in a line of transports leaving for safety.

The warden of St Nicholas's during this fateful time was the strong-minded, dynamic Walter Lynch, a cousin of John Lynch. The keys to St Nicholas had been stolen by Protestants in Tudor times. The day the Puritans were driven out of the city, two priests ran the length of the town to bring him news that the Protestant clergy had been taken as prisoners by Ulick Burke. The keys were retrieved and returned to Walter, who had been ready to break down the doors.

It was noted that Walter was never the same after he got into the church that first day. There he spent the night on his knees before the altar, attended by his exhausted clergy who felt a sort of madness came on Walter. He swore the church of their forefathers would never be removed from the freemen again. He had newly reinforced doors and locks installed and wore the keys on his person day and night and his constant prayer was that St Nicholas's would never again be lost to them. Walter read mass on the following Sunday when, for the first time in their lives, the mayor, corporation, freemen and women packed into the church to worship. They gazed around in awe at the pillars and aisles, the windows and the altars adorned in fabulous marble and embellished stone, work done by their own long dead ancestors.

Walter was not the only person who changed after that. Some of congregation went out the doors after that mass swearing the heretics would take their church again over their dead bodies. Others, walking beside them on the other hand, were busily calculating how they could build on and consolidate the money they were already making in new factoring, supplying army commodities hitherto undreamed of.

Walter Lynch found himself in a unique position among his fellow townsmen as they faced an unknown frightening future. *He* was warden of the collegiate church of his people, its fate lay in *his* hands now.

His dreams at night were haunted by images of his new responsibility and the catastrophe of failure. At dawn he prayed for strength to see his way and he knew he would do whatever it took to save the sacred beating heart at the centre of their existence, St Nicholas's Church, regardless of what Blake or the earl might think. The call of the church did not lie on their shoulders, however broad those might be. It was on Walter this great burden lay.

St Nicholas of Myra, the patron of sailors, protected the city and harbour of Galway for centuries. Every seaman of Walter's people prayed aloud to St Nicholas for safety as the outline of the church receded slowly from sight. And it was to their patron the first prayer of thanksgiving was uttered the day they returned to the quay, their business done.

The large, stubborn, twinkling-eyed face of Malachy O'Queely archbishop of Tuam appeared in every waking dream of Walter's and would not go away until he knew what he had to do. He would do the unthinkable. He would ally himself with Malachy and the risen Irish to save the church and the faith his ancestors had handed down to them to safeguard forever. He knew such a decision would be the cause of huge controversy among his fellow townsmen. But the call had gone out from Rome for an alliance of all Catholics in Ireland to fight the new heretical Puritan threat to the church and to their very way of life.

'The country is in turmoil, and no one knows what the future holds anymore, so what else can I do?' he said to himself. 'And the nature of such an alliance between St Nicholas's and Tuam needs only be temporary after all,' he concluded in his troubled thoughts. 'I will pray to our saint for guidance,' he said to himself for encouragement as he rose from his knees.

The following Sunday, in the newly liberated church Walter, after a night of prayer, publicly declared *for* the Rising. His sermon rose to the rafters, terrifying the congregation who began wailing and beating their chests at the sight of Walter in magnificent new robes marching back and forth shouting for holy war on the steps of the altar. His vicars, priests and scholars cowered in the choir. Those brave enough glanced up during the sermon to follow Walter's glare, giving them a clear view of the horror and disbelief on the faces of the Lynches whose numbers dominated the nave. The fury of Sir Richard Blake watching from his elevated position among the corporation had every eye spinning in his direction. They beheld these notables jumping to their feet, backing out of their seats in shock and bellowing at Walter, fists waving. They turned to rush out the main door, banging it shut behind them with an almighty crash that shook the ancient foundations. Walter was barely through the underground tunnel leading from the church to the residence before the earl's spy had slipped out of his seat. By the time Walter and his vicars had divested in the sacristy, this man was rushing for his horse at the Abbeygate to bring the news to Ulick of Walter's declaration for the war.

It was not only the house of Lynch that fell out. The freemen and women were split from top to bottom after Walter's day of drama. Word spread like lightening the next day that Sir Richard Blake and his cousin, Sir Valentine, had become sworn enemies overnight. A few hours after Walter's announcement, the independent-thinking Sir Valentine Blake also declared *for* the rising amid a great crowd of ecstatic, emotional supporters and weeping friars. Valentine, beaming and shouting, waving both arms, was shouldered like a hero down the middle of the celebrating crowds in Mainguard Street.

'That unspeakable fellow will never cross the threshold of this house as long as I live. He's an unprecedented disgrace to our family and I don't want to hear his name mentioned ever again,' Sir Richard raged, red faced at John Lynch, Lady Blake and his children in the beautiful parlour of Ardfry House.

Despite them all, Éamonn na Maor, fiery Walter Lynch, and the hero of the hour, young Kirwan, as well as colonel John Burke, the returned war veteran, and now Sir Valentine Blake, became the greatest men of their day in the opinion of most people. The poor and the Irish forming the bulk of the population outside the walls were behind them.

Colonel Thomas Preston was appointed the Confederates commander for the Galway siege. Burke and his men, aided by the warden's ardent followers, rising on a great wave of religious fervour, kept up sustained fire on the garrison still holding out behind their defences. The combined forces of *Gael agus SeanGhaill* besieged the fort of St Augustine for nine weeks under Preston's careful direction.

The garrison, commanded by the Parliamentarian Willoughby, despite receiving assistance from the Earl of Clanricarde, surrendered at midsummer. Preston's lifetime of experience in the Spanish armies had borne fruit during the siege of the fort. Burke, Dominic Kirwan and Éamonn na Maor had routed the soldiers, forcing them to fall back on the quays and finally abandon the city by frigate to avoid death or capture on land. The sight of the garrison's boats running before the wind out into the bay became part of the legend. Lads of Ruaidhrí's age who were too young to take part had to listen enviously to these great stories for years afterwards. The victorious insurgents, heroes in their own time, destroyed the garrison in the name of the king Charles I. The fort had long looked down on them from its height, a potent symbol of English rule with which their social and economic betters had for centuries gainfully collaborated.

It was said the hammering of pickaxes could be heard miles out to sea during the days the fort was being demolished and flattened, its stones being carted away to be recycled by the corporation in new projects.

In the aftermath, colonel Éamonn O'Flaherty and the Irish of Iar Connacht and Mayo, with their advisors, were finally admitted into the city to assist Burke and Preston on the orders of the war supporters at the Council of Kilkenny. This was against the wishes of the mayor and corporation. Unbelievable anathema to the freemen and women, this shocking news brought them out in force onto the streets in agitation, shouting and swearing.

Many witnessed the sight of the party of western Irish leaders and their captains in elegant dark coats and finely trimmed hats, grim-faced, attended by lawmen and priests, crossing the drawbridge into Lombard Street, escorted by a party of Burke's and the warden's men. They proceeded into Mainguard Street to disappear through the heavily guarded Tholsel door moments before the hostile crowd surrounded it. During the meeting all could hear the calls of 'traitors!'

coming through the windows as the crowd pleaded with the guards to throw down their weapons and allow them inside to execute justice there and then.

Their reception in town was a step too far for some in the Irish group after nightfall. Drink took hold and restraint was lost inside walls built specifically to keep the O'Flahertys and their like out. Arguments went out of control, leading to revenge being taken on people perceived to be occupiers who had driven out their ancestors. All settlers were seen as enemies by the dispossessed Irish. Violence is often the catalyst of change in human society, and it was no different in Connacht. It began when the crowd broke down doors to drag men and women from their houses and forced them to kneel in terror. Killing started, until priests in their vestments carrying the Eucharist aloft ran shouting through the streets to stop the carnage. The antipathy the town people felt in their hearts towards the natives of the western regions resurfaced on a mighty wave of trauma and terror. The Irish army left the city before further conflict could occur.

The alliance in the west between Irish and Old English against the Puritan English had been shattered by these violent events. Even the mutual spiritual threat of a new and powerful religious order could not overcome the bitter legacy of the deep temporal injustices which existed between them from the past, however great the misfortune into which together they were now all cast.

Different groups dividing on ethnic and religious grounds had started the long, terrible, ever-changing Confederates war.

In servant houses and pothouses in the suburbs Dominic Kirwan, Sir Valentine Blake, warden Walter Lynch and colonel John Burke were quietly praised for taking the Irish side with Éamonn na Maor. The poorer classes, mainly of Irish origin or relatives of merchants, were ground underfoot by the repressive rule of the freemen and women. Many of the students and apprentices, whatever their origins had been, gravitated naturally towards rioting and rebellion in a city state where a small oligarchy of wealthy families, secure in profitable trading charters, ruled iron-fisted for centuries. There also were many sons of freemen inclined towards the Rising, filled with religious fervour and new-found radicalism inspired by the news that the Old English had risen in arms and many allied themselves with the Irish throughout the country to protect their Catholic freedom.

Ordinary people under extraordinary leaders freed Galway from the Parliamentarians but they soon were mired in dispute with their fellow townsmen over which way to proceed. The foundation stone was taken from under them once civil war divided England. The Irish nobility rose up to get their land back and the church of Rome called for war to fight for religious freedoms.

An Irish government, the Confederation in the name of the king, had been established in Kilkenny to fight for religious freedoms for Catholics. The new Supreme Council and assembly controlled the bulk of inland Leinster and Munster, Eoghan Ruaidh's bases in Ulster, as well as Connacht, outside of Coote's occupied zone. Crucially the ports were mainly in Parliamentarian hands, except Galway and Limerick and smaller ports in southern Leinster. Ulster had been overrun by the Scots army and the army of the new British settlers.

In the liberated regions of the ancient colony of Ireland, a door was slowly opening to reveal the prospect of a strange new freedom for the Irish people, while the English were distracted in civil conflict.

Ruaidhrí was jolted in revulsion every time the memory returned of his flight out the city gate under bombardment from the English Parliamentary heretics.

He was on a *gearrán* cart laden with country people fleeing the town as fire swept through stricken buildings. He was returning to his sisters in Moycullen. From the rising road they looked back in horror at the sight of the evil light of the fires brightening the evening sky. The heretic militia were burning thatched houses in the suburbs, houses of the fishing people on the shore, setting fire to their boats and killing anyone they came upon outside the walls.

'It's come around again,' an old man sitting in the cart said as they looked back, 'the war of *Gael agus Gall*, when O'Neill and O'Donnell came down out of Ulster in the old people's time.

'The troubles began with Diarmuid Mac Morogh bringing in Strongbow and the Normans, giving him land and letting him rob and kill in the name of the English,' he added.

'The wars started when the Milesians invaded by boats from the sea,' the old man's wife sitting beside him said, uncovering her face. 'And drove the Fir Bholg into Connacht. They killed the Tuatha de Dannan, the good people before them.' She pointed higher up the hill on which the refugees had stopped to rest the horse.

'The dead of that race are under the hill above there,' she said, 'living in houses under the ground and no one will go near them. Those good people were seen lately on these roads — strange people driving their cattle on the road and going to weddings and funerals, large groups of them, men, women and children on foot and on horses, appearing without a word, passing by and never seen again.'

She pulled the shawl back over her face and they blessed themselves.

As they approached a cluster of houses, someone in the cart began to scream at the sight of bodies in the street, horribly violated and mutilated. The war had come to his home too.

'Where are you?' he called, running through the house. 'It's me, Ruaidhrí. I'm home.'

The place was empty. He ran outside calling, searching the brew house, the haggard and the grazing field, the woods, the plough field, the turf ricks, the cabbage garden, the beehives garden. The cattle and sheep were away at the booley houses for summer pasture. The place was empty of man and beast. He sat on a stone wall at the back door distraught, heart pounding, tears in his eyes, then ran in despair towards the darkening shore calling their names.

Distant shouting came from the lake. He sprinted through the trees in the dusk to the wooden landing place. A movement on the nearest island caught his eye, accompanied by shouting. It sounded like his sisters, he realised in a flood of happiness. A moment later he saw a boat putting into the water and pulling across the lake towards him. His sisters, aunt and Sean Chaití Éamonn were waving to him as they rowed. He waved back frantically, rushing into the water up to his waist to pull the boat in and tie it. They were all there, bedraggled and wet; hair and clothes in disarray, Honora, Bríd, Eibhlín and Máire, beaming, safe, jumping out to throw their arms around him and he cried from terror and joy.

'Hush,' whispered the aunt, clambering out of the boat, 'sound carries on water. Will you be quiet the lot of you! We don't know what soldiers are up the lake still. There's a power of people hiding on the islands.

'Is everyone alright?' he whispered trembling, thinking of the bodies he had seen, hugging his sisters in terror.

'I don't know,' replied Honora. 'Everyone in our house hid on the island. Is it safe to go back to the house? Did you see any English soldiers?'

'No, I saw none.'

'We weren't sure whether to join people rowing out the night before last or not,' Sean Chaití Éamonn told him from the depths of her sodden shawl, shivering and praying.

'None of them heeded the old story of the people who hid on the islands long ago and who were all killed because it was the first place the soldiers searched. Your grandfather's father said it was a death trap and they should have gone into the mountains. We thought of that, but we could see campfires inland and when it got dark we followed the rest.'

'Where's stepfather?' he asked.

'John is gone with his men to Clanricarde,' the aunt said, not meeting his eyes.

He looked out at the black expanse of Loch Corrib with its numerous islands and shuddered hearing the familiar old story, the past becoming the present. The family ate gruel that night in the dark kitchen and slept together at the hearth until the dawn awoke them.

The bodies lay unburied until Morogh returned with his men. The clattering sounds of hooves on the road carried to the people in their hiding places and brought them out, keening and terrified. The memory of the loneliness and the sadness of death that visited every house never left Ruaidhrí. Perceiving his parents' deaths in his childhood clearly for the first time, an inward-looking boy stared out at an incomprehensible world.

Deliverance

ohn Lynch explained to Ruaidhrí years later about the shock everyone received when Walter allied himself with Malachy of Tuam.

'I suppose we lived from day to day after the fort fell not knowing what Walter would do next when his new responsibility went to his head. I could see how he strove to outshine in holy and warlike fervour my archbishop, poor Malachy O'Queely, for I was — and still am — the archdeacon of Tuam, though distancing seas of exile lie between my jurisdiction and me. Since our church was opened in Galway, no incumbent of Tuam ever launched such an attack on the independence of St Nicholas's as did Malachy after he was elevated to Tuam. Malachy was the one who after all had never let up casting aspersions, both ecclesiastical and legal, on the documents of St Nicholas's. He had even insisted on the right of visitation within our walls, flaunting himself – and what a big man he was, too – under Walter's nose! Ah well! The wardenship and Tuam had disputed for centuries, hadn't they? It went back to the Old English distancing themselves from the Irish as our friend Mac Fhirbhisigh suggested more than once.

John Lynch continued, 'Suffice it is to say that in those years of which we are reminiscing, two Hercules ruled their jurisdictions like sphinxes guarding their own doors, eyeing each other in hostility, until they united, calling on their flocks to arms for the Confederation in defence of our faith!

'I had a foot in both camps, vicar of St Nicholas's in town and archdeacon out in Tuam. I kept my head well down and buried myself in the antiquities of our country, until circumstances led to my own elevation to the wardenship at the end of the war.

'A flame kindled in us those years of conflict and we sought the glories of the ancient saints.

'Poor, misguided, learned scholar Malachy, our suffering martyr!

'Tadhg an tSléibhte, the famous friar Mícheál Ó Cléirigh, had come to him with the Annals of the Four Masters which we had been able to read and discuss out in the peace of Tuam.'

After the forced withdrawal of the Parliamentary forces from the fort, the Lynches were no longer compelled to celebrate mass in damp city cellars or conduct classes in secret back rooms. They reopened their famous school and other schoolmasters arrived to take up teaching positions. Students who had borne arms with factions were expelled when the troubles ended. Corpses swung from the gibbet in the execution place following a spate of trials in the Tholsel of those deemed malefactors. Desperate men and women seized and found guilty of wilful murder, assault or theft during the riots were made a public example of as the freemen reasserted their authority with determination. The Jesuits emerged from concealment, rented a house and collaborated with the Lynches who controlled the school, especially Fr John Lynch after Walter broke away to join the Rising. Most, but not all, of Ignatius's men were hand-in-glove with Sir Richard Blake — the Speaker of the Assembly in Kilkenny — and with Ormond's army. The great bone of contention here was that James Butler, the Duke of Ormond, was a Protestant, the first of the family to accept the new denomination and by this secured his title and property. The duke was a kindred spirit with the conservative, propertied class of freemen in every other way. People from this faction were strong supporters of the negotiators for Ireland in the Confederation. Patrick Darcy, along with Geoffrey Brown, were Clanricarde's protégés, lawyers who sat in the assembly at Kilkenny.

Their city state, the most westerly outpost of the great European world, founded successively upon Greece and Rome, feudalism and the Renaissance, flourished for a while through all this. The townspeople lived in the fleeting freedom and independence won for them by the Rising during England's civil war. The routing of the garrison let in an unbelievable, unheard-of, wonderful light, never imagined or experienced in their lives. Gradually they realised in their hearts it might not last. Insecurity and fear underlay the joyous new freedoms. Like fearsome warden Walter they were all in possession of keys unlocking bright new wonders, while ordering new locks at the same time against misfortunes the world might yet throw at them. It was a unique time during which restraints were thrown off by the people in different ways as they sensed the ephemeral unreality of their situation. England and Scotland were divided in civil conflict following the Reformation, throwing their world into turmoil. Finally, the invasion of the army of the Scots changed the balance. Young and old realised that life in Ireland would never be the same unless the king protected his Catholic subjects. Militias, drilled under warlords, sprung up out of nowhere in the vacuum as war brought unrestraint and licence to the rigidly controlled civic life of Galway city.

New divisions were opening up between Irish and Old English, fuelled by mutual suspicions of treachery in a time of fear, change and insecurity.

The talk among Ruaidhrí's Darcy relatives visiting on Sunday evenings inevitably turned to another of his cousins, Patrick Darcy, the lawyer, their brightest star. As a family they delighted in debating current affairs, filling Cousin Darcy's comfortable room with loud conversation. Ruaidhrí grew up listening to them recount how the gifted Patrick had presented his 'Argument' before the Assembly of the Confederation, so Ruaidhrí knew Patrick's thesis by heart. Freedom of Catholics to practice of their religion was tolerated when the laws against them were suspended by the king's prerogative. Kilkenny was a loyal Parliament unlike the English Parliament, therefore that disloyal English Parliament had no right to pass laws for Ireland. In conclusion, only the king and the Parliament at Kilkenny had the authority to legislate for the Irish people. The power of his older cousin Patrick's speeches inspired all Ireland. The vista of Irish independence had appeared with the establishment of the Confederation of Kilkenny, their own independent Parliament under an English monarch, unlike the unrepresentative Parliament in Dublin. In this way their religious freedoms would be protected.

Cousin John's brooding oldest son, Dominic, and his two younger boys, Ambrose and Robert, listened blank-faced to their elders seated around the fire, made wordless signs at each other near the door when no one was looking and slipped out the back whenever the talk was loudest. They stole head down to the crowded Cross where they joined the high and the low in the glorious new adventure life had become.

Ruaidhrí understood how, in this world of danger and change, he was like his grandfather who had in his day, immersed himself in new thinking. His mother Elizabeth had reared Ruaidhrí in town ways. He was descended from both native and settler families, struggling to find his identity and loyalties in the turmoil of war and politics.

Although the Darcys and Kirwans were originally indigenous families, they were married into the city families for generations. Ruaidhrí was related to many wealthy Darcys and Kirwans, freemen on the town council and merchants, with connections to most of the leading families who had married into each other for centuries. Ruaidhrí was later to learn from the ollamh Mac Fhirbhisigh that the Ó Dorcadhaidh were chieftains in Partry at the time of Solomon's reign. The freemen and women were among the late arrivals who had come to the area with the Norman, English and Welsh settlers after the arrival of de Burgo into Connacht with his knights. He had interests on all sides, belonging to all and yet to none.

During his young days, the city people lived in a feverish insecure nightmare world, strengthening their defences against the threat of siege by Coote in Connacht and attacks by Parliamentary armies on Confederate garrisons in Leinster and Munster. They busied themselves in military and political matters in this new world. Conspiracies and wild drinking at night took hold among young people, tradesmen and poor tenants, willingly taking a new licence for themselves in the general distraction. The clergy and Confederate men travelled back and forth under armed guard to Kilkenny. They were active in discussions, law making and negotiations with the new, powerful men now directing the military campaigns and running the liberated parts of the country. Ruaidhrí grew up in the days of his wardship during the dysfunctional yet exhilarating final years of a proud, cultured city of old settlers.

At school, John Lynch was kind to Ruaidhrí, struck by his personality. Fellow scholars, townsmen, noticed this maliciously. They pinched him and kicked the ball hard at his head,

'Hillilloo, O'Flaherty na dTuadh!' they roared, mimicking that famous ancestor who brought in mercenaries to fight against the English.

Most townsmen were descended from the English of earlier times and spoke the English tongue as well as Irish. Better spoken than most, Ruaidhrí was more advanced in grammar, more fluent in Latin and Greek than his fellows when addressing the priests. They in turn began to take him aside for quiet conversations. This too was noted by his peers. This countryman was descended from the O'Flahertys of the mountains and the sea. His people had been long barred from entering the city walls. He bore a surname the town youths had heard from their mothers since infancy in tales of horror and evil. The murders committed during the violent days when the Irish army entered the walls of the city confirmed and reinforced that nightmarish fear for the new generation of city dwellers. Ruaidhrí represented otherness and created fear in their close-knit world, though he was one of themselves on the maternal side and on his stepfather's side, yet his name and place of birth went against him.

Dubhaltach Mac Fhirbhisigh's Road: 1643

On a bright summer morning, dawn beginning to dispel the shadows on the streets of Galway, the watchmen opened the gates at the appointed hour. Residents exiting in a steady stream onto Bóthar Mór met bare-foot country people entering noisily with carts. Among the residents was a tall man in his early forties of unusual appearance, riding a fine horse, his baggage packed behind his saddle. His suit was neat and respectable in the style of gentlemen of note. His brown curling hair, combed and gleaming, fell elegantly down his back from under his stylish hat. It was not only his attire that made him different. An air of distance set him apart, the proud set of the head despite a sort of aloofness or restraint, a sense of being faintly at odds with the world, like a fish out of water. This was a characteristic unusual among busy, outgoing, assertive officials of the law court, church or council to which his appearance suggested he belonged. He was a man whose passing was subject to close glances among strangers, obviously trying to place him.

The watchman recognised him though, saluting him as he passed out Great Gate.

'Are you for Kilkenny, sir?' the usual question these days to gentlemen heading out this side.

'No, I'm heading south to visit Sir Diarmuid's residence,' the man replied. This gentleman was highly respected and well-known in town. His mother was a wealthy townswoman, related to all the leading town families. It was no surprise that an outsider such as himself would call upon such a man.

The official, old and grey-haired, nodded his head approvingly, hat bobbing and, despite himself, bowed slightly to this outsider in the city but who was, nonetheless, well-connected in town and county. The man came from backward Irish parts and suspicion hung over him like a dissatisfied afterthought ever since the day he came to live with the priests at a time when the world turned upside down. The new fashion was priests and lawyers quoting antiquarian sources while listening to this fellow recite in Irish and Latin from old books. Sir Richard Blake was writing a play about his life. The man presented himself with the ease of nobility, it had to be said, and this more than anything saved him from being assailed in the streets.

A group of black-clad clergymen were handing their horses over to a stableman and gathering their bags outside the gate as the man rode through.

'Good morning, Dubhaltach,' they straightened to wave to him. 'Where are you off to?'

'I'm going to Munster for sources required by John Lynch,' he called down to them, reining in the horse. His strong, full-featured face broke into a pleasant smile, a face eternally young; a man who never aged, who kept alight with the inner tranquillity of lifelong reflection, study and writing.

'And I hope to visit the Franciscans on the way back.'

'God be with you on your road,' they blessed him, looking up at him, shading their eyes against the morning sunlight, feeling an awe the stranger inspired in them, the famous ollamh, Dubhaltach Óg Mac Fhirbisigh, patronised by the high and the mighty.

As for the ollamh, he was of an age when hopes and expectations that great things lay ahead of him had reduced to daily routines. The Rising and chaos following it swept through his home place upending life for everyone. It had brought him here to Galway city to work with the priests. Now his ambitions reformed into shapes twisted and unrecognisable when undercurrents of despair lashed upon his tranquil shores like *riabhach* days in Lecan or in dreams at night, when nameless fear gripped him. Grey mornings in the city brought overwhelming feelings of loss whenever he thought of his family and their ancient calling.

Wordless thoughts gathered to taunt him. He knew it was useless for him to spend his days forever looking back like Lot's wife. He must look to the future instead - a novel idea for a chronicler of genealogy, he said to himself with irony. He had to gather his strength to await the outcome of the war.

His friend and patron, the priest John Lynch, needing materials for writings, commissioned these research journeys. The well-known Old English clergy of Galway, teaching the classics as they had always done, were dedicated to historical research and writing.

Dubhaltach had time for reflection once he cleared the crowded houses and lanes of the suburbs and traversed the well-tended farms of the city's upper class which were tenanted by their kinsmen. Now the horse picked her way on the rough roads of Connacht. Green, rushy grazing land and fertile, well manured tillage plots of townlands appeared before him. Quiet dwellings of thatched roofs lay near the road where smoke hung over them in the still air, their pungent dung heaps outside. Women at the door stared at him silently and people toiling on strips laid out for crops surrounding the villages straightened up to stare at him. Roads skirted dangerous stretches of bogs where the unwary stranger could find himself bemired and drowned.

Mac Fhirbhisigh journeyed that day to the residence of Diarmuid O'Shaughnessy in Gort. He saw farming families in meadows, the grimness of starvation before their eyes, bringing in half-rotten hay ruined in the wet, stormy summer that had plagued the country. Aftergrass appeared among the black stubble on wet soil oozing over the people's feet. The harvest sun was shining too late. They waved a welcome to him, relieved by the diversion caused by his arrival as he rode the potholed road from Ardrahan, the wind in his face and his coat folded behind him on the horse. Wild young men with the madness of war on them came running for news at the sight of a stranger,

'How are they now down the country, *a dhuine uasail* and the fighting that has been going on?'

The women weighed up Mac Fhirbhisigh with appreciation from the fields and eyed each other speculatively before the strong smell of rot brought them back to the present. His arrival caused a stir in a quiet community burdened with bad weather, war talk and omens of evil.

Old people, when word was carried to them of Dubhaltach's arrival, started remembering passed days when people of the locality were collectively referred to as *Uí Fhiachrach Aidhne*. The better off among them began making their slow way to call on him at the big house that evening. They knew he carried in his head stories of each family group among them. News of his visit was relayed to young people sitting around the supper after the day, hearing from their parents how Dubhaltach's father and grandfather before him came regularly to enjoy the company, drinking at the hearth of the big houses to recite their ancestry. The ollamh enshrined the genealogy of the nobility and the saints, situating it within the entire community, reciting stories of many local events in the narrative. The wealthy families were most prominent in the genealogies and so the ollamhs painted intricate, intertwined images of long-gone kings and queens, holy men and women and strange, wonderful stories of their lives.

O'Shaughnessy was head of the leading family of the place, a well-connected prosperous farmer, trader and captain of the local troop. His bulky figure resplendent in lace-trimmed velour appeared smiling at the door to greet Dubhaltach, accompanied by his elegant wife in red flounces of silk and satin. The pretty daughters of the house, young, eligible girls among the nobility of Connacht, all ran out in surprise when they heard who was at the door and embraced him at the threshold of their impressive mansion.

'God and Mary and Patrick be with you!'

The women of the household caressed his hair, delighted to see him coming to visit, teasing him like a favourite uncle you could be free with.

'You are the fine-haired man from Killala,' they said admiringly, squinting at his linen collar, his suit of fine weave and shining leather boots, 'Look at you now, handsomer than any man in the town!'

He was refined and educated, yet was neither priest nor lawyer, he was just an enigma, someone different from everyone else. He loved the praise and attention of the women, bowing and greeting them all in turn, joking with them. When he was seated by the fire bantering with the children, the wife in a bustle of ordering the serving woman to bring drink, whispered to her husband at the door, 'That's a man who's come down in the world since he was last in this house, he hasn't a ha'penny.'

O'Shaughnessy nodded, muttering, 'It's as well old Mac Fhirbhisigh is dead before he could see this.'

An elderly, drunken, grey-haired harper entertained the guests in the room that night. Dubhaltach dined with the gathering, seated at an impressively rich table covered in dazzling linen, silver candlesticks and glinting crystal. Subtle echoes of money travelled through the candlelit room thrilling him. It was heard in the strong, confident voices of the diners, the grunting of the sleeping hounds tethered under the stairs, the exotic flavours and fruits in the food as dishes were laid down before chattering guests. Why wouldn't it be so in the residence of the kingship of Uí Fhiachrach Aidhne for fifteen hundred years? The rooms were sumptuous, as beautifully furnished as any merchant's mansion in the city, the visitor keenly noted every time he stayed. The view over the lawn and fields spread far across the townlands of the tenant villages into sloping upland woods. Guns were stored in chests in the weapons room, the door of which was proudly unlocked by O'Shaughnessy during a lull in the serving, to display the weaponry.

'You're well supplied by the factors in town,' Dubhaltach said to Sir Diarmuid as he was shown muskets, pistols, carbines and then brought him out to the powder-house to see the stores of gun powder barrels.

'I'm charged heavy prices by those same fellows,' the other retorted loudly. 'There's nothing cheap to be got in the town of Galway, they know well how to make profits.'

He owned half pikes, javelins, broad swords and shields in his collection, many of them made in his father's and grandfather's time, he explained.

Young men, officers in O'Shaughnessy's troop, relatives of his extended family, were examining their blades in the fire light to let everyone see they were armed as well as anyone. Dubhaltach took this cue to recite a war story of their aristocratic forefathers, his host self-importantly calling for silence, banging on the table when he began, and they cheered wildly when he concluded.

One of the young fellows, well-dressed and supercilious, stopped beside Dubhaltach's chair, eying him, 'We've seen through the wiles of the English you know, how they stopped the fighting in Leinster and Munster so they could subdue the Irish by settlement and supplant O'Neill by Ormond,' the young fellow said.

'Their aim is to corner O'Neill and flush him out of his strongholds. I heard with my own ears O'Neill declare it's vital that Connacht keep in the field to clear the English out and their supporters with them. O'More and himself will win all Ireland with the reinforcements coming from Spain through the western ports.'

The youths' eyes followed him whenever he moved from the table to joke and drink with the women in the small hours of the morning. They fell silent and watchful whenever Dubhaltach passed their huddled group in the corner.

'Do they not trust me?' Mac Fhirbhisigh asked the man of the house in displeasure when he confronted him at the table again, 'because I'm lodging in town? Do they think I'm a spy? I get a bellyful of that inside Galway's walls I can tell you. I knew that piece of intelligence they were boasting about since the start of the summer.'

'Young people don't know the former ways like we do,' Diarmuid said, squeezing his hand soothingly. 'Only the older, leading men around here have ever heard the history handed down, while this young crowd coming up are like town people, they don't hear the history. They don't understand what you're getting up to in the town since you obtained your position there, that's all.'

Dubhaltach found himself on his feet, shouting above the crowd. 'They're hearing the *seanchas* now! Every single priest and student in that place!'

Silence fell suddenly as everyone stared at him, taking in his unexpected speech. O'Shaughnessy in surprise, squinted up at Mac Fhirbhisigh and winced, regretting he had spoken. Dubhaltach did not know what came over him and shaking, sat down in shock, trying to compose himself after his frightening loss of control and decorum before such an ebullient, entitled, upper-class crowd.

His shout however triggered a right roaring, banging and clapping after the initial silence. Although no one understood what he had been saying, it did not matter, the entertainment was good and everyone merry with drink celebrating his visit. Dubhaltach scrutinised the heavyset face of O'Shaughnessy for signs of amusement, but his host was carefully looking into the fire so, thankfully, the moment passed. I must maintain dignity here, the ollamh thought, what's wrong with me that I'm like this? In the back of his mind, he felt the old, deep loss of standing that a man of his name should end up employed as a mere assistant to Old English priests of the town, even with the blessing of the archbishop of Tuam. It was only temporary until the troubles passed. He would not let it get the better of him.

Dubhaltach lent towards the other man and continued quietly, 'Every one of them is informed now. The wisdom of Amergin's children will re-emerge in the new fashion of printed books, following the example of the Franciscans in Louvain. Isn't that a great wonder! Look at their achievements! The times may have changed since the Tudor deprivations but so have the methods of handing down the branches of learning.'

The words were out of his mouth before he realised, they were John Lynch's words he was speaking, gaining a traction of their own in his erratic troubled mind after the drink went to his head. Frightening images arose from where he kept them suppressed.

'And are you content in the new ways of the town?' another of the O'Shaughnessys, older, louder and more uncouth than Sir Diarmuid, stretched his arm cynically along the back of the host's chair on catching Dubhaltach's words. The man leaned into the conversation to stare curiously at Mac Fhirbhisigh.

How could Dubhaltach, the ollamh, discuss genealogy and history with fighting men, parish priests and unlettered servants? His great pride rushed in like an equinox tide to drown any excuses he might have tried to make for himself, leaving him dignified, protected and silent in the face of such impertinence. Why should a man of his family have to endure the day when the learning was no longer handed down for the race of Fiachra? Instead, it was disputed in strange places, challenged and not accepted. Darkness had settled on his mind when the people of the *Uí Fhiachrach Mhuidhe* in Tireragh on the Moy fled from Hamilton's Scots in the shameful rout, abandoning houses, boats and livestock, the dead and dying left behind on the road.

Dubhaltach found himself standing up again declaring the lament on O'Dowd's defeat in Lower Connacht, and how it was the greatest misfortune of their times.

He should not have done it.

A heaviness settled and overcame the room until the family and guests fell totally silent. The set-back transfixed them as if a breach of social decorum had occurred, the unmentionable uttered. A stout, silent man at the table suddenly called out and as one they emitted their battle cry into the rafters, the ululating of the women rising above it. The moment passed and soon they were drinking to Eoghan Ruaidh who had encamped in Roscommon to join the war in the west, so everything was well again.

'We're mustered in strength from here to the Shannon,' the young fellows yelled, in their stride once more; 'and O'Dowd will rise again, will he not?'

The Rising had already brought a terrible, revenging army led by the hated Coote, along with Hamilton, across Lower Connacht from their base in Ulster, vanquishing his patron Daithí Óg O'Dowd, as well as O'Conor Sligo and their allies. Dubhaltach himself had been an inhabitant of that country during the Scots' campaign, whereas these boisterous, celebrating O'Shaughnessys had not been there for the aftermath. When the Irish army had retreated south, they departed with it too. Around Dubhaltach's home people went on the run, groups of the displaced population lying low in woods and ditches, their horsemen long fled into the hills. They were keeping away from roads and empty, ruined villages where the smell of death wafted on the wind. No one was safe with troopers and parties of drunken infantry soldiers scouring the countryside to seize food, livestock and survivors from the Rising — men, women and children. The troopers were directed willingly by a guide from outside the place who knew the area, or by a local captive on the end of a rope.

The Connacht army under colonel John Burke had begun a siege of Castlecoote, Coote's stronghold in Roscommon. This siege lasted without resolution until the Old English faction engineered the Ormond ceasefire. The satisfaction and relief of the Earl of Clanricarde was overwhelming when news of the Ormond peace reached Galway. The last thing Ulick Burke, Earl of Clanricarde, wanted in Connacht was to see the rise of the military presence of the Confederates in his own territory.

Dubhaltach's thoughts tormented him as he tried to sit up in his seat and steady himself. Wasn't it well for O'Shaughnessy to be safe on his estate, the Shannon between himself and the English and the Scots the far side of Eoghan Ruaidh's army? And don't these people see what is happening in this war?

'None will come after me,' Dubhaltach said by way of answering them, but it was in his head he said it, at once uneasy in case he had actually said it aloud — something he could not say in the roused atmosphere of the gentry.

What was happening to him?

'To O'Dowd!' he cried in a moment of insight and raised his glass to save the situation.

They roared and drank and Dubhaltach felt tension ease from the room.

Later women, young and not so young came over to embrace him, sitting on his lap, whispering in his ear, and offering him drink.

There was much speculation about his availability — an escalating, delicious undercurrent since his arrival which blended with the rumour of his financial uncertainty. Was he married yet? It was well time for him, as there had been some talk a few years ago. Or was he even betrothed before he left home? Whatever the situation, he was keeping it to himself due to the misfortunes of his family no doubt. This threw tradition wide open thrillingly. Unspoken desire permeated the place as laughing couples embraced in shadows and women admired the good looks and style of the unusual guest.

Dubhaltach closed his eyes in the confusion and came to rest in a dreamlike place, white-washed, thatched stone-built house on a lake peninsula in sight of Nephin's slope and fertile land stretching into the distance on the far shore. It was *Tír Amhlaidh* where people were saving hay and oats in meadows, herding cattle, sheep and pigs on the slopes, footing turf on the bogs, attending fishing lines on the lakeshore and talking at the open doors. He heard and saw everything they said and did and knew they were from millennia past. He longed for the manuscripts and books they were compiling, where the household followed the calling of Clan Firbhisigh.

He saw again that day in Lecan which still seemed so recent, when his father was *thar clár* in the kitchen. Women's unearthly death keening filled the street where men and women danced together, singing the lament while they played bodhráns and flutes.

He became head of his name in Lecan Mac Fhirbisigh beside Killala bay just as war cast him adrift following the defeat of his patron O'Dowd and the loss of his home and hereditary profession. Like a priest without altar was the scholar without patron. Thus, he remained until the employment by the church in Galway came in his hour of need.

Mac Fhirbhisigh rode to the Shannon escorted by a party of O'Shaughnessy's men through the country of *Uí Fhiachra Eachtgha*. They were greeted from fields and doorways as they passed. The crossing was marked by a sloping pebbly shore. They waited while the moon sank into darkness. Hunkered men silently cast dice in the moonlight beside the horses, long knives glinting in their belts. Lookouts surveyed the country stealthily with only the fox and the badger for company. Water lapped against its banks in splashing swirls over reeds and stones.

An elderly man of the place appeared silently on horseback out of the night to welcome them, his long white beard outlined in the moonlight, an old-fashioned mantle draped over embroidered trousers. He had a lively seat on a horse despite his age. The men who had accompanied Dubhaltach bade farewell, their task completed as the old fellow would lead him to the crossing and, mounting the horses, they turned for home. The newcomer greeted Dubhaltach graciously in confident, cultured tones and respectfully lamented the death of his father.

'Happy is the roof that shelters you from the Shannon to the sea, Dubhaltach,' he added warmly in conclusion. This man waited with him for the boatman to arrive after the moonlight waned on the water.

'Watch out on all the approaches to Portumna,' the old man said after a while. 'On the Munster side you're safe nowhere.'

'The traveller's passage is safe in the holy places,' Dubhaltach replied, 'where the saints' prayers fill the air since Patrick's time.'

'Hush,' the old man hissed at him, 'the sound of James Butler's guns fills it now! Regardless of truce or war!'

Mac Fhirbhisigh put out his hand and touched the dry dust on the clay-crumbling shore where they sat, hoof-prints of cattle and sheep dried into powder. The comings and goings of people on the river, voices of that country and music of the Dál gCais of a thousand years stretched behind him.

A boat soundlessly pulled alongside out of the shadows.

Mac Fhirbhisigh reflected on his ancient sources that indicated that here was the crossing taken by the kings of Caiseal leading the sons of Míl north against the strange Formorians, driving the latter into Connacht, to where the Fir Bholg were banished. Those earlier arrivals from hot eastern lands had brought their language, music and gods to the island. They interred their dead in strange mounds long before his own great warrior ancestors migrated in their sailing boats from the Iberian Atlantic seacoasts. They took the five provinces which they controlled ever since, assimilating with the old settlers and their ways. And now this nobility's day seemed to be facing destruction before Dubhaltach's very eyes, defeated by English and Scots from the neighbouring island. They were arriving with invading armies more powerful than had been seen in centuries, finishing what they had begun at the defeat of Kinsale.

He was in the boat bringing him through the darkness to Munster, the mare's head above the water behind, glistening as she swam.

The Ollamh's Story

ay, oats and rye lay ruined from the bad weather in the fields of Flann Mac Egan, the brehon. His house among its meadows and woods beside Loch Derg lay as solid as it had always been. Dubhaltach slept under a dry and sheltered roof in the Duke of Ormond's country. He arose and at the earliest opportunity, selected an old manuscript in the brehons' collections from which to copy. He could see the rich green grazing land and the bare, muddy harvest tracts of Úir Mhúmhan from his table near the window. The big houses and villages of the Old English nobles were under armed protection. Men patrolled the roads constantly. No travel out of the place was safe. Travellers were exposed to sudden attack from fierce militia troops of the English to the east. Armed troopers of the Mac Carthys were camped out permanently in the hills and woods, coming into houses at night for sustenance and information. Men from farms and fishing houses practised with pikes and swords by the lake in the evening. He could hear servants making a great commotion in outhouses while satisfying smells started wafting around the house. 'This is an old story,' Dubhaltach sighed.

As for Mac Egan's lawmen and scholars, they were few but acrimonious and unruly in their work, unsettled and excitable, their disputations on the precepts of the law were intricate and profound as they had always been, as he remembered from his own youth. Their discussions of the law cases never changed.

Following certain sicknesses, the swollen belly of a cow bursts forth with foulness in death and like this Mac Fhirbhisigh's temper erupted in the brehon's house. His companions clicked their tongues wearily and sighed, while women of the house and servants clustered around to take his arm as if he were Eoghan Ruaidh.

Old Flann Mac Egan himself emerged officiously to enquire, 'What in heaven's name is up with you, Dubhaltach?'

Dubhaltach was by then at the brehon's door with the vellum book ready for him.

'See this book which I crossed the Shannon to transcribe! Look at these pages and their binding! Some are so destroyed I'm unable to follow their chronicles fully or faithfully!'

'That is not the fault of the Mac Egans,' Flann was not slow to inform him in clipped decisive tones.

'I know well you don't have the number of transcribers your father possessed - may he rest in peace. In my own father's time, the son didn't have to engage in this sort of work I'm doing either.'

'Then why are you shouting fit to raise Munster?'

'How can I return to John Lynch in Galway with the excuse of an incomplete chronicle from here? From this house of such a reputation that even the lowest scribe in the town will tell me about you! I spend my days in that place defending the truth of our sources. I'll be compelled now to hand over an incomplete transcription to men who unfailingly question my authority over lesser faults.'

'There's nothing new or unacceptable in that,' said the brehon. 'You are dealing with those who are unlearned in our ways.'

'I am the one who has to stand before them arguing the absolute veracity of the sources.'

'We have been arguing the law against the precepts of the unlearned for three generations since the time of Elizabeth, that does not change in any way the laws which were handed down to us. There's nothing new or strange in that for your calling or mine.'

Dubhaltach had to return to his table with the manuscript. Mac Egan followed him after a suitable interlude, stood beside his chair tut-tutting and said eventually with a bow, 'We'll do everything in our power to obtain an undamaged copy of that manuscript and make it available to you. We'll dine tonight to welcome you on your safe arrival in Munster.'

They both knew no other copy had been heard of in years.

There was nothing further to say, and after Mac Egan had withdrawn, the lawmen commenced deafening him, trying to find out what the row with old Flann had been about. Dubhaltach left the scriptorium in mid-question and walked around the back to visit the haggard, his head aching, too shaken to work and too full of troubled thoughts. He sat on a wall with the setting sun in his eyes. Women milked cows in the enclosure, the calves lowing outside, thin as the beasts on O'Shaughnessy's acres after the unprecedented bad weather, the wet summer following a freezing winter.

He had lingered here in his youth with boys and girls of the place when they were released in May to visit farmers for summers full of long, hot days, a thing of the past in the cycle of shockingly wet, cold years they were now enduring. The dancing was on the green beyond where the fiddler played every night. They used to watch the sun rise from these walls in their schooldays.

Dubhaltach wondered bitterly was old Flann above in his room wondering 'Where are the precious leading manuscripts of Lecan now *a mhac*, the famous books, proud Mac Fhirbhisigh? You are lamenting the falling apart of our books, but at least we still possess them. Where is the great book of Giolla Íosa Mac Fhirbhisigh and the Leabhar Balbh, and the illustrious Leabhar Buí itself, written long before that by Giolla Íosa MacDonnchadh Mór Mac Fhirbhisigh?'

Dubhaltach returned to the old, broken book on the table, inconsolable heaviness weighing him down. Gingerly he turned the stained, disintegrating pages. They described the wars of the Ulstermen against the Leinstermen, the wars of Ossary and Laois, the wars against the Northmen, a history familiar since childhood. A robed and tonsured monk had written them with fidelity and reverence long ago, but soon the pages would be no more.

'Was anyone ordered to make a full transcription of this?' he enquired of an older man working with him in the room, indicating the manuscript.

'We're employed to transcribe legal documents for the law cases in hand,' the man shrugged. 'And anyway, plenty other manuscripts are in a similar state as the one you've in front of you.'

'The transcription of books is a primary duty in the law school, isn't it?' Dubhaltach insisted.

'Well, the roof might still be over the brehon's head, but the thatch is not as golden as it once was or money as plentiful,' the man said, tapping his fingers on the table. 'Nor are the foundations as dry since the defeat at Kinsale and the new land laws. People are turning to English lawyers instead of the brehons, new men who have no idea of our old family land laws, inheritance, marriage and all the rest. The titles given to our nobles are held under English law since the time of Elizabeth's father as you know, *a ollamh*.

'And we're all aware that the new land grabbers coming in will query our rights and titles to land, greedy for any property they see, even though they were granted to their occupiers by the crown under Henry. Land titles will be defended under English laws from now on. Why are prominent families in Ulster and the towns training their young men in law in London, only so they'll be able to defend their titles against new English who will surely come? The Confederation at Kilkenny is for this reason creating new laws for the regions under their control.'

Dubhaltach endured this talk silently, not having much choice as a guest in the house. He realized better than most how land rights were a concealed trap under the people's feet and so could not let this self-important fellow have the last word.

'Will the old laws fall out of fashion completely? There are still many chiefs of their name in Connacht holding their land under the brehon laws, my good fellow,' Dubhaltach announced loudly into the manuscript-lined, low-ceilinged room. 'And will these new laws of yours be permitted to the Irish in the heel of the hunt when it comes down to land ownership?'

'Will Eoghan Ruaidh defeat the English this time?' was the only answer he received, which was to be expected nowadays from such a fellow.

Dubhaltach was faced with the vista of a widespread, seemingly irreversible decline of Ireland's manuscripts. He understood Tadhg an tSléibhte's concerns about ongoing loss of sources, everyone knew the four masters were still talking about a crisis facing the old language and records and about the need to gather manuscripts into safe keeping for copying. The ollamh considered the sources to be intact as they always had been since the time they passed to the monasteries. Daughters and sons of pagan kings accepted Patrick's faith and built stone cells on cliffs and islands away from war and strife. In peaceful monastic solitude they could pray and write while the sun slanted his blessed rays through their windows as of old. The families of the pagan poets also became Christian and wrote new books to keep alongside the old. When the Northmen attacked the monasteries, books were guarded by the learned families during those centuries.

Important books were seized as prized loot during every Irish war ending up as valuable trophies displayed in the libraries of Old English nobility who knew their worth or who sold them on to the Elizabethans for a small fortune. It happened to his own family's books. Copies were made against such eventualities. Most of the learned families were concerned about the need for making copies and preserving their collections. He had never seriously considered that writings could be lost beyond recovery, however. Mac Fhirbhisigh's family were forced to gather their books from the library and leave the area. They stared back under the cover of upland woods to see its thatch burning, the enemy's army encamped on their fields, troopers' horses in the hay meadow and men and women hanged from trees in the haggard. That was only history repeating itself as the same had happened before over a thousand years. On this occasion one of Dubhaltach's uncles made his way back home to Lecan after the army had moved away. He returned in two days to the house in the woods where they were being sheltered with devastating news. One of the O'Dowds was in possession of the Mac Fhirbhisigh place and in the process of re-roofing the house, having witnessed his own seized by an officer in Coote's army.

Dubhaltach's family were compelled to move in with well-off relatives left miraculously unscathed and were able to store their remaining manuscripts on the loft at the end of the main room. Neighbouring members of the O'Dowds visited every night and said the king would defeat the Puritans and the ancestral estates would be taken back and all would be restored as before. This time Dubhaltach knew everything had got worse. The enemy attacks were more powerful than had been observed since the Normans, with the English greatly supplemented by the Scots who followed the new religion. There was nothing new in any of this except he found himself in a position certainly novel for the ollamh of Clann Firbhisigh.

The old brehon of course resided in comfort and plenty in his ancestral place. Where could the ollamh of Lecan maintain the library, conduct the school of history for youngsters learning the archaic, literary language and finance the transcribing and updating of the histories and genealogies of Connacht? His patron lost his lands and had no money to employ him anymore. Where could he earn his living until the tide turned for the nobility with the victory of the king? Nowhere, it seemed, Dubhaltach answered himself, except by hiring himself out to wealthy men who require his knowledge for their own research into the antiquities of Ireland.

Automatically his hand felt for his purse at his belt – the solid coins he received from the priests to present to Mac Egan as a token of gratitude to the brehon. Was his work as a keeper of genealogy over the day O'Dowd was destroyed? Surely not, but how could he continue in days of war and destruction? And how could any future written account of the genealogy survive when the guardians of that knowledge were not nurtured and protected from the woes of invasion and change?

Tadhg an tSléibhte, as the Brother Mícheál Ó Cléirigh was called, had seen this coming after all.

Dubhaltach witnessed the prophetic wisdom of the Franciscan's words finally in Ormond of the brehons. The seat of ancient power of the Mac Egan's was slowly being replaced by a new order. What could be more desolate than words that had vanished from the pages of a broken book?

Perhaps it had taken Dubhaltach until his forties to finally understand. He had lost the family house and land and he had buried his father. Was that it? Maybe it was the experience of living in Galway city among cosmopolitan, free, modern people that inspired and changed him. The idea came into him that the body of knowledge inherited down through his family should be secured, like the men and women at home who weigh down roofs and curraghs for the winter with ropes bound to heavy stones.

Sizzling, juicy mutton joints were slowly roasting on the fire since afternoon, their aromas mingling mouth-wateringly with those of the spiced smoked joints of beef and pork above the hobs, filling the house deliciously. Dubhaltach tried to relax beside the brehon's wife drinking good whiskey and wine with appreciation and listening to her news of people they knew — marriages, deaths and matches to be made now the harvest was in. However, he was busy as he nodded to his hostess thinking about the dream he had the night before travelling from Galway, in which he was late for a meeting with the O'Dowds the day of a celebration for a new-born child. In this dream a heavy curtain of uncertainty blocked his timekeeping, dulled his initiative and weighed his feet. Everyone he knew was already at the ceremony, yet he never ceased to feel he would get there in time. Where did such a curious combination of optimism in misfortune come from?

Mac Egan, watching Mac Fhirbhisigh closely from the corner of his eye amid the entertainment, came over after a time to sit beside him.

'Don't carry the weight of the world on your back, Dubhaltach,' he muttered into his ear. 'Does our hospitality not cheer you up, *a stór?*'

'It's wonderful, excelling all bounds. Generosity flows from your hand, brehon.' Dubhaltach raised his cup and drained it in one drink to please his host. Seizing the moment, he slipped the purse unobtrusively into the old man's hand and squeezed it.

'I'm not accustomed to these days and nights such as we spent long ago in genial company and which you still enjoy in your good fortune,' Dubhaltach added.

'You're not optimistic about the outcome of the Rising, in the way its affairs are progressing in Connacht, are you?' the other asked shrewdly, after he had stood and bowed his gratitude wordlessly. 'And you're put out because we've no other copy of the book from which you are transcribing. We extend our deepest apologies for that transgression to an honoured guest.'

Flann inclined his head gracefully to Dubhaltach, who ventured at this moment to admit to Mac Egan that he lacked courage with the war stalled and the loss of home and patron. It felt incredibly good, a feeling flowing from the bottom of his heart, to talk in a place like this of what had befallen him and share his burden with one of his own.

'Should I take up farming back in Lecan?' Dubhaltach laughed ironically. 'Maybe it's time for me to put my hand to the plough. The sons of Heber and Herimon are being reduced in the world to the point of being unable to function in their office.'

'Put your hand to your page where it's always been. You're not reaping too poor a crop where you are currently employed.' Mac Egan looked at him slyly, lips pursed and eyes shrewd. Then he leaned back in his chair and announced loudly, glancing at the diners, 'We've been hearing rumours that your services are esteemed in the highest and strangest of places. Certain people who know nothing about anything are going around Kilkenny declaring a new discovery of theirs! You! Your name has become well-known nowadays apparently. You are in greater demand than any of us!'

When Mac Fhirbhisigh raised his eyes, he realised with a start everyone was staring at him, listening to the host's words, taking everything in.

'It's *you* who is their big new discovery, not me, brehon,' he retorted. 'I seem to have fallen on my feet in the end. Is that it? And been saved from the fate of a clodhopper!' Dubhaltach said into the silence, a joke being the only suitable response he could think of.

47

'Well put!' said the lawmen and gentry around the table, smiling discreetly while the priest and the women laughed aloud and clapped.

Clad in dark cloth with lace at his neck, in keeping with his office, the dignified air of the brehon at the head of his table had never altered over the years. The hair tied on his back may have turned snow white, but the eyes were as deep and bright as ever. It was held that the brehons could never be shaken even if they were on their way to the gallows. They were reputed to be as wise as Solomon because they remembered the times of the Scythian ancestors from whom the people of Míl, having intermarried with the earliest occupiers of Ireland, were descended. The brehons were able to trace them back on their migrations through coastal sea routes from Asia.

In a rush, Dubhaltach put his frightful question to Flann, unable to contain himself any longer, the whiskey rising to his head in the heat of the fire and the loud, chattering, laughing company.

'What if all knowledge of the learning in all its branches, be lost without recall?'

So, he had voiced the words at last, clearly unambiguously into the ear of the chief brehon of the *fenechus* himself, the most learned and eminent of them all in jurisprudence, knowledge which had been handed down from Fithil over countless generations. The eyes in the brehon's long narrow face never blinked, the voice so self-assured it lay quiet on the soul.

'Ah, you are turning out like Tadhg an tSléibhte now, are you? The powerful factions are joined for the Stuart king, uniting *Gael* and *seanGhaill* - and including Protestants such as the Duke of Ormond,' Flann said. 'I see cause for some optimism in that. On the question you have raised, I note great interest among learned men of the new religion in the learning of Ireland and its ways, our schools, our books, our monuments, the native language of the Gael. Continue to look for new students and above all move with these changes. Take every advantage of the Old English's noisy new obsession with the Stuarts' genealogy, but continue recording the genealogy of our kings, the saints, the bishops and the *tuatha* at the same time.

'Lie your boat into the wind and never despair. We must have trust in God and in Patrick's promise to us, Dubhaltach, and keep hope in our hearts.'

'May you live forever!' the ollamh heard himself toast Mac Egan.

The man had the greatest patrons, yet all around in the old territory strong, swift, unprecedented currents were surely pulling at his feet, steady as they had been under Mac Egan for more than a thousand years.

'What vision is haunting you still?'

'The disappearance of Amhlaidh's descendants, Fiachra Ealgach's sons, pinned under the weight of new and hostile masters of the country,' a hollow voice from the distance was saying. It was his voice, sounding like an old echo in the cliffs above the shore.

'Our people survived slavery for forty years followed by darkness for over a hundred and fifty years during the Northmen invasions, hiding in forests and hills with the relics and books, didn't they?' the ollamh heard Mac Egan's measured confident tones, making him feel again the old shame over his descent.

The woman of the house, noticing Dubhaltach's agitation, got up and brought more drink for him. But Flann took it from her, to give Dubhaltach the cup out of his own hand and now he was telling him to drink.

'May you live forever!'

Dubhaltach realised at once the significance of Flann's action.

Dubhaltach's father explained to him when he was a child the ancient protocol of inaugurating a king. It was the duty of O'Caomhaoin and Mac Fhirbhisigh to publicly proclaim O'Dowd to kingship on Amhlaidh's hill before the crowd. The privilege of the first drink was given to O'Caomhaoin by O'Dowd. O'Caomhaoin was not to drink until he first presented it to the poet, to Mac Fhirbhisigh. The king's arms and battle horse were not presented until Mac Fhirbhisigh called his name and moved the ollamh's staff over O'Dowd.

Past blended into present as Dubhaltach took the cup from the brehon and drank the fiery whiskey and with that he saw the future. The genealogy would not be lost while the breath was in Mac Fhirbhisigh and his feet travelling Fiachra's roads, because now he knew what he had to do, and the noise of the room faded into nothing before his thoughts.

'I need to gather in the genealogy of Ireland and put it down, solid, clear and easily read, in one great book, as the four masters did for the historical and ecclesiastical annals of the country. It will have an index like books have nowadays and a preface to set out the aims of the book. Why not get it printed with many copies that can be read far and wide when the Franciscans at Louvain return to Ireland bringing us the printing presses? Wouldn't *that* preserve the inherited body of Clann Firbisigh's records which I am now left solely in charge of?

'I would have to supplement our own books and exemplars from other sources held here and there, the way we always do. I will read Stephen White's books of those recommended continental antiquaries who are applying the latest techniques, which White teaches are necessary in modern scholarship. My work would have to be summarized and concise, considering the quantity to be put down. Recensions would have to be made and a fortune spent on good paper and ink. The cost of the printing and binding would surely be borne by the priests. Above all, the old literary language of the ollamhs would have to be translated into a more modern readable form. The Jesuit warns about the importance of the primary sources and the need for exactitude and fidelity, exactly as our own laws of transcribing lay down for the ollamhs.'

During the merriment Flann leaned towards Dubhaltach, his clever eyes bright in the light of the candle he was holding so he could see into the other's face.

'Books like the one from which you are making your extract were written from originals in the monasteries which were lost or destroyed during earlier invasions, words as sacred as the early books of the Testaments. Their wisdom and truth, the wisdom of an age-old, sacred law, survive like the forests covered by water during the very earliest ages when our old pagan gods lived in stone habitations underground. A truth that is with us forever.'

Dubhaltach rediscovered his path in the ancestral place of the brehons. An indescribable brightness appeared in his mind, held up before him by people long gone - long gone on the way of truth.

Next day the ollamh approached his work with a new peace. He took up his pen to write,

'*For my friend John Lynch, in the name of God and Mary, Patrick, Bridget and Columcille.*' He took a long breath and continued transcribing annals of turbulent days when the holy men and women had shone their light to illuminate the darkness.

'God is wide in a strait,' he thought when he finally placed his pen in its pot for the evening.

Dubhaltach left the brehon's house when shortening days set in with terrible bouts of cold and rain, to make the Shannon crossing into Fiachra's land. Back on the Connacht side, he took the road to the Franciscan Abbey of Cenel Fechín where the abbot himself came out to escort him into the parlour, sending a lay brother to stable the mare at the back with the order, 'Give a *gabhál* of hay to the ollamh's horse.'

In this holy place on the slopes of Sliabh Aughty the famous Leabhar Breac was held, the object of Mac Fhirbhisigh's visit.

'I have a new undertaking that brings me here today, brother,' Dubhaltach told the abbot. They were partaking of bread and mutton washed down with ale in the silent, airless room.

'I need to copy some pages.'

'It does not seem that many years ago when we had Brother Mícheál himself here for the very same purpose,' the abbot replied, looking at Dubhaltach curiously. 'You and your illustrious family are heartily welcome to our house of God and everything in it. Let me show you the books. We keep them in the room beside the sacristy under lock and key.'

The abbot felt under his robes and produced a key on a chain as he stood up.

'What are you looking for?' the brother remarked as he escorted him through the cloister to the church.

'Details of saint lore I require to supplement my work on the lives of the saints. And I want to consult Cormac's Glossary as well while I'm looking.'

After the abbot unlocked the door, Dubhaltach found himself in a small room full of light flooding in from windows overlooking the countryside to the southwest. The passing clouds moved in the distance before the winds of upper Connacht to unveil the autumn sun. At his smile of delight, the abbot said as he indicated the table and chair under shelves of volumes, 'Brother Mícheál said the light of heaven lit this room, did you know that? And that a person could write for hours in it. Here are the books you need, *a ollamh*.' placing the celebrated volumes on the table before Dubhaltach where they shone in a pool of sunlight.

When Dubhaltach was satisfied with his copying, he took his leave of the Abbey and turned for the road to Gort. He looked forward to spending some time again with O'Shaughnessy to enjoy his hospitality and hear the latest news from the locality.

Having found his mission, the ollamh was a changed man as he set off on the high road to Galway city.

Back in the city once more, he was relieved to be able to present John Lynch with the extract as soon as he met him in the parlour of the residence after Sunday mass. Mac Fhirbhisigh explained straight away before John could say anything that he had run into some small difficulties with the exemplar above in Tipperary. The latter, who was skimming through the pages rapidly, looked up at him, patted his arm and beamed.

'Oh, my goodness, don't fret over that, my dear Dubhaltach. You have what I desire. My eye running over this copy tells me at once!'

Dubhaltach smiled back in relief and relaxed for the first time since the upset during the summer in the brehon's house.

There was something about John Lynch that he liked, though it was hard to put a finger on it. They were exact contemporaries, both driven by passion for research, debate and writing about the antiquities of Ireland and each were burdened by the need for solitude and contemplation. They approached their learning from different viewpoints. Mac Fhirbhisigh saw life from his ancient, hereditary, rural ollamh position. Lynch looked at the world out of the eyes of his centuries-long, urbanised Anglicised church ancestors set within the classical European world. It was Lynch's solid and single mindedness, maybe along with his unfailing kindness and practicality in dealing with every aspect of life, that was always comforting, even when they disagreed. His heart was in the right place. One knew where one stood with him. Dubhaltach felt the priest was his anchor in a passing storm. What else would a descendant from an age-old line of boatmen of the Uí Fhiachra be?

Practicality may have been an old cliché about the worldliness of the townsmen due to their legendary business and political acumen. Yet Dubhaltach recognised keenly another gifted side of the priest, that of the chronicler immersed in organizing his own world of the past, so much preferable to dwelling on the chaotic troubles of the present.

John for his part was fascinated by the otherness of Irish learning, the beauty of the Gaelic as he explored Geoffrey Keating's work *Foras Feasa ar Éirinn,* and the inner self-containment of the ollamh teaching him the complexities of the language. He drew increasing comfort and guidance from the lives of the early Irish saints being made available through the door Mac Fhirbhisigh was opening for him. Even arguing with Dubhaltach about where the origins of the Lynches lay was enjoyable for John. Like Keating, he felt that assimilation of all races on the island trumped the exclusiveness of the ollamh's claims, shifting him from self-perceived superiority to defensiveness.

John thankfully said not one jarring word of criticism. He shared his blessings as he always did, his love of research and writing, his gift of faith in adversity and his understanding of the new learning. Although the two men were to disagree throughout the years of collaboration, their paths had by now irreversibly crossed.

Lynch, with satisfaction, brought the transcripts with him to Tuam to study them.

Mac Fhirbhisigh, time on his hands in the collegiate residence, looked around at the new ways as the brehon advised him. He pondered deeply the needs of the *seanchas* in these awful times of change. In summary, he said to himself, he had to continue gathering the best genealogical sources both lay and ecclesiastical. He had to write down the records of the kings, families and saints of Ireland. Seeking necessary employment wherever he could get it was essential for this endeavour. Above all he should continue this unprecedented collaboration in the antiquities of Ireland with the priests of Galway.

Beyond in Britain and Europe the ecclesiastical records seemed to have moved into a new, complex controversy. They had begun circulating in erroneous Scottish church histories, written and printed by hostile Protestants from the time of the Reformation. These new books were bent on twisting the truth about the Irish saints, bishops, monasteries and abbots of Scotland. This controversy was the centre of everything the old Jesuit ever discussed with Dubhaltach or with anyone else. The priests and Dubhaltach heard first-hand the latest news from White about the Irish Franciscans teaching in Louvain - Colgan, Ward, Mac Aingeal, among others. White's mind ranged from Clonfert to Iona, from Lindisfarne to Prague. His knowledge of Irish manuscripts abroad in Europe was fascinating and exciting and he maintained a correspondence with John Colgan until the end of his life

Dubhaltach, deeply moved, listened one night in the parlour as Stephen White told them how the Irish school in Louvain struggled in their counter battle against the heretical Scottish and English authors, whose books had firmly gained the ear of people abroad. Gerald de Barry of Wales — that old irritant in their sides — served to make matters worse, being reprinted some years earlier and read far and wide. Scholars abroad were treating *him* as a reliable primary source of Irish history, recommending him to foreign university men who were forever looking for copies of Gerald! Only the Irish Franciscans abroad knew the extent of this threat facing the history of the Irish church, until the government in Kilkenny, on being brought to awareness of it, ordered a refutation of such errors.

For a long time, unspoken thoughts were taking troubling form in Dubhaltach mind. The body of knowledge he had inherited was vulnerable before the world in new, modern, undreamed-of ways; both from challenges at home and now from abroad. An opaque, shapeless anxiety seemed to be always present when he moved among these well-travelled clergy, listening to their erudite arguments and far-seeing viewpoints — an anxiety which he hid from himself as he sat with them wondering what he would hear next.

Seeking the light of peace and reassurance, Dubhaltach left the city to visit houses of friends or retreats at abbeys and churches. Around this time, he began in earnest collecting genealogical sources throughout the province and beyond, and then returning to his life and duties in the city as the dark years passed.

The Tribulations of the Amanuensis

plashing river water sounds carried across Lombard Street and filled the house during calm days when the priests opened the widows facing the river. An underlying tang of latrines drained by the swift flood wafted over after matins. Dubhaltach's young servant, Tadhg Mac Seáin wearing his respectable new coat, entered the residence of St Nicholas every morning by the side door on the Bóthar Cam. The graceful, green-marbled front entrance of St Nicholas of Myra's church with its lofty roof and bell tower filled the space in the bend of the busy Bóthar Cam which connected Lombard Street with Market Street.

The young man climbed the flight of narrow side stairs and knocked on Mac Fhirbhisigh's door.

'Come in, *a mhacín,*' muttered the ollamh.

'Good morning, sir,' Mac Seáin said, awaiting the usual, 'What's the day like out?' as Dubhaltach sat at the table against the window, trying to clear a space between the piles of manuscripts covering it.

The view from the ollamh's window was dominated by activities up and down Lombard Street which could be heard on this side of the house — bustle from the fine merchant habitations across the road: people calling out noisily, shops opening, students going to school, carts coming in at the Bridgegate nearby, the watch patrolling. Here Dubhaltach had found himself accommodated when the priests invited him to assist them, living among clergy and students at St Nicholas's college house or residence, as it was called. He was living under a patronage he would not have countenanced even a few years earlier. These priests were descendants of Old English town merchant families or families who had long ago decided they were. The priests needed the ollamh's assistance and support for their research into the early Irish church, a major part of their efforts in the Counter Reformation. The leading families were exceedingly wealthy from trade, land and tenants, and their daughters were married into practically every lordly Gaelic Connacht family. They were committed to Rome for centuries, through holding high church office and maintaining convents, friaries and schools.

The usual question from Dubhaltach did not come however, causing the young man Tadhg to turn in surprise towards the figure sitting immobile, hands clasped in thought.

Eventually Mac Fhirbhisigh said, 'The friars of Cenel Fechín sent me word this morning after refectory, letting me know that pages I need transcribed are ready for me up the country. I'm leaving today to get them and to meet scribes they arranged for me to see.'

The young servant nodded, listening. The ollamh had made such journeys before he had employed him. There was nothing unusual in that, but he wondered suddenly in fright where that left his job.

Was he being dismissed?

'However, I'm very behind in transcribing my own work here,' resumed Dubhaltach distractedly, tapping the table with his fingers. 'I want you to continue writing these lines from this book.'

Mac Fhirbhigh picked up a work from which he was copying over the past few days. It was Mac Seáin's job to call out the line while Mac Fhirbhisigh scribed it in his clear hand, muttering to himself often while he closed his eyes in thought, sometimes correcting the boy's pronunciation, changing old words into modern Irish and summarising. Dubhaltach would be searching in the exemplar for where he had left off, having to double-check against what he had just written. Tadhg, as his attendant, would be ready to point out the place he was at in the work being copied.

Dubhaltach was pointing to the line they had stopped at the night before, saying, 'Continue into here,' while he pulled his writing from the chair beside him, to indicate where the next line was to be put. He left his own composition between them, tapped on the page again, then very slowly and carefully left the frail, old vellum book, the exemplar, resting on top of a heap in front of him.

'There you are Tadhg, my right-hand lad! Let me read out to you the lines you'll do for me.'

Dubhaltach read it aloud in his clear diction, the poetry of the old Irish genealogy just like it had sounded when the young attendant's grandfather had read to him in his childhood from old books, while he wrote in Latin and Irish.

Tadhg was bright from a young age and destined for the priesthood, his father's wish back then - before his life changed irrevocably in the borders of what the English call the counties of Leitrim, Sligo and Roscommon.

'Now you read that back to me yourself,' Dubhaltach moved the pile over to Tadhg without disturbing the vellum manuscript. The servant looked at the old writing with its abbreviations, a part of a genealogy. He read it aloud without pausing. When he had finished the page, he sat back and looked anxiously at the master. There was a little smile of pleasure on the latter's face as he began calling out the modern version of the lines, then Dubhaltach asked Tadhg to repeat the modern version for him.

'They taught you well below in Roscommon. There're very few can read the old Irish, your *Daideó* was one, of course. He came from well-known people. Even fewer can remember the modern words on one hearing.'

Tadhg beamed in pleasure. Once he had read a line he remembered it forever — the deciphering of the old Irish writings that stumped the other boys, the glossing of Latin, the lists of rules — he could remember them all. He could not remember however his father's instructions on how to weave a *súgán* that would not fall apart the minute you bound the sheaf or tied the horse's load with it. Nor could he answer his mother's questions on which heifer was in season after she had sent him down the land specifically to find out.

Tadhg's strange gift came into its own in the blessed retreat in the ollamh's room when he obtained this position.

'You didn't want to take holy orders though?'

The question hit him with like a blow, bringing him back to earth. He looked at the table, at the heaps of work that carried onto the windowsill, even all over the floorboards.

He felt the pat on his shoulder.

'Ah well,' Dubhaltach said with a sigh, 'the priest's coat would be too heavy for you maybe. You are a lad unto yourself with your own ways. You've proved your ability in the scribing for me like no other man in these parts,' Mac Fhirbhisigh said. 'You are uncommonly well recommended by the learned people who educated you in Connacht. You've certainly lightened my load since I've had you here. Now I will leave my book in your capable hands to keep on with the work while I'm gone.'

The lad was staring at the ollamh stunned.

The ex-seminarian, ex-lay brother, ex-teacher who had lately become the servant of *dubh 'gus páipeár*, of the copying and reading aloud, *he* was to write in Mac Fhirbhisigh's book! He was the one who had to carry loads from suppliers in the city and who had to bow to the supercilious, sneering old brute of a lay brother under orders from the warden to wait on the ollamh's needs! Tadhg stared at Mac Fhirbhisigh open-mouthed

The ollamh read his thoughts.

'From now on you will take on the duties of my amanuensis. Here's wages of four shillings for yourself for subsistence until I return,' Mac Fhirbhisigh was taking the money out of his purse.

Tadhg had never possessed so much money in his life, four weeks' wages.

'Take it,' said Dubhaltach. 'You will need your rent ongoing, won't you? To pay Master Blake, the chandler where you are lodging, who will shortly be demanding the half year's grace.'

Mac Seáin nodded at this piece of wisdom which had been obscure to him until the ollamh put it like that and slowly put out his hand to take the money.

There was a knock on the door which was roughly opened. The cynical, scab-covered face of Brother Benildus poked in at them, his cold eyes raking the room.

'I have the black mare ready for you beyond at the Abbey gate, sir,' the brother announced to Mac Fhirbhisigh in his harsh voice.

'Thank you, Brother,' the latter replied, rising gracefully. Without warning Dubhaltach placed his own special quill in its ornate ink pot at the other man's place with a wink. At the same time, he reached for his coat while placing his bag and baggage into the arms of the brother who scrambled to hold them together. Then Mac Fhirbhisigh swept out the door ahead of him without a word. This wonderful attribute of sailing through the people like he owned them was not a gift possessed by his newly appointed amanuensis. The lad was left hastily rising to his feet, receiving the end of a grin of yellowed teeth stumps from the old devil Benildus. This fellow was doing his usual deliberate surveying of the room behind the ollamh's back when he noticed Tadhg was looking at him, eyes wide, nose wrinkled in distain. Then, tittering and clattering noisily in his clogs down the stairs, he followed Mac Fhirbhisigh, cursing under his load.

Tadhg was left alone in charge of the ollamh Mac Fhirbhisigh's important work - his own man for the first time in his life and with a fortune in his pocket to accompany it.

In the midst of the deteriorating situation in Ireland, a new pope, Innocent the Tenth, was elected in Rome and he was determined to help Irish Catholics in their hour of need. He sent the suffering country his best man, laden with bags of gold, huge supplies of weapons and with orders to take over command of the military campaign on the Supreme Council. This churchman, sent as papal envoy or Nuncio into the swamp of Irish affairs, was the unfortunate archbishop of Fermo, Rinuccini. The Pope's man in Ireland soon found out the situation among the Catholics was far from straightforward. Every step he took, he found he had wandered into a hidden thicket of divisions among the faithful that ensnared him in every part of the country. Gradually it dawned on him that he was a saviour to only some Catholics and for the rest he was bad news. In all his days dealing with ecclesiastical and legal matters in Europe, he had never been so challenged and troubled.

In June three strange churchmen, two of them dark foreigners in beautiful robes, marched at the head of a wildly cheering crowd all the way up Quay Street and Lombard Street before coming in the front entrance of the residence. Tadhg Mac Seáin was with a group looking from the windows. The scene would be forever imprinted on his mind because another crowd was assembling rapidly from the direction of High Street, chanting a terrible, unbelievable, shameful thing:

'Rinuccini go home! Rinuccini go home!'

The warden's men were blocking that end of the street to restrain the frenzied charge. After the commotion died away behind the locked front door, the warden welcomed the foreign bishop, introducing him to the clergy, students and servants of the house. Tadhg was squeezed at the back of the crowd in the visitors' reception room, when a party of angry, rain-splattered clerics slipped into the room from the back entrance. While everyone else was craning to look at the dark, sun-tanned face with the cobalt eyes, these troublemakers were panting loudly, whispering and muttering roughly right beside Tadhg. The proud carriage of the noble-born prelate, the elaborate hand waves, the laughable, singsong accent of this vision in the heavy, red fur-lined cloak and ornate, red leather, gold-buckled shoes dazzled the assembly in the room. Tadhg fell to his knees with the community of St Nicholas's for the blessing from the Pope on the faithful of Ireland. The agitators knelt quickly too, nudging each other, and glaring from the corner of their eyes. By the time it was Tadhg's turn to kiss the ring, these clergymen had long fled from the reception room, nearly knocking him over in their rush for the back entrance. Why were some town people against the foreign bishop? How could they behave like this? What was going on? The lad was too troubled by these thoughts to notice the offensive odour of Rinuccini's breath mingling with his strange perfume that was the talk of the students for days. All Tadhg remembered afterwards was the incessant shivering of the Nuncio and the ice-cold feel of the ring on the shaking hand. The scribes and servants were the last in the procession out the double doors into the front hall, himself the last, while warden Walter, his vicars, priests and seminarians brought up the rear with their guests. Rinuccini was moving out, guided politely by his host. The Nuncio's Latin was foreign sounding yet the ollamh's lad understood every word Gian Baptiste Rinuccini was saying to Walter Lynch.

'I'm directing the cause of the faithful in a country, not only divided but full of suspicion of treachery, and no one is able to untie the knots.'

And with that he fell into a fit of sneezing and coughing so that he was barely able to make it over to the oratory where he would pray for Ireland. As soon as he could, Rinuccini requested to be shown to his room to rest after a chilling, blustery, raw sea passage up from Limerick, wilder than anything he had ever experienced. In the quietness of his room in the residence of St Nicholas, Rinuccini had prayed that the Connacht faithful might turn the situation around. His mixed welcome in Galway that morning had not been promising. Here in this city was the end of the road, where either success or failure awaited him.

Tadhg felt a horrible shaking of his shoulder and realised the hardness under his face was the floor.

'Wake up lad! Wake up will you!'

He could recognise the ollamh's voice anywhere.

'God of Graces!' the boy shouted. 'I thought it was that villain Benildus! And they say the warden has gone against O'Neill.'

He rolled over on his back shouting, tears streaming down his face.

'When was the warden ever a supporter of the Prince of Tyrone's kingship ambitions, aside from fighting for religious freedom, might I enquire?' he heard Dubhaltach ask in his clear, educated voice.

Tadhg sat up raving, shuddering, nausea rising in his throat. Crying in drunkenness, loss, terror, and sadness, all the voices he had been hearing were going around in his head like drunken dancers on a fair night. He struggled up dizzily and collapsed on his chair. Dubhaltach was sitting on his bed looking at him, his eyes sad, eyebrows raised, clothes dusty, his long, curling hair falling dishevelled around his face after his early morning ride back to the city.

'I'm sorry,' Tadhg said. 'I fell in with some foolish students and our apprentices from the chandler's. I'm no man to be in your service, master. I have let you down! I am a fallen hazel seed, that's what I am, carried on the winds of Eireann! And in calmness when the storms die down, I will settle, take root and flourish!'

'I wonder now who told you this about Walter?'

'Father John Lynch told me that, master. He was searching for his lads who were in the drinking house at the wall, and I suppose he noticed me there, fallen from grace. He came looking for me afterwards. He is my confessor now. He gave orders I was to lodge here in your room until you returned and one of the seminarians downstairs, Patrick Bodkin, is to be my guardian angel and prays with me in the oratory every day.'

The lad pointed to the rolled-up mattress under the ollamh's table. He must have been looking for it when he passed out on the floor. Blurred pictures came back to him of conversing in the pot house with his friend from the lodgings, Richard Athy, and how his acceptance by Richard was a changing moment in his life, something he found difficult to explain even to himself. Maybe it went back to the time he joined Richard's world, an invisible dimension of their own, catharsis that made existence possible.

'Ah! I thought that sounded like something John would say,' Dubhaltach said.

61

'I didn't know you were coming back to town today, master,' he managed to continue, his head spinning. 'I encountered John Lynch at a time I was not behaving as I should. I had seriously gone astray. He knew of course who I was from my time with the Capuchins and that you've taken me into your employment. He laid my life before me as it is. He heard my confession and he absolved me. He is the kindest priest I have ever encountered anywhere. I could never be as holy as he is. Don't let on to him I was on the *seachrán* again last night, master!'

Mac Fhirbhisigh nodded in thought.

'Are you informing me *students* are consorting with apprentices and the lower classes in rough drinking houses?'

'Yes, they are,' he looked up from the floor, 'and I saw important people there who're in St Nicholas's every Sunday and soldiers from the watch were in it toasting the king, sir.'

'This place must be falling apart,' the other muttered slowly, getting up, going over to his book-laden table, and gently pulling his own work towards him, all the time looking questionably at the amanuensis.

'I couldn't believe it when John Lynch said he quarrelled with you a few years ago over the work,' Tadhg continued drunkenly. 'You didn't argue with that godly man, did you, sir?'

Dubhaltach looked at the amanuensis's entries into his work. He sat down and very quietly took up his pen, dipped it and made some entries, correcting spellings no doubt. It was only what he could expect.

While Dubhaltach worked, he said, 'Is this all you have done for me, *a fhear óg mo chroí*? John Lynch and I didn't argue! Now, I wonder what word did he employ? Was this conversation in Latin or Irish that you engaged in with him?'

Tadhg collected his tormented thoughts and said, 'It was in English, sir, in the prison beyond at the Tholsel where I'd been detained. The gentlemen in charge spoke only English to Lynch when he came in to bail me out. Yes, we spoke in English, a language I have only been practising in these latter years since I came here, as you know, master. John spied me looking out the window one day when he was passing by on the street. He told me things about how he'd known you for years.'

But Dubhaltach had dropped the pen, turning around in alarm, giving him his full attention.

'John Lynch paid me out and brought me here, the week before last it was, I think. No, it was this week. I suppose *disputation* was the word he used for what had gone on, argument, debate.'

Tadhg put his head in his hands, he could not bear to look at him.

'John Lynch said we all have a dark side in our lives and that we must all strive to overcome it. He said I was not a bad person, only foolish. The master of the prison bowed to him on hearing all this and agreed to my release.'

'That applies to us all in this earthly place, doesn't it, that we all have a dark side?'

The lad waited in misery for Mac Fhirbhisigh to dismiss him from his service.

Dubhaltach only said, 'Inform me all about this dark side of yours tomorrow and maybe I'll inform you about my collaboration with John Lynch, our *disputation*. Go home now, that is, have you still lodgings left for yourself within these walls?'

'John Lynch paid my lodgings with Blake until you returned to Galway, sir,' he confessed in shame, his body heating and chilling frightfully in turn.

'But I have spent nights here. Patrick Bodkin lets me in if I tap on his window, you see. And he doesn't tell Benildus anything, seeing as Patrick slips out at night himself too, you know. You won't let on to anyone I told you that about Patrick, master? I really have no proper recollection.'

'And what does the warden's night watchman have to say about outsiders like yourself carousing within the walls of this town?'

'Oh, the watchman's quit the warden's employment, along with a couple of other fellows from the kitchen and stable and he's gone off to seek work with the Blakes and Lynches on the boats.'

'What is this? When? Why?'

'A few days ago. They said they didn't like the big foreign bishop from the Pope who's staying in the guest quarters. They're against him, they never had a good word for him and the next thing they're gone! Even the warden really doesn't want him staying here but he is not letting on, some people are trying to make out. Can such an awful thing be true, sir?'

Tadhg stopped his foolish babbling with the look on Dubhaltach's face.

'He's *here?* Rinuccini is in the residence?'

'He has a name like that,' the boy said, afraid of the look on the master's face. He could not stop himself talking or control the whirling of the world around him. Noises in his head prevented him from listening, dizziness in his eyes impaired his vision when he was upset.

'Excuse me, sir, but are we *for* or *against* that … that … Nuncio from Rome, as they call him. People keep asking me.'

Something told him to leave it at that but the impulsiveness that was always within him, was urging him as usual to say more, to his constant misfortune.

Fortunately, Mac Fhirbhisigh was not listening, busy muttering to himself, unloading a pile of manuscripts and papers from his bags and looking for a free space for them. In the end he had to put them very carefully into a corner on the floor.

'In the name of Patrick and Bridget, will the place be fit to remain in? Walter's play-acting at war again putting up the Nuncio Rinuccini here, whom they ran out of Limerick city in no uncertain terms. We should have known there would have been nowhere else for him to go at this stage except Galway, but right here in a guest room!'

'Three guest rooms he has,' Tadhg interjected, 'for himself, his chaplain and his secretary from Kilkenny.'

Dubhaltach said nothing and silence filled the room. The young man could no longer hold back the question that troubled him more than anything else.

'Why are some people in the town saying the foreign man is really the devil come amongst us in disguise, master?' he said.

Dubhaltach glanced at the young man impatiently. Then, seeing the expression on Tadhg's face, the older man sighed, left down the books he was organising and pointed to the table and chairs. They sat down in silence. Near to tears, the lad remembered, too late, that Mac Fhirbhisigh did not ever want the war discussed in his room. Despair at the thought of losing his job eclipsed the images of hell which haunted him since the Nuncio's arrival.

Then John Lynch's calm, kindly face appeared before his eyes, the sound of his low voice in his ears.

'I will ask John Lynch why people are saying these terrible things, if it pleases you, sir,' Tadhg heard himself say next.

Dubhaltach glanced at him, shook his head, folded his hands on the table and spoke.

'The Catholic hierarchy of Ireland are divided on this war. The powerful and wealthy among the Old English royalists are in favour of Butler the Duke of Ormond leading us for the Stuart king in the ceasefire. Ormond and his Protestant faction are close friends with freemen and certain clergymen of Galway. This faction is selling out Eoghan Ruaidh O'Neill and the Irish armies by negotiating a ceasefire with the Parliamentarians. They hope this will protect their land first and foremost. They're denying these actions will lead to loss of religious freedoms for Catholics, themselves included.'

'And why do they say the Nuncio is the devil?' Tadhg asked with trepidation.

'Rinuccini is telling them not to negotiate any ceasefire with Ormond. The Supreme Council discovered Ormond even held back on secret treaty concessions to Catholics that the king was prepared to make. Rinuccini is the most outspoken person in the country against the same James Butler, Duke of Ormond. He declares that Butler does not want to see Catholics being given unrestricted freedoms and in addition he says that Butler's supporters have been plundering church lands since the war started. Rinuccini has also said some hard things about this town and has made a lot of enemies here. That's why they say around Galway that he is the devil.

'Our warden Walter Lynch and the archbishop of Tuam are the only bishops of the church backing him in this part of the country.'

Mac Fhirbhisigh straightened up and leaned back heavily in his chair with his eyes closed.

The misfortunes of the Supreme Council and Eoghan Ruaidh compounded the day the English royalists were defeated at the Battle of Naseby in the English Civil war, he thought sadly.

Everyone knows now the king cannot defeat the Parliamentarians. Does this mean Charles Stuart will have to abandon giving concessions to Catholics here if he wants to make any settlement with the Puritans and Scots over there? What can Rinuccini do from now on to save his flock?

And where did all this leave him? They'll be saying he was collaborating with Rinuccini for O'Neill. What would he do? What could he do?

To keep the conversation going and the silence at bay, in the interlude, Tadhg remarked,

'You've brought back a great many manuscripts, I see, master.'

'That's because I have a great compilation to make.'

After a pause Dubhaltach said, 'So you are still in possession of your lodgings down at the sea? Well, go and sleep there now and let me do the same here! I have a great deal of work to get done and no time to waste. Be here first thing tomorrow. From now on we will be working from dawn to dusk. And tell no one about this interlude of yours if you can get away with it. Say you were gone away with me. There are so many strangers in town now, men at arms everywhere, not to mention the returning exiles. It's hard for the locals to keep abreast of all that's going on, although they make a good fist of it. Hopefully, you may get away with your indiscretion - we'll see. There was a time before the Rising when you would be ejected for sure out of here before you knew it. And I in need of all the help I can get!'

Dubhaltach continued after thinking a bit. 'And so, His Excellency, Walter is still a busy man, charged now with trying to put an end to the wars when he is aiding them above in Kilkenny in their negotiating with heretics. That is, when he is not accommodating in his own house in Galway the war party determined to fight to the last for our faith, freedom and stolen land. Time will show which way the apple will finally fall. And that applies to our own John too, I'll have you know.

'And listen to me, if anyone asks you whether you, or me for that matter in light of the situation I'm in now, are *for* or *against anyone* or *anything*, you are to reply - let me see - you are to say. *'I will ask Master John Lynch for his advice when I may.* Now repeat back to me. What will you say when they ask?'

The boy did so perfectly, although his head reeled. He stood up and walked uncertainly towards the door.

'Here, take these', the ollamh said, 'that are after falling out of your pocket.'

He handed Tadhg his playing cards silently. His shame compounded, the boy opened the door in misery. As he was leaving Dubhaltach said, 'We were all young once, *a Thaidhg a stór.*'

His heart collapsed and wept inside him. Outwardly he said, 'I am nearly at the age of ordination now, sir, had I persisted.'

'You'll do,' the other said. 'You'll do.'

Outside on Lombard Street, the boy pulled his coat tight against the wind as he walked. He breathed a sigh of relief when his conversation with Mac Fhirbhisigh came to mind.

'Thank you, Oh Lord, for the forgiveness of the ollamh and the priests,' he prayed.

The thought of returning to his lodgings at Blake's, the chandlers, came uneasily into his head as he walked.

'I hope the Blakes do nor pass much heed over my absence. John Lynch would have told them I was engaged in the ollamh's work, anyway. And I cannot tell Richard Athy I was in the jail in case he carries it! I'll inform Richard I was working for Mac Fhirbhisigh since I last saw him.'

Tadhg laughed quietly to himself.

'Is it unfair to deprive our Richard of news such as the jail? But I have to be careful and mind my position here, like John Lynch said. Well, never mind, no doubt Richard will have plenty news himself. He has to mind his position in the world of finding out everything.'

Richard Athy, who shared the lodgings at the chandler's, was on the same pilgrim path as Tadhg Mac Seáin, a stony, uphill, twisting road full of strange people and their ways. Richard was the only person who ever understood Tadhg's afflictions and who could meet him in a place beyond confusions where quietness fell, and they could talk. It did not matter whether this place was situated in the chandler's back rooms or the church, the taverns or the Cross, drunken or sober, among the poor or the rich. Richard sat at the right hand of God, even if it was only Tadhg who could see this.

Richard had saved his life when he fell into the sea at Blake's boat a few summers previously. Tadhg stood one fine morning with the lads on the quay watching Blake's men, among them Richard's father and brothers, unload French wine casks onto mule carts bound for depots and townlands far inland. Images of southern lands under hot sun, that once were ruled by Rome, and where the wine was made, rose before him. Tadhg reached out his hand to touch the side of the vessel that brought in the cargo crossing magical, fabled seas. The boat felt the tide under it and moved as he did so, so he lost footing and plunged headfirst into the cold depths, sinking down into blackness. He rose to the surface. Above, Richard was shouting, throwing a rope from the berth.

'Take hold of that!' Richard was calling as if from a great distance and Tadhg's flailing hands found it. The lads seized the rope with Richard and drew him up on the dock where he lay on the wet stones retching.

'Ah, sure that fellow never saw the sea in all his life until he came here,' someone was saying with contempt. He opened his eyes gasping to behold melancholy, searching eyes, scanning his face. Richard took his hand when he stumbled to his feet and led him into the house to help him cast off his wet clothes.

'Tell me what you behold when you fall into thinking the way you do,' Richard asked as Tadhg recovered, still shivering in the blanket from his bed. The *bacach* was staring into his face with the sort of curiosity he possessed about a world around him, from which he too was excluded.

'I see the wonders of the world lying beyond our shores,' the amanuensis replied, blubbering and shivering from the sea, hardly knowing what he was saying.

'I see the ancient lands of the Romans where the Celti tribes in those parts were overrun by their legions. Niall of the Nine Hostages came from Ireland to fight with his allies, braving the legions and hostile tribes and took Patrick to Ireland as a slave on one of his raids.'

This was a story Tadhg had once heard from the strange student Ruaidhrí Óg Mac Aedh O'Flaherty when a group of boys and attendants were lying in the sun during recreation one hot day in the collegiate garden. This fellow was odd because he only talked about things he had read or learned. Apart from that he had nothing to say and could not have a conversation with anyone without going red in the face.

The ollamh himself taught him, Ruaidhrí Óg added, that all the principal families of Connacht were descended from Daithí the last pagan king in Ireland, a myriad of septs and tuathas to whom Mac Fhirbhisigh's ancestors were genealogists, historians and poets.

The story was so vividly described by Ruaidhrí that Tadhg dreamed at night about Daithí's raids in France, how he was struck dead by lightening at the foot of the Alps, how his son Amhlaidh beside him in battle carried Daithí's body back. The forced marches through foreign forests and swamps, running along the fine paved roads the Romans had built. These warriors were painted and fearsome as described by St Jerome, who witnessed as a child Irish warriors with their war chariots passing near his home in Illyria in the heart of the empire. Our people were engaged with the Romans everywhere, narrated young O'Flaherty, his eyes closed dreamily under the shade of the trees. Ruaidhrí continued telling how Irish men undertook their sea crossing in *báid mhóra* from Europe and around the British coasts back to Ireland. Amhlaidh brought his father's body all the way down the western high road to bury him with his ancestors in Rathcroghan of the Kings.

'I will never reach their ports,' Richard listened keenly in sad silence to the story. 'The task of the *bacach* is to keep to the land and sprinkle sawdust.'

Tadhg walked down Lombard Street with its noisy passers-by, handling carts and loads. Disgusting, stinking rubbish was everywhere underfoot. He would never grow accustomed to this place if he were to live here a lifetime. Maybe that was why Mac Fhirbhisigh rarely went out when in town only to mass or visits to the religious orders. The bells of St Nicholas of Myra pealed for daily mass. Hood squeezed tightly on his ears, looking around surreptitiously to see was he being watched, his pace increased as the noise of the bells went through him, striking every nerve in his body. By Quay Street, the bells of the Dominicans on the hill, the Franciscans and the Carmelites were also ringing mercilessly. Since childhood Tadhg could not endure the fearful riot of bellowing cattle at the fair, or the men's endless yelling and clashing hurls at ball play on summer evenings.

Tadhg's father declared making a priest of him would cure him of his nonsense. His mother would only say he was touched by the hand of God when he was born. An old aunt of his father cried out from the *cailleach* bed on hearing this that the good people had taken the real son of the house and left a changeling child in the cradle. She declared she had heard them open the door and come in a week after his birth.

At the priests' house where his father sent him at fifteen to become a priest, misfortune struck. During his very first year he had a fainting fit in the church at an all-night vigil marking the start of Lent. The fever lasted until Easter. He was unable to speak, read or study, lying under a heaviness he never had experienced before. When he got up and walked into the cloister, aided by a seminarian, his legs collapsed under him, and blackness engulfed him. His father was sent for finally and met him at the priests' entrance, where he stood looking at him, shaking his head when the superior said farewell.

'I suppose seeing as you were never right from childhood, what happened below when Coote destroyed the home place finished you off entirely' his father told him bleakly.

The father brought him back on the *garrán* without another word, until the house was in sight, when he said, 'It would be unfortunate to waste all the learning you've had. I'll see if the monks in Galway will take you.'

Tadhg knew there was nothing for him in the sod house his family built on an empty place by the side of the road. This became their home after they fled with other refugees from the murderous attacks in his birthplace. Every nightmare came together there whether looking for food by day or lying on the clay floor by night.

The first morning at the Capuchin house in Galway the boy heard a horrific clamour break out across the city and ran into the linen house sobbing until he was discovered.

'Those holy bells have not rung since the treacherous Elizabeth's time and now the Rising has rid us of the English and restored our churches,' the abbot thundered in Tadhg's ears while a lay brother and the prior dragged him into the reception room.

'You'd better take yourself off to the schoolmaster beyond at the wall and use that great learning of yours to find work there if they'll have you!'

Tadhg found himself engaged as a monitor in that feared tyrant's schoolroom. At least there the noise of chanting was quelled frequently by the master's stick, as that old man launched into lengthy, ferocious corrections of what he was hearing. When the master realised his ability in spoken and written Latin, Tadhg was given bedding and sustenance in the servant house. No wages were forthcoming after the master unfortunately spied a pair of howling older boys shoulder him out the door to tip him head-first into the street. On the strength of this, no money was paid during the first half year. Time stood still while he was on probation as the seasons blended into one another until the day he finally found the courage to ask the master for his wages.

'Aren't you after eating me out of house and home and you nothing but an excuse, incapable of conducting a gaggle of geese across the road,' the old master shouted and dismissed him.

Tadhg took shelter subsequently in the Franciscans' side entrance, huddled with beggars waiting for food, his mind blank, barely conscious of his surroundings. Somehow word must have been carried to the ollamh, Mac Fhirbhisigh, who sent a monk with the message for Tadhg to meet the ollamh on the street. That day his luck changed. Mac Fhirbhisigh knew who he was before he could say a word. He beckoned Tadhg to follow him to his residence, where he brought him up to his room, employed him and found him lodging.

Approaching the Strand, the clean tang of salt water was in the lad's nostrils, the wind fresh and strong. A big boat was being unloaded on the dock, its sails furled, the stabbing peal of the bells replaced now by the winching of pulleys swinging huge rope-bound loads over the side operated by shouting seamen under the squinting eyes of hard-faced merchants and factors, their agents on board gesticulating in vigorous deal making. Oak wine kegs were rolling down the plank with great noise, manhandled by the skill of the hardy, leather skinned, rough-mouthed seamen running with them, directed by merchants waving and shouting. These were loaded onto waiting carts at speed. Next came out pungent, weeping salt barrels to be dealt with in a similar way. Suddenly a barrel spun out of control rapidly, plunged on the shining stone surface of the dock and shattered in a great burst of black powder, to alarmed shouting and quickly suppressed swearing. Consternation raged as the factor shouted orders to gather up the scattered contents. It was gunpowder, not salt, in some of the barrels being taken off.

Loads wrapped in leather and bound with rope appeared next, swinging over smoothly towards reaching hands. As Tadhg drew nearer, he recognised Colonel John Burke's men mingling with Sir Valentine Blake's seamen, taking charge of this merchandise, loading it onto handcarts. The heroes who had run the English out of the fort and vowed to lay down their lives fighting against the Puritans of the Parliament ever retaking Galway city were eminent in the defences. One of them was engaged in opening these loads and counting the contents, including muskets and pieces for the armies still at war, awaiting uneasily the outcome of the Ormond truce. Weapons for the town's own reinforced defences were being received by the corporation's men in their distinctive insignia. Tadhg peered around curiously to see which apprentices he might know before he remembered the words of warning just given in the ollamh's room. Instead, he hurried into the lane to the side entrance of Blake, the chandler's, house. Already the first barrels were rolling behind him where cellarage facilities were rented out to merchants by Blake.

He had not reached the kitchen quarters in the courtyard at the rear when his friend Richard Athy accosted him. Richard missed no one coming or going, never mind someone who had been on the *seachrán* with him over the last week and who had subsequently not shown up at the lodgings. There had been neither sight nor light of him since. It would take less than this to exercise someone like Richard Athy.

Richard was the only person Tadhg had ever met in his erratic existence who felt the same about the world as himself. The first week in his new lodgings at the chandler's, while the pair of them lay awake before dawn among the sleeping apprentices, they talked about life in Blake's as experienced by Richard since childhood. Tadhg answered the many questions about his own life coming from the curious Richard.

Richard was short and square, his jacket and trousers shapeless, with his lame step. Their landlord, Blake the chandler, to whom the *bacach* was related, favoured him and protected him. He took full advantage of this. Richard had been slipping out the back window at night for years, flinging his stick out before him and wriggling through the opening like a worm. After Tadhg had got to know Richard, he asked him where he went at night.

'I never miss a night of the cock fighting and baiting by the river,' the other replied cheerfully.

'Is it good sport?'

'Brilliant sport, *laidín*. The crowds are great, coming from all over the place, bringing the news of the world and the gaming is worth a lot of money. The women are friendly and well I know them all. But that's not all, country lad.'

'What else is there?'

'The apprentices are drilling there secretly at night in case they are required to defend the town in time against the Parliament's heretics.'

Richard knew an outsider like the ollamh's man would not inform the Blakes about these terrible things without repercussions for himself. The master of the house strongly favoured Ormond's side and the truce, like his prominent wealthy cousin the famous Sir Richard Blake. Tadhg picked all this up from the talk of the women and men in the back kitchen when they ate their gruel crowded around the large wooden table at dusk.

Richard Athy taught him dominoes and backgammon in the evenings and a strange eastern game his father brought him from Cadiz. He, in turn, showed him the card games he played in his youth with the boys learning their Latin from the old scholar in Leitrim his father sent him to. He was taken in by the ollamh and got lodgings with Blake through that old man's connections.

The very next night after the *bacach* confided his secret nocturnal life to Tadhg, the pair of them lay hidden in the bushes eavesdropping in a garden where a hooded man placed a letter into a militiaman's hand. Afterwards Richard brought him to a tavern where the conversation of the *bacach's* friends opened new images in his mind of bravery and conspiracy, loyalty and treachery. The strong ale went to Tadhg's head in an explosion of heightened reality, only to be replaced by sickness and darkness in the lodgings. Different to the rest of the world, they recognised a deep sense of alienation in each other. Tadhg found a strange comfort in Richard's endless scheming in the cold, draughty apprentices' quarters.

'You're back again, 'mo Thaidhgín Dubh 'gus Páipéar! Well, well, well, well!' Richard was grinning expectantly, quivering with curiosity. Without another word Richard seized his arm. He hobbled with intent straight down the yard, heading behind the latrine house dragging Tadhg, working his stick as fast as he could through bushes on the blind side of the wash house until they were hidden. There they were overlooked only by the servant house at the end of the garden which was empty during the day. It was a private place, but one still had to whisper due to the comings and goings of women bearing great loads for the washing lines.

Their dash to cover gave Tadhg a minute to get ready what he would say. Remember what the ollamh said to you, boy! warned the voice in his head.

They sank down together on soft, damp, leafy clay, leaning against the stone wall which formed the periphery of the chandler's property, protected by trees and bushes from prying eyes at upper windows overlooking the garden. The *bacach* pulled his helpless leg straight and threw down his stick, putting his head close.

'Where have *you* been?'

'Master John Lynch, the ollamh's friend, vouched for me to the guardsmen who took me, and he even planned for me to stay in the ollamh's room while Mac Fhirbhisigh was away. He's after returning today. Did the guardsmen arrest you too?' he asked innocently.

'Faith, I may be walking on a stick but I'm quicker than yourself with your two legs. Wasn't I one of the first pulling myself up into the thatch when the word went out the watch, blast them, were at the door and me looking around for you to follow me before I went out the hole and through the window next door? Didn't I inform you in the clearest terms possible about that secret arrangement the first time ever I brought you over there? You were one of the few in the place that night who even knew about the bolt hole. What did I see but you making eyes at Úna, the Browns' girl sitting beside you however *you* managed that? You didn't even hear the lookout at the door call out! I did not have you to help me get down next door's back stairs to the street afterwards, did I? Thanks to your little romantic antics you ended up being taken with the rest of them.'

Tadhg had forgotten about Úna the fair-haired, freckled young woman working at the student Francis Brown Fitz Peter's house. He started to laugh, and Richard dug his elbow viciously into his ribs to quieten him, shaking with suppressed laughter as well.

'I'll be leaving you here in your bed the next time I sally forth in the night in case you meet a woman,' he whispered. 'You're the greatest *óinseach* I met in a long time! Yet you've come by a lovely girl just sitting there with your mouth hanging open like you do always!'

They snorted and gasped with laughter until they lay against the wall in exhaustion. Happiness flooded through Tadhg Mac Seáin on being back in his old friend's company again. They never discussed anything in the apprentices' lodgings except the doings of friends and neighbours both high and low, along with wry observations about their wealthy master and mistress. But life was tinged with adventure and intrigue whenever he was with Richard, who was driven by an all-consuming curiosity. The *bacach's* irreverence towards everyone, his love of nocturnal outings and his unshakable spirit, despite his misfortune, was a bulwark against the upheavals of their times. He was the person who had introduced Tadhg to the secret life of the disaffected young people of Galway, bringing him places he had never even known existed.

Richard must not have heard Tadhg had been incarcerated in the jail or he would have referred to it. There were few members of the merchants' households sitting on the rush-covered floor in the stinking, miserable rooms that he could recognise while he was there. Poor people filled the place from the county and suburbs. A sight of strangers who did not belong to the city begged him for the price of a crust of bread when they saw his dark coat and polished leather boots.

Richard must not have heard how Tadhg had fallen in with the students the previous day. These young men saw him as one of their own since they began slipping out too. Tadhg would prefer if Richard did not know he had moved up in drinking society. At the very least he might be hurt, at worst he would be looking for news that he could carry.

'Tell me all about yourself and Úna. I met her at mass last Sunday and made it my business to ask her, How's himself, your handsome lad the ollamh's man, *Dubh 'gus Páipeár*? and she went all red and laughing. Delighted with herself over you, that girl is.

Aren't you the fine fellow?' poking him so much that he pushed him off, trying not to shout.

'There's not much to tell,' he insisted while Richard pulled faces and made rude signs.

'And I'd wager a month's wages you have no idea she has been pining her heart out for you this long time? Do you even know where her mistress's house is situated?'

'How would I know that?'

'If you weren't such a gawk you'd know her place is just across from your master's on Lombard Street. She's been watching your comings and goings there.'

Tadhg caught Richard's stick and waved it dramatically over his friend's head to quieten him.

'But your master isn't slow to smile when she's at the old grandmother's window upstairs. He has a sharper eye than yourself for a good-looking girl and he must be twice your age!'

'What's that about Mac Fhirbhisigh you're saying?'

'Only that herself and the ollamh smile across the street at each other from upstairs windows, which is more than can be said for you!'

They fell silent contemplating the wet leaves and branches, breathing the acrid smell of the ashes heap while Tadhg wondered about the veracity of anything Richard Athy ever said in his life.

'Here, where was Mac Fhirbhisigh gone off to, then? You said he had been away,' whispered Richard eventually, as the amanuensis knew he would, getting back to the main activity of his life — news.

'Gone off to visit teachers to discuss the history of Ireland,' he replied.

'What? Which? Who wants to discuss the history of Ireland, I ask you! What place was he in? He's an Irish spy, isn't he? The whole place knows that.'

'He doesn't inform me where he goes.'

'What does he and John Lynch discuss when they're together?'

'The history of Ireland.'

'Ah!' Richard waved his stick in annoyance then continued with a vengeance. 'It's a soft job you have reading and writing for him, mixing his ink and buying his paper at a merchant's where no local who believes in minding their money would dream of setting foot. They see you coming in this town, that's for sure. And yet you learn nothing about him! Not like me, carrying messages, making dowels and plugs for the Blakes for the rest of my life, sharpening tools at their beck and call, holding planks for sawing, while my brothers are years serving with Daidí on the boats.

'But I learn about *people*, unlike an *amadán* like you. The *bacach* is left ashore of course. Blake's frigate is docked from France this morning and I'll have to listen to their tales all over again of what they saw and did in foreign ports. But it's me that'll have the news of the town for them better than anyone else!'

Richard tapped his stick emphatically on the ground making this point.

Tadhg pitied the poor *bacach,* his only friend, getting older like himself and no further in life, who once said if the amanuensis had his head and he himself had the other's legs, they would be a man between them.

'Oh yes, indeed I just saw her unloading. A barrel of gunpowder fell and split open on the dock when I was coming in here and there was great consternation.'

'God in heaven, I hope it wasn't any of my crowd that let it fall, was it? Blake would let a fellow go from his employment for less.'

'I didn't see who did it.' He was sorry he spoke.

'We'd better go,' Richard said. 'You go into the latrine house and wait until I am well back in the shop.'

Tadhg entered steamy back rooms from the garden, chaotic with women cooking, stoking fires, washing and shouting at children. He was keeping an eye out in case Mistress Blake might be walking the rooms with her heavy step, watching the servants and might notice he had been a long time away. He had got safely into the passageway without encountering the mistress when he heard a familiar hissing noise from under the stairs. It was Richard listening to conversations audible from the open door of the first-floor dining room.

He hobbled out, face flushed, beckoning Tadhg into the inner shop room where they slept with apprentices under the carpenter's bench. They flopped down on their mattresses.

'You never as much as uttered a word to me that the Pope's Nuncio, who put in on the tide this week, is lodging beyond in the priests' residence! Everyone thought he'd be with the friars or Franciscans who are praying and agitating for the war, hot and heavy, morning, noon and night!'

'Oh, that's so,' Tadhg said casually, wondering where this was leading.

'That foreign devil has come to direct the war from here to decree that we must not parley with heretics. He's hand-in-glove with O'Neill against Ormond,' Richard said with the authority of the seasoned eavesdropper. 'And will be the ruination of us all if the new army defeats us in arms,' he concluded importantly.

After a moment he added an afterthought, 'Have you seen his horns, his tail and his terrible cloven feet yet? Andrew Fitz Ambrose is after saying in the shop that he met someone at the Cross this morning who saw the hoof prints burned into the road by that devil walking up Quay Street from his boat.'

'I saw him arriving with the people cheering for him, but the councillors and their men were shouting from the street for him to go home. He never leaves his rooms since.'

The boy paused in thought then added in wonder, 'The Nuncio has a man full-time running out to the turf stack seeing to his fire, who told us he shouts something foreign when he sees him coming with a load of turf and starts waving like a madman.'

'Why would he do that?' Richard pulled himself up to stare round-eyed at him.

'His secretary explained he wants wood for his fire not turf.'

'Does the man not know the price of a load of wood over at the river quay nowadays?'

'I bet he doesn't, seeing as he has to have a fire going day and night in the month of June.'

'Day and night! The summer might be bad but what state would he be in during the winter, a creature out of hell? What does he look like anyway?'

'Dark and foreign like the merchants from Spain and France that visit Blake and Blake Mór.'

'Do you know the room he is staying in?'

'Yes.'

'Does he speak in a foreign language?'

'No, he speaks Latin.'

Richard slapped him on the shoulder with satisfaction, about to speak when Blake's deep voice could be heard shouting in the shop, looking for *the bacach* and he scrambled awkwardly to his feet.

That night Richard woke the amanuensis and whispered in his ear.

'I've been thinking all day how Latin is a language you speak as well as the priests, Mistress Blake says. Isn't that why she makes you hear her sons reciting all day on Sundays? Well, you'll have plenty news for me about what the foreign fellow is up to, won't you? And I'll arrange for Úna Ní hEidhin to meet you at my grandfather's out in the fishing village any time you want. I'll set up a meeting next holy day at the well for a start. She's the same family as us, she's a first cousin to me and it was my brothers who were escorting her from our place back to master Brown's house when they fell into company that night in the pothouse. And it was no accident she ended up sitting next to you either, it turns out. It was our Philip who had to run for Blake's factor to speak for them to the guardsmen.'

Tadhg was struck with wonder at this revelation. 'I thought all this time you were a town man.'

'I'm town on my father's side and Irish on my mother's from out the Claddagh village.'

The stress of all this was weighing heavily on the previous night's drinking - his secrets, the ollamh's work, the endless wars and cessations and the news about Úna Ní hEidhin.

'You fell asleep last night like a candle quenched,' Richard complained afterwards, 'and me in the middle of telling you about Mamaí's family. They sent her to be a maid to Blake Mór's wife because she was the most beautiful girl in the place, unequalled in sewing and singing. She was hired on sight and Daidí married her a few months later'.

On the Seachrán

Tadhg had wandered out that previous evening with a few students, Darcys, Deanes, Kirwans, Morrises and the strange Ruaidhrí Óg, among others. He encountered them in the courtyard outside the oratory, and they were very friendly to him since word of his scholarly prowess went about. They waved and called him over, sounding in great form altogether.

'When the master's away the mice will play,' one of them winked at Tadhg when he approached them shyly.

'Mac Fhirbhishigh's up the country on his research work and the Lynches are all gone out to Ardfry for a big meeting about the truce,' O'Flaherty explained smiling in the quiet off-hand way he had that attracted people to him.

'Walk with me, *a Thaidhg*,' Ruaidhrí said then, 'so we can discuss the master's research and you can tell me all about your work with the ollamh.'

In the young lad's eyes, Ruaidhrí appeared a dark, handsome youth, serious and engaging, wealthy, beautifully dressed and well-spoken in a manner few could match. Yet it was the soft, uncertain way about him that was strange, making the young aristocrat almost like himself, on his level somehow. He was even a few years younger than himself.

'Oh!' the other lads hissed. 'Forget about books, will you both, the night that's in it, in the name of all that's good!'

They strolled slowly through the city before the gates closed as people from outside were leaving. Shops were shutting their doors as business in the town died down. The watch was changing on the towers. Master carpenters and masons on the fortifications were overseeing their apprentices gathering up the tools after the day. The works were nearing completion.

The angelus bell pealed six o'clock from the bell tower of St Nicholas of Myra, followed by those of the other churches. The usual overwhelming urge to cover his ears against their piercing sounds overcame Tadhg but, knowing the world, he had learned to clench his fists in his pockets and recite his prayers. The students broke off from their petulant complaining over their fathers' refusal to allow them to join the militia while they prayed the Angelus. The porters and watch at the gates called out, captains of militia shouted orders to the sentries who responded, muskets in hand. They passed St Nicholas's church, closed and locked after last prayers. Arm in arm, they ambled down Middle Street until they reached the quarter defended by the Lyon's Tower. There the engineers and masons were finalising the strong new bastion defending the gate. A maze of rancid little laneways was situated here. They were so narrow that two persons could scarcely pass each other. They were full of small, thatched dwellings, thrown up against each other by the encircling lane. These cabins housed a large population in a space, confined by the leafy perimeters of Blake's Garden and the line of tall houses in Little Gate Street.

The group entered the low, overhanging, dripping doorway of a drinking house and were greeted in the interior dimness by the man of the house, who bowed while seating them at table. A solitary old, weather-beaten seaman was slouching on a broken chair at the far wall drinking ale, his outline visible in the fitful light from the door. The host served them dark, strong beer from the brewery on the river. then sat on a barrel in the back watching until they drained their cups and smacked their lips. Rising, he refilled the cups to their loud chorus of appreciation. The seaman shouted for *uisce beatha* and was silenced by threats and oaths from the man of the house.

Later, the restless, merry lads bade him farewell and left the house to seek further entertainment. They jogged through the black, empty streets in great form, unchallenged despite their laughing and singing. Suddenly, without warning, a pair of armed youths were marching on each side of them. They hushed them, slowing them down. Left right, left right, they marched behind the beacon held by another man who rushed ahead through the maze of the streets. They marched swiftly into a house shrouded in darkness, the beacon-bearer having disappeared. Tadhg found himself stumbling after the others down broken stone steps into a noisy cellar. A packed scene of men and women drinking and shouting in a dark, hellish, evil smelling place appeared like a bad dream. Rush lights flickered on rough walls, barely lighting the murkiness of the cellar. The floor was wet, foul-smelling, straw-covered clay. People were coming and going on the faintly lit stone steps rising against a wall on the far side of the room. He guessed hazily this was the fabled passageway into a house outside the walls. Richard Athy had once mentioned this place to him. Was he in the cellar dug under the city walls during the time of the wars of the Earl's sons? Reports had it that the breach of security it offered had caused it to be blocked up long ago!

'Why has the corporation not closed this place?' Tadhg asked Ambrose Fitz John Darcy, another of the leather merchant's sons - kindly lads who were cousins to Ruaidhrí O'Flaherty. They stood staring at the strange people in this outlandish hole while Tadhg's fists clenched against the shrilling uproar.

'The corporation don't know of its existence,' Ambrose replied grinning.

'Of course, they know well,' one of the Browns contradicted him sarcastically, winking knowingly. 'They know if they seal it up someone will simply open another passage to the suburbs to take in strong drink for selling. They have planted a spy in here to see what's going on. He'll report every word of it to them before he goes to bed. He'll report what sort of people are in and what news he's after hearing. No one knows for sure who the spy is, but there's endless speculation. It allows them to find out information about what the warden's men and the apprentices are up to. Not to mention Burke, Kirwan and the rest of their crew and especially if undesirables sent by O'Neill are getting in and who they're involved with inside.'

'They collect a fine healthy tax for themselves from Master Potboy there, you see,' his brother added with a sly wink, nodding towards the elderly, balding man in charge of the serving, who was taking the money and shouting orders at serving men.

'Drink!' Francis Fitz Peter Brown said to his brothers, bringing two large, brimming pitchers of ale to where they were clustered at the end of a table. A man following him with tankards.

Later Tadhg recalled the profligate Francis telling a story he had heard from his grandfather.

'On the northern coast of Spain where my people owned land and wine depots, there was a great, white building in a garden full of fruit trees. My grandfather, a young boy on his first visit abroad with his father, saw the tall white house as they neared land and immediately took it for a palace. He tells the tale to this very day, how loud a seaman laughed at this and declared, pointing at the building, That's a hospital for seamen with the pox, lad! Keep on the outside of that place, if you know what's good for you!'

Toasts were raised by the apprentices, 'For the king Charles Stuart! For the Confederate Catholics! For the Nuncio from the Pope!' And all drained their tankards.

Tadhg wondered did he really imagine there was a passage through the walls or maybe it was that the students were filling him with lies, mocking him because he was from humble origins outside the town. In the midst of the merriment the quiet eyes of O'Flaherty looked down at the floor when things became too sharp, too uncivilised; a self-protective gesture he himself instantly recognised and he saw this in his troubled dreams for years afterwards.

Tadhg woke that night in the early hours to find himself in an upper room, roused by a stiff sea breeze from an ill-fitting window. He was lying between the brothers Dominic, Ambrose and Robert Fitz John Darcy, squashed on the bedstead, and the Darcys' cousin, Ruaidhrí O'Flaherty, at their feet - the woollen bedding pulled up to his mouth, with Oliver Morris the far side of Robert Darcy. Intricately carved wooden presses were outlined against the far wall. On a table in the corner, he made out in the moonlight an empty wine jar and the remains of bread and cheese upon which they had dined. He drew himself up to the window, opened it and looked down to behold the familiar vista of Cross Street, its house fronts gleaming under the full moon. He realised he was in John Darcy's house, cousin of Ruaidhrí's. He knew also he should be in the priests' residence under John Lynch's orders, not here in the rowdy company of students, sons of freemen, drinking and straining to go to war for faith and country, mainly because their fathers were in favour of cessation and settlement.

'Shut the window,' one of them shouted with a curse.

He shut it at once and scrambled over them and went out the door carrying his boots. He stepped quietly down the stairs in the darkness and was fumbling with the lock on the back door when, to his horror, a shape arose from between two bags of turf in the corner, whispering roughly 'Will you quit rattling that lock you *amadán*, before you bring the master down on top of us all,' and he heard the man turn a key stealthily. He rushed through the door and breathed again in the dim light of the lane as the door was locked behind him. Only then did he vaguely recall the arrangement the sons of the house had made with Ulick Óg the factor's son, whom they smuggled into the house to let them in when they returned in the early hours of the morning. Sickness came over him in waves and he nearly collapsed with the effort of pulling on his boots. Never again, he said to himself, hurrying around to Lombard Street where he was able to climb over the wall now there was no watchman around and knocked on Bodkin's window, praying he too was not abroad.

A warning tap on the window inside told Tadhg his friend was there, and a minute later Patrick opened the back door to admit him. With finger on lips and tiptoeing quickly past the locked stores of the gun room, he beckoned him into his narrow, ascetic cell containing only a bed and a crucifix on the wall, so they could talk.

'Aren't you my fine hearty fellow after all, to be drinking in the pothouse at the wall last night?' Bodkin said wide eyed, grinning, looking him up and down. 'I saw you there early in the night with lads from the school, the last person in town I expected to be out after all you've been through lately with John Lynch.'

He stared at him miserably, shaking with nausea.

'Go up to Mac Fhirbhisigh's room, very quietly mind! and I'll come up behind you to hold you in case you fall and wake the house with the clatter.'

He had no further recollection of kindly Patrick the guardian angel getting him up and into the room where he collapsed on the floor, in which unfortunate position Mac Fhirbhisigh found him the next day.

Ruaidhrí O'Flaherty:
Adolescence

he priests praised sea winds that aired the streets and soothed the boys' burning faces in times of fevers. The age-old cross borne by town dwellers since the days of the bible struck at will. They played down the infectious diseases, ever threatening in the stench of the back lanes and sewers, and the teeming, overcrowded suburbs.

Ruaidhrí, grown taller since his summer out in the fields, sat on brand new benches in the freshly distempered, high-ceilinged room of a fine house along with the students to read Latin and Greek. He made numerous imagined travels to storied places in those blessed years. The more his imagination ranged, the more everything around him seemed unreal. The masters brought the students through the *ratio studiorum:* syntax, the authors from Caesar to Horace, English, mathematics, history, geography, sacred doctrine, until they were poised at the door of the great orator Cicero. Outside, the old city walls were undergoing repair as they were raised and reinforced by the corporation.

The masters threw open the windows in fine weather. All had to listen to the lecture during the early years straining their ears above the unholy tumult of the works outside on the walls. Stones were raised higher and higher under the direction of the foreign engineer who had fought with O'Neill's regiment in Flanders. The width of the walls was greatly increased, and the defences of the gates strengthened. Sweating, ragged masons, porters and carpenters cursed and swore on the pull of the ropes, singing as the stones came up, oarsmen of the scaffolding. They cheered the mayor, short, angry Francis Fitz Oliver, when he clambered up on the ramparts with the councillors and officials, to praise or admonish them,

'Throw up those stones, ye *traithníní!* For the one true faith,' he shouted, 'for town and king!'

His muscles stood out like a bullock's as he dragged up stones and earth single-handed in buckets while the men shouted for him, 'She's up, in the name of God!' as the load came to rest on the rampart. The friars, brown and black, came daily from their nearby houses to recite prayers over the works, blessing the stones no heretic would ever breach.

Prepare yourselves to fight, they concluded each prayer, prepare for your death in defence of faith, king and town.

The most radical toilers on the ramparts and among the friars were undoubtedly the warden's men. Some of the students paid more heed to the business outside than the grammar and syntax of the orators. The top of the room was where Patrick Lynch instructed the rhetoricians, big fellows hunched on their benches, knees up to their chins. These lads rushed to the windows at the recess after the bell rang when Patrick Lynch had turned his back and left the room. They were like Persians before the Greeks, expert engineers of war assessing the repairs to the damage and the progress of the new additional reinforcements. They could gaze from the windows out at the fortifications from west to east and beyond to the English garrison's fort, now levelled. They revised every detail of the English treachery and bitterly lamented they were too young at the time to follow their hero, Dominic Kirwan. Older youths, grown men already, bent their heads before the wisdom of Aquinas and Aristotle in Stephen White's philosophy class and were too pious and stilted most of the time to pay much heed to the antics of the room next door.

They could see luckier friends out there promoted to captains, even Walter Óg himself, patrolling with the apprentices, cocks of the walk with musket, shot and sword. Their elders tried to admonish them for unfilial behaviour. Rowdy outbreaks continued to disrupt the place in this new world. The English were so unexpectedly driven out after keeping them crushed under their heel since Elizabeth's day, that the times went to their heads. Jack is as good as his master, now lamented the merchants every time they looked up and down the streets to be struck by the changed walk of the people, never mind the way they spoke every time they opened their mouths.

The freemen were fortifying the northern perimeters and the walls outside the school quarter quietened down. The older rhetoricians under master Patrick Lynch were tense and single-minded. Some turned against the others. The most radical were the seminarians from the college house who fell under the warden's influence.

Sometimes the Lynchs' man at the door ran in with his heavy blackthorn to drive fellows out of the house. They could be heard below in the street shouting in heated argument, the watch coming for them at a run, and they'd take to their heels like the sea wind coming in over *Ceann a' Bhaile*. If the monitors were slow to quell a riot in the house, the Jesuits' retainers could be seen with the glint of their swords as they ran towards the schoolhouse. The watch would come no further than the walls when the Jesuits were under arms. Ignatius's priests spread terror and awe with their powers and learning. Boys trembled at the threat of their wrath. Worst of all was the curse of a Jesuit. The old professor, Stephen White, whom they seldom saw, was said to be able to cure maladies and make prophecies. After he came into town the black sickness passed.

Ruaidhrí lodged, as always, with his mother's kinsman master Darcy, the merchant in Cross Street. His yard was full of casks and baled skins loaded between the servant house and tenancy, his leather shop dark and rank. Ruaidhrí had numerous relatives of his mother's kith and kin, the Darcys, freemen of the town. His maternal grandmother's people, the Kirwans, were strong in the town too. He had plenty connections, but he was not a seminarian bound for holy orders. Those youths kept inside the residence, prayed endlessly with the priests and fell out with no one, at least until they turned to open militancy. He was heir to his father's house and estate, a ward of the crown since Aedh had died before he could know him. He had to take his place in society, obey the law and mingle with good company. He kept his terrible vulnerability suppressed and hidden, receiving his instructions with bent head every year on his birthday when his self-assured and talkative guardians from the corporation met him to monitor his progress.

In quietness John Lynch addressed them. He held Ruaidhrí's attention like music, capturing the spirit with the gifted power of oratory which lives within. The voices of the ancients spoke to him when Lynch, his shiny face glistening in the heat, interpreted their words. The class was immersed in the writings of Caesar who witnesses the wars in Gaul and north Africa; in the historians Tacitus, Livy and Homer, who described the events of their day. Above all they embraced the eras of the world following the light of Christ in the works of Augustine, Tertullius and Ignatius who are the foundation stones of faith, the rock of the church.

One day, during the recreation in the yard, Ruaidhrí was deliberately struck at ball-play, a form of persecution which had died out once he had been accepted after his first year. Society within the walls had coarsened noticeably since the Rising, especially among the young men. Gangs at play shouted and clamoured on the day Ruaidhrí was assaulted violently by John Font, aided by the latter's young cousin, Oliver Skerrit. They charged him falsely with fraud over a matter concerning his family and with adherence to one of the factions outside town. This was not his affair, but he was vulnerable as he was not born and raised within the walls. He was accused of being a spy for the Irish who had returned from the continent with Eoghan Ruaidh, to lead the Rising, win religious freedom and recover church land seized by the Old English Protestants. Ruaidhrí had to challenge Font and they fought with fists. The priests stopped the antics when the commotion was heard in the oratory.

Font disappeared from town soon afterwards, moving north in O'Queely's party. Fortunately, Ruaidhrí's connections were excellent and his patronage in the school remained secure despite the incident.

The salt air of the bay was strong and sharp in their lungs when, on fine days, the students spent recreation outside the walls at the boys' swimming place. This was west along the canal bank where Gaillimh, the ancient chieftain's daughter, drowned. Across the bridge and fosse, the diverted channels of the river were cool and inviting,

The deep, rich, fermenting odours of the malting house competing with the stink of the river latrine waste brought him back to the present. Water rushed through dark rocks in shining cascades, its roar endless in the bubbling pools. Near this place the O'Hallorans traded in the port and his western ancestors maintained their fortification until the Normans seized it and built their settlement.

The big houses of the Blakes, Lynches, Morrises, Browns, Frenchs, Athys and Martins had armed men on their land out in 'the county of the town of Galway' and were so strong in the council that every word was carried to them. Warden Walter Lynch had turned St Nicholas's into '*a wooden horse,*' as a crowd called over the residence walls on one occasion, regarding the students to be all in Walter's party. The freemen saw to it however that the iron fist of Walter Lynch civilised his boys and kept the peace within their school room, regardless of what faction they were in. The pro-war faction was forced to conceal their military preparations outside the city. Walter struck terror in his students. Those destined for the priesthood coming up through Patrick Lynch's class wept at the thought of their future when they would be subject to the even stricter will of the Jesuits.

Ruaidhrí was adrift in an unsettled world from which he increasingly felt at odds.

One day Ruaidhrí visited his kinsman the wealthy Morogh na dTuath O'Flaherty in Aughnanure some miles along the lakeshore. Ruaidhrí sat at the table near the fire, feeling the fine linen of the tablecloth. Máire sat across from him smiling and happy to see him once again. The daughter of the house was grown up now, elegant and beautiful. They would be married when he was old enough to inherit his father's estate. Ruaidhrí had played with Máire many a summer during their childhood in the peaceful idyllic years before the war disrupted their times. Happy memories were treasured by an increasingly lost generation of which they were part. Yet the changes in her drew him to her, grown up like himself but still the same companion to whom he never had to explain himself, even from their childhood days.

'Tell us the news of the town, *a Ruaidhrí Óg Mac Aedh*, where you're the big scholar, well esteemed by the town people, as you say,' she said teasingly.

'Aren't you only a ward of the crown in that place?' her father interjected sourly. 'They gave no town privileges to your grandfather, who was a more learned man than any of them.'

Máire's mother, Síle Burke, spoke up to side with him.

'Isn't it all changed now with the red fighting of war bringing Gael and Gall together for the king? Hasn't the old Earl of Dungannon's two-handed sword been sent from Rome and a crown of gold is being crafted for the head of Eoghan Ruaidh?' Síle declared loudly to Morogh who only grunted, raise his eyes to heaven and said nothing more.

On his departure, Máire accompanied Ruaidhrí to the *bán* where he mounted the black stallion. He turned and waved goodbye to her at the gate and crossed the land back to Moycullen, grand and handsome as anyone in town.

The greatest news of all came when Malachy O'Queely, united with Walter and the Irish at war under O'Neill, announced their joint intention to launch an attack on the Parliamentary forces in Sligo. Events were overtaking them, and people felt the world was coming to an end.

In summer Ruaidhrí lay in the meadow reading the *Agricola* of Tacitus and met again the Celti tribes that Julius Caesar had known in Gaul during the exciting days of the Gallic wars. Here in Germania, a far cold northern land, other Celti tribes lived, people of the Gael witnessed by Tacitus. No one around the house bothered him with requests to bring cattle to the boolying or bring down sheep. He took no part in weapons practice outside the haggard with the young men and no one asked him to go hunting with the hounds. He was left in peace with his books, going on to explore the work of Titus Livius, the historian of Rome. Words and phrases appeared before him filled with insight and unity, moving in symmetry and beauty, shaping together images of the past gradually assembling into one.

Cicero was their hero and exemplar. 'Sed pleni omnes sunt libri, pleni sapientium voces, pleni exemplorum vetustas, quae iacerent in tenebris omnia, nisi litterarum lumen accederat.' He heard the words with pleasure, moving his eyes from the text on his knees to hear Lynch's rendering of the supreme orator's argument for the study of literature. 'Quam multas nobis imagines non solum ad intuendum verum etiam ad imitandum fortissimorum virorum expressas scriptores et Graeci et Latini reliquerunt.' Lynch continued reading the lines he had set for the construing. He had to shout above the noise of the other classes in the long, dark, low-ceilinged room. He raised his head and swept his eyes over his silent students, some of them tall as grown men.

Lynch nodded towards the towering, hunched bulk of Dominic Fitz John Darcy, sitting squeezed in beside Ruaidhrí and Francis Fitz Peter Brown, the slight, sharp-faced, ferret-like figure of great mischief and inquisitiveness.

'What is your interpretation of these lines of Cicero, Dominic Fitz John?' Lynch asked.

Dominic floundered lamely, clearing his throat while he frowned at the book on Ruaidhrí's knees, having lost his own crossing the river. Dominic stumbled to begin the denunciation, nudging Ruaidhrí for help.

Lynch prompted him, then said in encouragement as Dominic came to a full stop, 'See how you are presented with a declamation of power and cultivation, Dominic Fitz John. And note well the master's use of reason, of argument employed with force yet with such ease! In like manner you too will be called upon one day for disputation in the conduct of public affairs and to defend the true faith against the learned wiles of Satan.'

The priest's eye, wandering around the faces of the boys, fell on Ruaidhrí and he thought back how Ruaidhrí excelled at the disputation the last half holiday. Now the brightness in the lad's eyes revealed the fire concealed beneath the introverted exterior, eyes that were on his books, unlike poor Dominic Fitz John beside him.

'What do you say to our author, *a Ruaidhrí Óg mac Aedh?*'

Dominic Darcy sank back in relief as Brown's giggle was audible to the nearby boys but obscure to the master's ears in the din of the room.

'From Trooper Darcy to his cousin Aristotle O'Flaherty!' came the whispered riposte. Those who heard grinned and shook with suppressed laughter. Brown, a most troublesome lad, was busy whispering into the ear of the student seated on his other side. The sharp eyes of the master swept the row and Brown subsided in silence into his oversized jacket.

Singled out now, Ruaidhrí knew better than to reply that he preferred writers who described the events of their day, such as Caesar and Tacitus. Although they did not write with the power of Cicero, yet their greatness lay in the witness they bore to contemporary history. Fellows in the front row turned around to hear his reply, some winking at him in derision, knowing Lynch could not see their faces.

For safety, he repeated the often-heard statement,

'Cicero is one of the most outstanding of the orators in style and of the rhetoricians in his use of language, master.'

The master lit on this reply immediately, 'Is he not *the* greatest of them?'

Lynch moved to stand near where Ruaidhrí sat on his left in the middle row. Beside him Brown pinched him hard and trod on his foot, while his agile face stared up blankly at the leaning master. Ruaidhrí attempted to elbow him away. Put on the spot by Lynch, he felt his way slowly into his reply.

'Cicero is the greatest of the orators without doubt, but others such as Caesar, Tacitus, Livy are also great authors excelling in handing down the affairs of their times.'

Lynch seemed to understand. 'Would you not rate Livy to be the greater of those historians you mention?'

He watched carefully along with the silent class, while Ruaidhrí, singled out, gathered his courage to reply.

'Their style is not the most developed in argument or embellishment in rhetoric. But their strength lies in writing what they saw, so that their value lies in their authority as historians.'

A few boys muttered agreement when they heard this point, nodding and whispering among themselves. Lynch held up a hand and walked up and down in the confined space between the rows of boys and the wall. Ruaidhrí let out a sigh of relief and tried to kick Francis's foot away as Lynch answered him.

'Rodericus Flahertius has raised an important, though of course debatable, point. He refers to the distinction between the style of the author and the witness he offers of the affairs of his time, that is the content, in this case of history. But many authors past and present write of sacred doctrine, mathematics, science, medicine, geography and so on, for their content. Some achieve superiority of style and power of language, others do not.

'Now consider this carefully: is an argument or a factual account more effective if couched in powerful language? Or is not? And if your answer is, it is more effective, then consider *what* makes it effective. And finally consider Cicero's use of language – how is it rendered powerful?'

John Lynch encouraged frequent debates in this way, giving all the boys an opportunity to take part. Was Livy greater among the writers of antiquity because he bore witness to his times? Is authority elevated in historical value? Wherein does the power of speech lie?

'Syntactical skill!' they shouted in reply to the latter question. 'Learned references! Multiple clauses! Balance! Rhetorical questions! The marshalling of argument!'

Lads of the Darcys, Lynches, Deanes, Morrises, Frenchs, Kirwans were seldom defeated. One of them leapt to his feet and shouted, 'The structuring of points so clearly that refutation is forestalled!'

'No, no! sureness of weight and truth as Rodericus has said,' their brothers shouted, pushing and jostling rowdily until the monitor came over to quieten them.

'How will you defend your gift of the true faith against its enemies if, unlike Cicero, you are unable to defend it in argument?' Lynch cried as usual. 'Observe well the reasoning, tactics and style used by the master - argument of force couched in ease.'

He continued, 'I have always asked you to bend your young hearts and minds to the eras of the world in which Peter's rock of faith, hope and love was founded. This troubled modernity stirs the foundations beneath us while our enemies gather against us. The heretic hoards from Britain and the Continent are attacking our native church, denigrating our records and the lives of our saints. All authority and all argument come down to us from God, the true source, the one argument.'

Ruaidhrí noticed Dominic Darcy walk from school in the company of Edmond Fitz Oliver Skerrit, son of the locksmith. Whispering close together, they hurried into Oliver's shop located in the same street as the school. Ruaidhrí did not know the consequences of the headstrong Dominic's latest piece of mischief that fateful day. Dominic never confided his plan to Ambrose and Robert, the younger brothers. Later they blamed this on the fact Dominic would have been afraid he, Ruaidhrí, would hear them whispering and carry the news to their father.

A few days later when the lads rose at dawn there was no sign of Dominic in the bed. It was clear he had gone in the night. Suspicion and terror filled the house and threw the business of the day into chaos, until Cousin John's stableman, Ulick Óg, came running and shouting to confirm the worst. Not only had Dominic Fitz John fled to join O'Queely's campaign but he was gone on one of his father's horses. No one discovered for a long time how Dominic had managed to get out that night. It was when Ambrose and Robert's friends discovered the delights of the drinking house at the wall that the two lads decided to check the windows in an effort to get out to join them.

There it was a sliver of metal inserted in the lock of a back window which prevented it locking properly. Then Ruaidhrí remembered Dominic's surreptitious visit to the locksmith with Edmond a few days before he ran away to the war.

Ruaidhrí progressed in his studies through the school ranks with honours. In the summer days he went home to see his family. One summer holiday, during the latter years of his schooling, John Lynch announced he would visit Moycullen. 'I would like to accompany you Ruaidhrí on your visit to your family.'

Ruaidhrí looked surprised. Lynch continued, 'I want to hear the language of the mountains again which I heard abroad in France in my youth. I held many a conversation with priests from the rural west. I would like to visit the holy churches and wells of the ancient saints of the diocese of Tuam.'

Lynch was on a personal journey into the old Irish faith that summer. Ruaidhrí understood this when looking back on it years afterwards.

'We'll take the horses instead of going on the Woodquay boats,' Lynch said. Ruaidhrí's heart filled with happiness and pride as they set out across the river one fine, sunny morning through the western gate over the drawbridge, the dew still on the grass.

The household met them at the door to welcome Lynch, who delighted in hearing the language of the country people all around him.

'I don't come out to these beautiful parts often enough with the vicars. I hear them always praising the beauty of the countryside and the hospitality of the people when they return from their duties out here,' he told them.

Lynch slept soundly and happily in a simple feather bed in the guest room. Next morning, he swam with Ruaidhrí in the lake. He visited the old and the sick in the houses followed by a crowd of the local people hearing of his visit. On Sunday he blessed newly married couples and celebrated mass in the village.

'The old hospitality is the best of all,' he cried, drinking buttermilk and savouring fresh salmon at the table when they returned from the church.

That summer together they traversed Ruaidhrí's patrimony, West Connacht from the lake to the mountains and down to the sea and its islands, the old divisions of Gnómór and Gnóbeag. The priest heard with his own ears stories from local priests of sacred places where saints once lived and performed their miracles.

He knelt down in his good black silk coat on the heather to drink holy well water and he prayed with such fervour in the ancient church ruins that when the strong sea wind whipped his hat from his head he did not notice. Ruaidhrí became alarmed.

'Why are you praying so earnestly, master?'

'I'm praying to the early saints of the west for strength to carry out my mission in the coming darkness.'

Lynch's grimness froze Ruaidhrí as he sat on the turf bank outside the old cemetery, wind blowing in their faces from the sun-filled sea and sky. The lad had heard terrible news of the church's enemies abroad, the followers of Luther and Calvin who attacked its very foundations with relentless determination. This was the first indication he heard that their glory days of freedom might not last forever.

They walked the horses down a dried, stony, hillside road where women with children descended, bent under the load of bags of turf roped on their backs. Soon the sun shone on John Lynch, and he looked around for his hat. Ruaidhrí had it in his hand and wordlessly gave it to him. Lynch did not speak again until they returned to the house and a cousin brought him wine. He lifted the cup to Ruaidhrí, saying, 'One day you will wear my hat, *a Ruaidhrí a stór,*' addressing him in the indigenous way.

'Will I be a priest, master Lynch?' he asked, wondering with dismay who then would succeed him in his father's place where they were sitting, looking out over fields full of cattle.

'You will walk in the ways of learning under the light of the Lord. You will follow the mission of our church in the refutation of lies presented against our saints by heretics in Britain and Europe.'

He fell silent reading his prayer book, while the dogs of the house scratched at his feet on the shiny, fresh rushes covering the floor.

Ruaidhrí had first learned his Latin and Greek in his father Aedh's house in Moycullen from the priest who lived with them. The grammar was in the small, black, leather-covered books. New ways and wonders were piling up for him, knowledge gathered up in sweet-smelling ricks, stored dry for the winter, new words shaping themselves.

Town men and women frequently came ashore on the lakeside quay, carrying out their dealings regarding rentals, cattle sales and land stocking - relatives of his who always visited the house. They brought words in the English language, sounding stuttered, loud and unmusical to his childish ear. He did not remember when they began remarking that he was like his grandfather. It seemed to have become a general agreement wherever he looked.

One terrible summer's day, his father's relatives, in a fever of determination, brought him down to a field beside the river that flowed into the lake. Near it stood a shambles house, where animals were slaughtered. They wanted to show him the exact spot where Ruaidhrí Mór's father - the original Morogh na dTuath and a great warrior - had cut down the men from across the lake in a decisive and bloody victory. The relatives had long awaited to arrange Ruaidhrí's encounter with his family's history and their present expectations of him. The occasion was now right as his stepfather, John Bermingham, had left to visit his family's residence in Tuam. He had supported Clanricarde in opposing the Rising in Connacht and was deemed highly untrustworthy by his late wife's family.

This battle was the reason Ruaidhrí Óg's family were still in possession of their stone house and arable land on the western shore.

'Let you remember who you are lad, for your own sake and for all of us who are facing this new war,' they said sternly, as they stood around him, staring in hostility.

Ruaidhrí was told, yet again, how, years before, this Morogh had hired gallowglass mercenaries. Whoever could afford to commission these fearless soldiers with their long-handled battle axes had success in armed conflict. This earned Morogh the title Morogh of the battleaxes. His cousin in Aughnanure, in turn, was also so named. Ruaidhrí's relatives talked pointedly for hours about the former Morogh's success, the debt they all owed him and how the hour of need had come around again. Their war talk rang in Ruaidhrí's ears, filling him with thoughts of failure and disaster as he fled as soon as he could.

During late autumn, when the street outside the shambles house ran with blood, he thought of the killings in that river meadow as the carcasses and hides were sold and the rendering fat in the tallow vessels was boiled. Its odour sickened him, and the men smelt of blood afterwards at mass.

Ruaidhrí's teacher, John Lynch, began spending more time in his residence in Tuam when St Nicholas's famously became 'Troy of old,' as opposing groups shouted and wrangled in the streets. He lived for the sake of peace and quietness in the archdeacon's house near the cathedral, travelling in and out to town for his duties there. He was a man who stood outside society as it reshaped itself into opposing factions. He read the mass in the big house of Sir Richard Blake, the leading man in town society, out in 'the county of the town of Galway.' On the Blake estate Lynch was chaplain to the family where he had his own room and stables. In town he carried out choir duties as vicar of St Nicholas's, as well as teaching his classes in the school.

War had been swirling around England, Scotland and Ireland when circumstances brought Dubhaltach Mac Fhirbhisigh to Galway. Ruaidhrí remembered the day he first heard Lynch speak of Mac Fhirbhisigh. He had heard references to the Mac Fhirbhisighs long before from his father's friends. These people were celebrated hereditary chroniclers and genealogists, recording for numerous families descended from Daithí throughout all Connacht.

Lynch said of Mac Fhirbhisigh, 'If we did not have Livy we would have understood extraordinarily little of Rome's history when the rock of faith was established in that city.' Later Ruaidhrí understood what John meant by this comparison.

One day after mass, Lynch come over to him to shake hands and enquire about his family and how his studies were progressing. That was when Ruaidhrí asked him how the ancients of Hibernia could have known about the keeping of calendars.

'There was no Roman calendar before Caesar, Rodericus,' Lynch explained. 'But civilisation didn't begin with the Romans. They built upon what had existed before them; earlier writers who had dated their years, noted eclipses, storms, plagues and the reign of kings, wars, invasions, as Livy did. The Egyptians did this, as did the Jews, the Syrians. In the case of the Scoti or Gael, who occupied Ireland and Scotland, we must apply similar reasoning. The ancients before them had a way of calculating time which subsequently became obsolete.'

'What was that method, master?' he had persisted.

'We don't know, but as the ollamh Mac Fhirbhisigh tells us, the method was carried out with exact precision, whether they used a solar or a lunar system or both.'

The Opening Door

One day when Ruaidhrí was in the upper rank of his schooling he lingered after class waiting for John Lynch in the garden leading onto the street. As he became older, he felt increasingly driven by curiosity over the question of the native historical sources being studied and debated by his elders. He wanted to learn more about what it was about. It was late afternoon while he delayed in the company of youths whose habit it was to pray and talk, sheltering in dry spots beneath trees surrounding the courtyard.

Listening to their conversation was disquieting. These fellows said Malachy O'Queely, the warden and the Irish at war under O'Neill were gaining such strength and influence that soon they would convince town and county into uniting with them in all-out war against the Parliamentarians. Encampments were growing in the regions north of the city as their numbers grew. The dogs in the streets know O'Queely has no chance against Coote, they cried.

'All his crowd will achieve is to brand us all as rebels and destroy our only hope, the truce under Ormond.' They became more and more worked up.

'My father said they have taken over every single crossroads from Tuam all the way into Mayo, so his factors down that country can't travel the roads anymore without being robbed with knives put to their throats,' one of the lads said. 'Our agent abandoned his house beside the depot and fled into Galway with his wife and family after his life was threatened.'

'They are creating an unforgivable barrier growing higher and stronger against the truce, throwing all of us into danger, the loyal, such as ourselves, as well as the rest,' another student declared. 'All they want is to see the Parliament's army destroy us so they can seize the country.'

They shifted and fidgeted full of nervous energy after a day pent-up in the class hall and glancing frequently over at him as Ruaidhrí sat on the edge of the wet bench against the wall, as far from them as possible in the confined garden.

'Blake sent his chaplain, John Lynch, out to Tuam to spy on that recreant Malachy and report back to himself in Ardfry, so he can keep our allies in Kilkenny clearly informed of their treachery,' said one of the Skerrets loudly in a carrying voice. He nodded his head towards the opened door of the school where Lynch was conferring with the masters in the passageway. Skerret simultaneously rolled a jaundiced eye towards Ruaidhrí.

'And then what do we see? Only this country fellow over there eavesdropping, spending his time listening at doors to everything the masters say. He can report it to his savage relatives out in the bogs and let them in with their knives during the night,' Skerret added darkly.

Every head turned to stare at Ruaidhrí in a most unfriendly manner, their eyes narrowed and hostile. He sat up a little higher on his bench and declared strongly that he did not gather any information or carry any messages whatsoever to anyone. He had to appear unafraid, calm and collected in company such as these young men, greatly disadvantaged as he was by not being born among the freemen. They didn't believe his reply, needless to say, jumping up and throwing their books at him, jeering that the O'Flahertys were allied with O'Neill, that Malachy was raising all Connacht attempting to destroy the Duke of Ormond's representations for Ireland with the king.

'They'll overturn our chance of peace,' Skerret said, pointing his finger at Ruaidhrí threateningly. His family was part of the powerful faction lead by Sir Richard Blake. The group under the trees grew angrier, snatched up their scattered books and soon left in search of the warden's men, 'to break some heads', they shouted.

'The spy can watch Lynch's affairs and send the news out to Morogh na dTuath, his kinsman!' they sneered.

'The curse of White on you!' Ruaidhrí called after them, roused into anger. '*Marbhfháisc oraibh!*'

He was fortunate they kept going, leaping and jostling through the garden, shouting insults until they disappeared down the street. Ruaidhrí had seen White, the professor, one day in the walk on the Strand, as old as Methuselah enveloped in his Jesuit gown, the Lynchs supporting his unsteady steps. The old man had the calmest face and the clearest eyes as he gazed at the world, not the eyes of the devil. Sitting under the wet trees the boy wondered how peace and happiness could ever be found in this world outside the cloisters of the religious who had turned their backs on its dreadfulness. This option could never be available to the heir of West Connacht.

When he saw Lynch eventually emerge, he arose in relief and asked if he could talk to him.

'You may Ruaidhrí. I'm going across town now on business but do accompany me,' John said, heading briskly towards the gate with his energetic stride. As they turned the corner of the street a young militiaman hurrying from the other direction collided into them with an oath. On seeing the clerical clothes, the militiaman pulled himself short with a muttered apology and shouldered his way head down past them into the adjoining lane.

'Who was that?' Lynch was staring angrily at the man, disappearing into the gloom of the narrow lane, 'who passes so boorishly through these civil streets?'

Lynch looked at Ruaidhrí.

'I didn't recognise that face. Did you?'

'No, sir, I didn't either.'

'I take it he is one of those young cocks who nightly crow on the walls, flapping their wings and stretching their necks to let us all know they are there looking down on us. I will find out who he is and have him censured by the constables. Such insubordination that has come into this town has never been known before in our records. The corporation is passing new by-laws to hopefully contain this unprecedented unrest.'

The neglected aspects of the streets obviously displeased Lynch greatly as well. He began a monologue about Galway's former days of trade and prosperity when its houses were first laid out and embellished and cargoes in great numbers were transported in and out of the quays before Wentworth's time. He was recently witnessing a lack of civility among strangers mingling with the population since the fighting had erupted, he declared. The priest greeted his fellow town people kindly whenever he passed them in the street or glimpsed faces at their doors as they hurried by. The smell of the fish market near the western gate carried through the streets as they passed, cartloads of fish brought by men working on weirs under the bailiff's supervision not far upriver from the walls. Housewives and white-aproned servants examined the display of eel, salmon, trout, shellfish and sea fish fresh off the Claddagh boats. Wretched, poorly dressed, barefoot women from the country sat on the ground beside baskets of mackerel. Beggars and the poor of the suburbs moved through the bustle aimlessly. Robed friars coming out of their house nearby in pairs, beads swinging from their belts, were immersed in the overwhelming odour of fish as soon as their door closed behind them.

'Every age has been troubled in some manner, I suppose. It would be difficult for the young to know of respect when clergy and religious are brawling with each other in the streets in broad daylight,' Lynch said, steering Ruaidhrí through the market when the boy nearly walked under a water-carrier's cart, confused with trying to listen to him as he hurried along.

Lynch had his finger on the pulse of the world.

'Business has declined since trade routes in the enemy areas and depots fell into the heretics' hands. Trade is reduced to local exchanges of essential supplies which are scarce at that. Dubious vessels, on God only knows what business, are being reported arriving and departing in darkness on Trá Bhán down the coast. Our Confederated Catholics control the country only in Leinster and Munster where mass is read in the churches again. The Supreme Council's barely cresting the stormy waves in Kilkenny, split between Ormond's faction and the war party, and if we don't tread carefully, we'll all sink in the depths together.'

'Yes, master'.

This was not what Ruaidhrí wanted to discuss with Lynch.

'We in Connacht are still fortunate to be able to get on with life. For the present anyway.'

Lynch fell silent, brooding, and this gave him the opening to ask, 'What are you reading these days, master?'

Ruaidhrí had his attention at last, causing him to slow down, looking into the lad's face silently. This gave the beggars, another new sight, the chance to crowd in front of the priest in supplication. Lynch gave them some coins and they blessed him and left their path.

'I'm studying the history of the Irish church, its saints, dioceses, monasteries, bishops and abbots and its missions abroad on the Continent in earlier ages. Keating's account needs to be subject to a fair amount of critical expansion and additional sources need to be obtained to aid us.'

The priest was suddenly interrupted by cattle being driven down the lanes from the market to the shambles. They were herded by tall, black-haired and red-haired men of the Joyces, strong as oxen themselves, who greeted Lynch as they ran. Lynch and Ruaidhrí stood in a doorway until they passed. Strange people ran behind them, barefoot, never speaking and faces of new lodgers peered from doors of carpenter, wheelwright and shoemaker shops, averting their eyes when looked at.

'I knew everyone here in my boyhood before I went to university in France,' Lynch told him wistfully, looking up and down the street. While they sheltered in the doorway from running beasts, Ruaidhrí said to Lynch,

'I'd like to learn more about work on the historical sources, if it please you, master.'

'Is that so, Ruaidhrí? I'm glad to hear that and not surprised such an outstanding student would be so interested! I marked you out from an early age for the work in the refutation of heresy. Did I not tell you once that you would walk in my footsteps! I'll find plenty work for you transcribing, in faith!'

'I would like to examine the history of the Celti as well,' he said, persisting.

But Lynch was staring at a man and woman with a cartload of turf concealed under straw, half hidden under an archway.

'Those rogues are selling way above the settled prices on account of the scarcities,' he muttered, studying them. 'Hoarding and profiteering since the war has got out of hand.'

Lynch peered towards a group of men watching the couple from Cross Street.

'I declare the constables are on to them but they're not challenging them. Ah! I see the regulator coming from the gate to check their licence. The Celti, you say? Come with me, I've business with James Fitz Andrew before the gates close.'

'I've heard there are disputes about the ancient Irish historical accounts,' Ruaidhrí said, not without hesitation, wondering would he too appear to be getting above himself like the young militiamen, involving himself in the business of his elders. A smile lit the priest's face however at this question and he replied with pleasure in his voice, 'That argument is being debated by some of our professors, so it's not surprising you've been hearing it. We have the foremost of the antiquarians here, well capable of making a lot of noise between them!'

The last of the cattle ran through the narrow streets, loud bellows and shouts of the men filling the foul-smelling air. Lynch pulled some loose pages from books he carried under his arm and occupied himself with them. When the cattle passed on their final journey before entering the shambles, Lynch waved the pages and tucked them away carefully.

'These pages are from the hand of Dubhaltach Mac Fhirbhisigh who ploughs the unturned furrow in our field, enabling us to light the early darkness,' he said. 'He is our Livy, our native historian of the early Christian and the pre-Christian eras of Ireland.'

Then Lynch lifted his coat to rush through the ordure of the wet streets, muttering in unpriestly language about the laxity of street sweepers, while Ruaidhrí ran to keep up with him. In the next street Lynch called over his shoulder for him to admire a house they were passing, something he often did.

'See that!' he pointed to an imposing doorway elegantly set into the beautiful front wall of a three-story house.

'Italianate!' he cried, 'marbled and castellated two hundred years ago by our ancestors. Look at those carvings and engravings!'

The city's buildings were a well-known wonder.

They hurried on. After a pause, Lynch continued, 'We have examined the classical authors who bore witness to their contemporary events, Cicero, Plato, Homer, St Augustine, Caesar, Tacitus, Livy. A great debate is underway among the masters since we began in recent years examining native Irish authors in our work. What's happened is we're forced to cast serious doubts on the historical veracity of many early accounts. We are up against the assertions of the heretical authorities such as Camden, attacking our early accounts and unfortunately, these heretics have the ear of the learned men of Europe. We are conversant with the modern works of writers such as Scalinger and Helvetius and the way they opened up ancient eras for us with sound reasoning. Their work in its exactness is admirable, even if it champions the Protestants.

'Our aim is to employ in our work the fruits of all existing modern research and scholarship from whatever side of the divide. We hope when our various works are complete, they will be printed and distributed far and wide abroad.'

He shook his head, clutching his books, saying, out of breath: 'The trouble is some of these guidelines validate the ancients' accounts and some of them don't!'

Ruaidhrí said, 'The classical authors in their accounts witnessed the Celts, the Suebi, the Picts and the Gauls. When their accounts are examined considering our native Irish accounts and if they differ, what then is the truth? And what if no foreign writer witnessed our early events? Or if they wrote falsely about our history?'

The lad followed the priest into a wider street away from the markets where the houses were of the sort that excited Lynch's admiration. At that moment, the master had other worries.

'So how can we find the truth if the classical authors haven't concurred with the native authors of this country?' Ruaidhrí tried again.

'If we knew that we'd have the debate settled in the morning,' Lynch said shortly. 'I'll tell you the kernel of the problem. It is that no one can be certain of the reliability of the earliest accounts except those of holy scripture. That's the centre of the storm that's blown up in Galway, whether it is when early Romans are describing what they saw or whether it's the early Irish historians, we must take careful stock. We ought to approach all such chronicling with humility, reasoning and wisdom.

'The work of the professors in Galway is enlightened, comprehensive research of the Christian era for the absolute glory of the one true faith.

'Listen', Lynch continued, 'we can only pity the darkness and idolatry of the pagans who lived before the time Christ walked among men. The illumination of God, cast on the world in reflected glory by the Son, flourished in the centuries on our own island after Patrick's mission began the early growth of faith.

'Of course, we don't ignore the strange heathen days of early antiquity nor the many accounts of those eras. We can examine them all, in various parts of the world, from the accounts in the Irish sources, the far northern regions, imperial Greece and Rome, the migrations of the Jews, the eastern tribes, the fables of the southern countries.

'But truth? You asked me about truth! I'll tell you about truth! Truth lies only in the witness of the prophets and the saints. We must treat the early Irish chronicles before Patrick as eras of which no man can be certain, Ruaidhrí. The exact same as the pagan classical accounts.'

105

They were by then approaching the merchant James Fitz Andrew French's large, beautiful house, its wares displayed at the door. Great rolls of cloth were beacons of colour lighting the greyness of the street.

Before Ruaidhrí could say goodbye to Lynch, the latter took hold of his arm, saying,

'Numerous fascinating accounts are handed down to us in this country of the days of darkness. Our own native Irish teachers are versed in many interesting, detailed, complex accounts and stories of the strange, early, heathenish eras. That is fact and we do not ignore those early annals. We subject them to modern critical study. It's also true the Romans never conquered Ireland, calling us Hibernia 'the isle of eternal winter.' The Romans left us bereft of eyewitness accounts of the tribes on our own island, they who knew so well the European tribes. However, it's by no means improbable they did visit our shores and may even have established trading posts. We know Christians were living in Ireland before Patrick's mission, we may speak of Palladius and also St Ursula in this context.'

The merchant's wife, a small, elegantly dressed lady, peered at them from the entrance of the clothier's shop. Behind her tailors and apprentices were busy with paper designs and materials while seamstresses sewed, heads bent at the window.

'The Greeks as well as the Romans knew about us too, of course. Let me see. You will read Ptolemy, the second century astronomer and geographer of Alexandria who described and mapped Ireland. Have you heard of him?'

The name thrilled Ruaidhrí. 'I've heard him praised as a great authority, master.'

'Hum!' said the master, 'that's another day's work! Procure the text in the collegiate library. You'll have my authorisation for it. We'll see how you get on with our friend Ptolemy for a start and then we'll talk again. We might raise a disputation on him yet with some of the students!'

The woman stepped into the street, small children holding her skirt of deep green velour as Lynch turned to her and bowed. She was short and plump, fair hair escaping from her fine lace headdress.

'I bid you good day, mistress Catherine! I crossed the street to see master James. Is he within?'

The lady curtsied.

'How pleasant to see you, master John. Too seldom we see you! I trust you and all your family are keeping well. We hear you're occupied a great deal in Tuam and in town with the students. Yes, indeed, James is home.'

Mistress Catherine was busy by then looking Ruaidhrí up and down.

'Who's this? I know the face from mass!'

'The young man who's heir to Moycullen, Roderic O'Flaherty, the late Elizabeth Darcy's son.'

'Ah, sure I knew her well and all her family, may she rest in peace. A most graceful, tranquil retreat, your residence by the lake!' The woman's head nodded, her eyes still on him.

'So, this is the lad! A grand, tall lad! Step in!'

Ruaidhrí had entered the hidden ways of the Irish antiquarians.

He also entered the realms of the wealthiest freemen because before he knew what was happening, Lynch had seized his arm and escorted him through an archway beside the shop, just as he was about to head off on his business. From the stone courtyard they were shown by a servant through a hall to master James's room. It was richly furnished and comfortable. A beautiful, patterned carpet covered the floor, and the head of a great antlered stag was set in magnificent dominance above the fireplace.

James Fitz Andrew came in, strong, stocky, grey-haired, impeccably dressed, bidding them in English to be seated. The weak sun shining between the showers gleamed on his large window which was draped with blood-red curtains. The servant who had shown them in reappeared with wine which he served in large crystalline goblets more beautiful than any Ruaidhrí had ever seen. Master and servant both had the characteristics of town people: practical, definite, self-assured, cultured, more for this world than the next, their strength in their hands and their calmness of head.

Ruaidhrí soon fell into a daydream sailing before the winds of the Mediterranean Sea with Ptolemy pointing to the evening star and taking readings with his compass. He sat in a comfortable chair beside the window half-listening to the talk, savouring the heavy glass of wine.

'I'm right glad to see you, John!'

'Thank you kindly, James. Good health!'

'Good health John! Because we're all agog for any crumb of news from the Supreme Council, and I declare to the highest heavens if Blake isn't avoiding us like the plague! Surely to God, he hasn't taken it into his head that we've joined the band behind the skirts of his cousin, the *gom* Valentine, and placed ourselves in Walter Lynch's militia! Speaking of which, since archbishop O'Queely rose out with his rabble, heaven protect us, Walter, and his allies, not to mention certain rowdy, lowly-bred Franciscans and Capuchins, have organised militant crowds who assemble every evening at St Nicholas's and these gatherings are growing more riotous and unruly every day. Our complaints have gone before the mayor and by God, another is on its way to Tuam, I might add. I'm indeed glad to be able to say it to you to your face, John. Our misfortunes are piling up around our ears in town and county, thanks to Walter and his ally, Valentine Blake, and I could name twenty more in that faction who should have no business being seen dead among such a crowd. See here! Let no nose from Tuam poke its way into our affairs to make a bad story worse.'

'Ah! I ...'

'Yes, yes, forgive me. I am wholeheartedly assured that you of all people support the truce. But we don't hear your voice being raised aloud in condemnation of the unlicensed rabble such as we are hearing loud and clear from your kinsman Francis Kirwan. We want your condemnation of them raised at Kilkenny and sent to Rome. Here, let me pour you more wine, drink up, good health! The lad! Hold out your glass, young Moycullen! Good health! So, my dear John, what do you suppose the people around here imagine you're getting up to in Tuam, cossetted out of sight with your mad archbishop?'

'The projects of studious works we've on hand will take us several years yet, James. The Supreme Council has pressurised us to get our refutations into print as soon as possible. Every available assistance has been acquired for our work. We've been like the hare before the hounds for a generation, that's the extent of the lead the heretics have on us now. Yourselves in the corporation know about heretical assaults only recently in comparison to us, for as you know James, we are soldiers of the Lord! If we don't get ourselves into print soon, it will be too late in the heavenly battle for souls and the avoidance of scandal at home and abroad. I would need to be seconded from the school, but circumstances make that impossible with the increase in students. I'm pressed in my engagements to Blake and Lady Blake these days. In fact, I've got here…'

'I agree heart and soul with the refutation of heresy! I wish to God all the clergy confined their activities to such pious worthy labours …what have you got there?'

'I have here a document outlining details of a request from the Session to be submitted to Galway corporation. It's merely a letter that Sir Richard wants forwarded for the freemen's consideration. He bade me put it into your hands…excellent claret James.'

'Blake is unable to come in with it himself, is he? What in God's name is this?'

'News of another loan mooted by the Confederation in their desperation for financial guarantees. They are offering good terms as you can see.'

'We are robbed blind and stripped naked until we haven't the shirt left on our backs! Do they consider the one thousand sterling my lord Clanricarde levied on us before he lifted his siege? That the dog Willoughby burned every house from here to Oranmore above our tenants' heads and drove off every beast? That we have boats in dry harbour under repair after the attacks on us? And what about the fortune being spent on the new fortifications?'

'Yes, yes. We are witness to terrible times.'

'And what exactly is the latest news from Kilkenny, from one that has the whisper of the Speaker of the Council himself Sir Richard Blake? Seeing as our sheriff and bailiffs must collect the rents to invest straight into that crowd's purse, I want to know what exactly *they* are doing for us in return?'

'The hierarchy are still at odds over the articles of peace and therefore there is no progress. Elsewhere good news: the king's offer of complete religious toleration has been confirmed recently. The churches will remain open, public office will be open to us, Parliament will be called to ratify the treaty. The rumours of late have all been confirmed.'

'Nevertheless, all I see in this part of the world of late are rabble-rousers who find these terms unacceptable and committed to advocating all-out war on England.'

'That is so. Opposition is gathering to these terms. They've heard in Kilkenny that the envoy from the Pope, residing here with us in Galway, is expected to maintain his unwavering position in urging Ireland to reject the treaty out of hand. That this person will never countenance a settlement in which Ormond is appointed Lord Lieutenant of the country, without compromise, because he is a Protestant. It's unbelievably difficult, this situation we find ourselves in.'

'Why has that Nuncio been let in here in the first place? Who is responsible for that piece of misfortune? Walter Lynch of course, who else! Isn't O'Neill the Nuncio's client general in the field and he is pouring the Pope's money into O'Neill's pockets? I wonder is the bold Walter looking for a share of that gold too. We've no other hope of peace or settlement except Ormond, even if he is a Protestant. The truce settlement must be legalised. We have no other position if we are to retain our land and standing!'

'It's difficult to comprehend the point of view of the archbishop's faction, leading men into battle against far superior forces that cannot be defeated in military terms. O'Neill is in the field in contact with them, and he is trying to raise support abroad in Spain and France, another great uncertainty.'

'We don't want that man declaring himself king of Ireland. Ormond must be the one negotiating for us to keep O'Neill out of the picture. Neither do we want O'Neill bringing in invasion forces from his friends on the continent. We will do everything we can to block him bringing in foreign forces into this country.'

'The Parliament will sweep us before them if they take us in arms. The Ormond peace has to hold, so we've room to manoeuvre before things come to that.'

'That is all we need to give ourselves a chance. Do you know, we'll soon all be branded as rebels? The innocent as well as the guilty! I can't sleep at night anymore, John. Well, it's enlightening talking to yourself. How is it, though, whenever anyone asks John Lynch for his opinion, he inevitably replies that he abhors war but is wary of negotiating with heretics?'

'You can never believe all you hear, James,' said Lynch levelly, rising and bowing to his scowling host, who unceremoniously bade him sit down again and drink with him.

Ruaidhrí too quickly sat down again.

He was soon sorry they had not left at that point because mistress Catherine came in serving even more wine and came straight over to him in his corner beside the window, sitting down beside him and pulling over a chair. She stared into his face as if she had never seen a person before, muttering, 'I can see resemblance to your poor mama in your face, yes, just as you turn towards the light.' He cringed.

She began then asking him question after question about his stepfather, caressing his arm as if he were a child and paid him so many compliments his head was spinning, already muddled with wine.

'You are the eldest boy, Roderic?'

'I'm the only boy, mistress.'

'How old were you when your poor father died?'

'I was two years old.'

'How old are you now?'

'I'm going on seventeen, mistress.'

'And you were made ward of the crown. Have you any sisters?'

'I have four sisters.'

'Four young ladies in your house! And how carefully you're being brought up and educated! Remember me kindly to your cousin John Fitz Stephen. Where've they been hiding you? You must dine with us soon, my dear Ruaidhrí.'

And mistress Catherine slipped gracefully into the Irish, as fluent and as natural as her English.

When it was time for Lynch to get going before the shutting of the gates, they arose to Ruaidhrí's relief, full of good wine and conversation, unsteady of step.

Ruaidhrí asked to be shown to the small house as they were taking their leave. James Fitz Andrew's servant brought him down to the back door and pointed it out to him. The man waited for him until he returned from the privy, talking over his shoulder to people in the kitchen, falling silent on his approach. The lad heard his name mentioned through the open windows giving out to the garden as he drew near. Following the man indoors he noted two women were peering from the kitchen door who blessed themselves as he passed.

Within the gloom of the kitchen a voice could be heard declaring,

'Who let the likes of that into a Christian house?' and face burning, he hurried up the stairs after the silent, expressionless servant. I will never be accepted in this town, he thought, heart

111

pounding, the haze of wine blending into anger and humiliation in his head.

The happy face of John Lynch beamed at Ruaidhrí, his cheeks crimson and eyes bright while putting on his hat, his hand out to take his arm. The beating of his heart slowed as they hurried off into the heavy rain. Ruaidhrí's breathing calmed and the pain of mortification eased. He had his own friends who accepted and understood him and that was all that mattered in this vale of tears. He accompanied Lynch as far as the northern gate before the clock above it chimed the hour. Lynch's man, Turlach, waited with the horses.

The sun broke out through the clouds over the sea as the rain lifted.

'Wouldn't it be grand, Ruaidhrí,' Lynch said light-heartedly before he mounted, flushed, mellow and smiling, 'to be out in the boat under sail for Aran running over the waves with the wind in our backs and singing Columcille's holy song! Anyway, I'll head away for Tuam before nightfall.'

Lombard Street: 1645

he masters were waiting impatiently for the publication in Louvain of John Colgan's *Life of the Saints*, the first part of the projected work that would assist them in their own research.

By the time that book appeared, the hand of doom was reaching for them. Fights broke out on the streets, nightmares disturbed the students' sleep and households prayed for long hours on their knees. News of the fall of archbishop Malachy O'Queely of Tuam in the battle to repossess Sligo from Sir Charles Coote, commander of the Parliamentary army in Connacht, spread like wildfire. The frightened people huddled at their doors like cornered foxes. Women with infants wrapped in their shawls and children at play in the streets paused, struck with unspeakable horror.

'It's just a lie spread by the devil Coote's men,' someone shouted in Market Street, lighting a flicker of hope in their hearts.

Darcy's house in Cross Street was in upheaval with weeping and terror. Not a word had come from Dominic since the night he disappeared to join O'Queely's campaign. Cousin John sent for Ulick Óg, the stableman, to come to the house. No one could not miss this fellow whose hair stood out from his head in a red frizz.

'Take the young stallion and ride to Sligo. Search for news of Dominic and don't come near me until you have found him.'

Ulick Óg's eyes shone for an unguarded instant before he bent his head to the master. The sharp eyes of Cousin John had seen the look on the young man's face.

'If you take off in the army on my horse like that son of mine, if such a notion should enter into your head, yourself and your father and all belonging to you will never darken this door again.'

Ulick Óg stared at him red-faced and cried, 'Indeed I have no such notion, master. I'll find Dominic and bring him home.'

Survivors of the battle began arriving after a few days into town, rain-sodden and exhausted. The students rushed out along with everyone else to see them at the Cross. It was all too true about the archbishop's fate. Attempting to besiege the town of Sligo garrisoned by Charles Coote, the initial, erroneous reports had it that Malachy was in the vanguard of the Irish attack that became a rout on the wet river fields nearby. He fell under an English sword crossing the river with his men! The water ran red with his anointed blood! The men wept on their knees as they described the awful carnage.

Malachy in fact, like Brian Boromha at the battle of Clontarf, was killed in his camp. The archbishop and his companions were surprised by Coote's cavalry, who cut them down without quarter.

Factions of the town started yelling for revenge. Fighting erupted when the watch attacked them, trying to push them off the streets. People ran into their houses and locked the doors, country people gathered their carts and streamed out the gates in a run.

Soon curiosity drew the young people outside again. Ruaidhrí O'Flaherty was with fellow students who gathered to pray for Dominic's safety. When they heard the news next day, they agitated at the Bóthar Cam entrance to the residence. Inside St Nicholas of Myra's church nearby, the vigil for the archbishop was packed to the entrances, the opened doors blocked by the kneeling crowds thronging the yard and out onto the streets. Praying could be heard the length of Lombard Street. Ruaidhrí was listening to the loud talk and rumours when whom did he see rushing down the narrow street, but John Lynch accompanied by priests from Tuam.

'Where's the master Mac Fhirbhisigh gone off to now?' Lynch demanded the minute he saw Ruaidhrí.

Before he could answer him, Lynch called to the students, 'Come with me to the chapter house, come away off these streets, in the name of God!' and he set off.

Despite the fact the residents in town were unarmed, the watch was losing its grip on authority and unable to keep weapons out. Plenty men around the place had muskets and pistols hidden on them. About a hundred men, yelling and threatening, gathered all day outside the jail where men who had been arrested by the watch were incarcerated. Enemies of the war faction with similar dark intent outside the chapter house entrance on the Bóthar Cam side, which was locked with armed guards outside it.

In the rush Ruaidhrí informed Lynch that master Mac Fhirbhisigh had gone out to walk by the river. Ruaidhrí felt no desire to go near that centre of unrest, the chapter house. He wished he had the good fortune to be gone off like the ollamh.

'I've just *seen* master Mac Fhirbhisigh flying around the corner like the wind, his head completely covered by his hood on this mild

October day,' Lynch shouted in annoyance. 'I called out that I wished to speak to him, but didn't he cross the bridge at a trot that accelerated when he heard me! He's being difficult again, as if he were the only person in the place having a bad time! We're all having a bad time and we have to face up to it. And I hope he's in good form again before the gates close or he'll find himself locked out for the night and it wouldn't be the first time that's happened to him.

'Look at the misfortune borne by myself this day! What has the ollamh got to complain about in comparison, I ask you? I have to see our Walter about the funeral, God help me,' Lynch continued bitterly when he caught his breath.

'The archbishop of Tuam is lying slaughtered below in Sligo, his body held in heretic hands and our hearts are truly broken these last two days. Didn't I arrive at the main gate with Sir Richard Blake yesterday, after riding the fourteen miles from Tuam, seeing as no news about the funeral arrangements had been brought out to us of course! Only for the two of us to find the gates of this, our own ancestral city, shut in our faces by some lowly dogs laughing and cursing down on us! In the name of God, whatever is happening here? Then someone on the wall started firing on Sir Richard's men, who had to flee the shooting the length of the Bóthar Mór through the suburbs, myself in their midst. My good friends inside here let me in today. I've just heard the watch have imprisoned the impious misguided rogue and his cohorts who fired on us yesterday, may they rot over in the jail.'

Lynch pulled a book out of his bag as they hurried. That was the first sight Ruaidhrí had of John Colgan's famous work, Lynch waving it in front of him distractedly, panting and yelling with tears in his eyes,

'Malachy collaborated in Colgan's book and now he's dead in the very war he himself incited this past year in the west! And he would take advice from nobody, the stubborn, unyielding, misguided fool! He will never hold this publication in his hand or turn its pages for the greater glory of the ancient Irish church!' Turning to heaven, Lynch continued. 'Poor Malachy, scholar and bishop turned soldier! What good will your death do, the pawn of cruel warlords, cut down by Coote in a hopeless skirmish at Sligo? Parliament will destroy our king and leave us friendless before its fury.'

John led them through the courtyard to the oratory. The warden's armed men were on guard here. On seeing from the porch John Lynch's black-robed group of clerics, the men made way for them silently and grimly. John's group had to pass through the threatening, agitated crowd at the entrance. They reluctantly allowed them into the oratory and from there a narrow side door lead into the back of the chapter house. Armed men stood just inside this door, hissing when they saw the group coming in. One of the vicars of St Nicholas's admitted them, stony-faced.

The meeting place was full. Warden Walter Lynch sat in council at his table, assisted by his secretary and vicars, surrounded by representatives from Kilkenny and notables of the belligerent party from town and county and beyond.

'Come in, come in, my dear John,' Walter cried. A strange other-worldly light illuminated his face, seemed to gleam on his purple coat and the large golden cross on his chest. The new arrivals stood in a panting, breathless bunch at the end of the hall, not having been bade sit down. Ruaidhrí felt his heart pounding as he gazed at the scene and the figure at its centre.

'We are afflicted with great grief at these tidings, John,' Walter cried shrilly from his end of the table. 'The heretics are gaining ground everywhere, but no news comes so terrible, no word more dreadful, than that of the archbishop's death. We extend our heartfelt condolences to Tuam, John.'

'Thank you, Walter. I am here to receive the latest news from you, kinsman.'

'We've received letters from the abbot of Kilmallock travelling in the campaign with our soldiers. It seems they were surprised in their camp outside Sligo when Malachy and those with him were killed. And there is more …

'Coote discovered vital letters on the archbishop's body. These are the letters from the king to the Earl of Glamorgan, his delegate, to the Supreme Council. So, the most terrible piece of evidence of the king's secret concessions to the Catholics of Ireland has fallen into the Parliament's hands. Now the Parliamentarians have learned about the Confederates' secret plans with the king to send thousands of Irish troops over to England to help Charles, in return for getting our religious freedoms. 'And the enemy's holding the body awaiting ransom.' Walter nodded at papers on the table in front of him. 'We've sent messages for further information and have heard nothing since.'

John Lynch lowered his head a moment, then said, 'I see. We would like to know what Your Excellency intends doing on this matter.'

'Let it be known I've sent envoys to Sligo to ascertain the position first-hand. Inform all we intend to have the remains conveyed to Tuam for burial, John.'

'Then let us discuss the conduct of the funeral with candour. The great need now is to have a private burial for the archbishop,' John Lynch said the words with emphasis, looking directly at Walter. 'The whole place is in turmoil since the news of his lordship's death. They're holding vigils in the cathedral in Tuam, wailing and lamenting in the street. They're lighting bonfires at crossroads and drinking all night getting ready for the funeral. They're forming bands for pillage and plunder at night, attacking houses in the countryside, driving off livestock, taking what they can lay hands on. This will only achieve the destruction of the Ormond Peace, the greatest need of our day. Shouldn't the avoidance of giving our opponents any excuse whatsoever to end the truce so hard won, be our main purpose from now on? A public funeral will trigger rioting and worse.'

Walter Lynch responded emphatically, 'You should know that the taking up of arms in defence of the faith is the greatest need of our day.' His words echoed around the silent room, the men around the table nodding, no one daring to move.

'The negotiations at Kilkenny cannot and must not be jeopardised at this crucial time,' John Lynch replied into the silence, from the end of the room. 'Ormond has the king's ear and is strengthening the royal side in Ireland while we still can before it's too late. These days now are too important for anything to destroy our chances of building on our gains already won. This war in Connacht is only playing into our enemies' hands.'

Narrowing eyes, the warden replied, 'Listen to the words of John Lynch! Where have you been while your archbishop wielded the sword of Christ in defence of the faith? You have holed yourself up like a rat in a cellar! You intrude yourself into this town to spread your sedition among the students. Who sent you in here today with your puling-mouthed petitions? I wonder would that be your patron

Francis Kirwan issuing decrees from his new elevation in Killala? I am warden of this church and collegiate and, should the need arise, I will do as O'Queely, and rally the faithful in battle for Christ.'

'Our greatest ally the Duke of Ormond will stand by our guarantees for religious freedom before the king and the Parliament if we stand behind him,' cried John.

'Don't say the name Ormond to me! He is a heretic,' Walter bellowed in rage, 'one in whom we cannot trust our future. And all the other opportunists crowding around him. You are so blinded by the luxuries of your patron, Blake, that you cannot see the truth before your eyes. There can be no further negotiating with Ormond.' Walter sat back in his chair and folded his arms.

'Know that the conduct of the archbishop's funeral rests in our hands, that is the news you can convey to your vicars and congregation,' he continued shrilly. 'And while you're in here, I want your support to ensure the successor will bear the banner of Christ in the field before our enemies. That you will oppose the preferment of that horrid backslider, John de Burgo. I intend to do everything I can to keep a lickspittle of Ormond out of Tuam!'

'I've given no thought to Malachy's successor in these days of sadness and cannot answer that question,' John replied.

'Nor do you want to answer it, either! Let that be as it may! The Holy Father in Rome is praying for us.'

'His anointed majesty the king will never forget the loyalty and support of his Irish subjects, Walter. I beg you let circumspection rule you while the English and the Scots are divided, until we learn the outcome of their negotiations and our own negotiations with them. Ormond warned the council of this again recently, that we must not compromise ourselves at this time.'

'Who have ever been more loyal than we in Galway?' Walter Lynch finally fell silent contemplating the irrationality of existence, the unpredictability of this life, the awfulness of the times.

The thoughts were going around Ruaidhrí's mind that if anyone should know the latest news from the Confederate council and assembly, it had to be John Lynch. John was getting it from Richard Blake, the Speaker in Kilkenny, everyone knew that. It struck him John was bringing a warning from the Old English faction this day into St Nicholas's to his cousin Walter.

118

Walter's face was terrible to look at, grotesque and glistening. In the silence, John Lynch began again, saying what had brought him in to run the gamut of the brawling streets.

'There is urgent need that the archbishop be buried quietly to avoid a public funeral with the outrages that will surely erupt in its wake throughout the diocese.'

Walter jumped out of his chair on hearing this and threw back his head to shout,

'His lordship has died a martyr's death on the battlefield for the one true faith. We will see to it that he will be buried with all due honour and respect before his mourning flock!'

The men at the door cheered loudly and waved their guns in the air. More of them pushed their way into the room hearing this.

John bowed low to Walter finally.

'Then we'll send messengers from Tuam to discuss this matter further,' he said, taking formal leave. The priests and students followed him quickly towards the door.

Walter dismissed him with a wave of his hand, saying, 'Go with God and may he protect you, you and all in this town who fail to understand the nature of the Puritan enemy confronting us. You refuse to accept the council of our church of St Nicholas, but we will pray for you. You desecrate your archbishop's memory. Let us not all hide ourselves in a backroom in the countryside until the enemy burns the roof over our heads!'

John Lynch turned sharply on his heel with this insult. They saw the anger the students recognised of old in the master's face, the clenched fists as he shot out at Walter, 'That will be our certain fate if you and your followers persist with your policy of madness. And I lament O'Queely's death until the end of time and all other deaths. Our faith survived clandestinely for generations under harsher persecutions. We will reach a settlement with the house of the Stuart king. Do not tear asunder the new Confederate brotherhood.'

Ruaidhrí was pressed near the door in John Lynch's party, trapped between the crush of men and the fear in his heart but he never forgot those words of reconciliation Lynch threw before Walter.

The students heard Walter's roar, telling John Lynch to go back to his books and stay with them and that it was himself who was trying to split the Confederates.

119

They ran after Lynch through a furore of yelling and blows to gain the street,

'Traitors go home! Blake's lickspittles! Clanricarde's spies!'

They made it finally into the back of the residence from the Bóthar Cam side, the porter locking up rapidly behind them. They did not consider themselves safe even there but had no choice except to remain indoors until the menace and anger in town subsided after nightfall.

The students stayed in prayer with Lynch in the empty library for hours. They dined frugally in the refectory when darkness fell, where bread and all other food was scarce. Afterwards they discussed the situation with the priests in a dark, cold common room near the kitchen. They were still there when a pale faced, dark-robed seminarian came looking for John Lynch with the message, 'Dominus Firbissius is awaiting your pleasure in the parlour, sir.

They followed the light of the lad's candle along a passage into the parlour, wondering as usual about the erratic comings and goings of the ollamh. He was often away on business for the masters, looking for manuscripts, affairs which took him off on long journeys. There was an ever-present suspicion among the boys that Dubhaltach had a secret way in and out of the town, one of several rumours circulating about him. Here he was in the sedate, austere surrounds of the wood panelled, candlelit room, elegant in his bright jacket and collar of lace, his hat and cloak on the back of his chair. He was seated at the guests' fire with three travel-splattered clerks who were staying the night in the residence. Lynch thought as he went over to sit down with him that Mac Fhirbhisigh even seemed tranquil considering the times. But the ollamh was good at hiding his feelings, he knew.

Mac Fhirbhisigh took Lynch's hand and bowed to the lads who sat themselves down on the floor, backs to the wall, prayer books opened in their cold hands and eyes everywhere but on the page. The guests whispered about the disasters from Sligo, warmed ale at the hearth and passed brimming cups to the two masters.

Mac Fhirbhisigh and Lynch started immediately into their usual discourse about the early books of the Irish annals - an edgy, heated disputation that had been going on for some time. The students were used to hearing it but the strangers at the fire fell silent in wide-eyed amazement. Leaning over their shoulder suspiciously to this talk, they shrugged with disdainful incomprehension, shook their heads and returned to their discussion of the war.

It was the opposite for Ruaidhrí. The masters' arguments resonated in his thoughts, and he lost himself in their allure and logic, their vast ancient families and landscapes. This was infinitely preferable to treading the dangerous path between the violently feuding families of the freemen and merchants, their employees and tenants. Equally, he was treading a lonely path of his own away from the muster of his people under colonel Éamonn Mac Morogh na Maor O'Flaherty who had also gone north to retake Sligo under the command of the archbishop. If Coote and the Parliamentarians were left in possession of Sligo, all Connacht was vulnerable. The notables of Ruaidhrí's family rode as lieutenants and captains with Éamonn. Everyone was gone on the doomed campaign except him. At home in Moycullen they believed he was strong in representing them in the warden's faction, whereas in town it was thrown at him that he was Éamonn's and Morogh na dTuath's spy or it would be cast at him that he was John Lynch's spy and an Ormond man.

When the historical arguments were in full flood Ruaidhrí felt an incredible peace, a place where none harassed or derided him, and he knew this was where he really belonged. His road lay among learned men where he was discovering his own unique way to labour for faith and country in dreadful times - a gleam of light over the mountains when storms are passing far inland.

'We're bogged down in swamps denser than the brine of Loch a' tSáile, Dubhaltach,' Lynch was saying to the ollamh while sipping ale together, heads close, feeling the tensions of the day easing somewhat in Mac Fhirbhisigh's company.

'What we seriously require are relevant materials to complement our existing sources. I'm not maintaining that the provenance of many dioceses doesn't yield up considerable sources on former abbeys and monasteries but that plenty of them give up nothing. I wish to heaven Ware's work contained more details for other dioceses as well as Cashel and Tuam,' Lynch added.

'I'm searching far and wide for those,' interrupted Mac Fhirbhisigh, somewhat tetchily. 'The priests and monks *themselves* have in their possession such records and scrolls in distant parts of this country and abroad as we know. Meanwhile, until you obtain for yourself more church-held resources, you must continue examining our own books, as I have explained.'

'Where will I find time for all that reading?' Lynch interrupted him. 'I've made it quite clear my objective is to take aside the fifth and sixth centuries, the holy eras when the light of Christianity was brought to the Dalriadans on both shores of the northern sea of Moyle and issuing from there to the glories of Iona!'

'I rejoice in the work of that time too. But pay heed now to me, John. In all things you can truly start at no place except the beginning. That's where we begin, at the beginning! As to where the beginning is, I'll not dispute the first Irish origins any further, having already done so for years inside this town until the cock crows. when dawn sees me taking to my bed with my head spinning.'

'Ha ha! You can still bring a smile to my face even with the archbishop slaughtered, the diocese in uproar and the house here in turmoil!'

'Ah, but there will be no joy left after this.'

'And you know well, Dubhaltach, I *have* read the early Gaelic chronicles. I've explained clearly to you that I can't present saints getting up to Lord knows what! Such as bringing their stolen cow back to life again after she was slaughtered and skinned. Imagine elaborating this episode before the most illustrious, most sceptical and most famous scholars of Europe! Oh Lord! And hundreds of other similar tales that give little or no glory to the one true church! Or how the dioceses were the *tuatha* of ancient kings divided up so weirdly no one would listen to me! I will henceforth concentrate instead on the blessed glories of the Christian era.'

Lynch paused, overwhelmed by indignation, while Dubhaltach raising his voice, put down his cup with a thud.

'Everyone on both banks of the Shannon will tell you the story of the theft of Ciarán's favourite cow to this day. It's still clear in the memory of the people, John, who could show you the very house where the hide was drying, hung over the door while the thieves were butchering the carcass on the grass. They didn't notice Ciarán and his monks — who had seen the brown hide gleaming in the sunlight from across the river — rowing over after them in fury to the Connacht side until they were upon them and slaughtered them. And how the saint in his miraculous power from God brought his cow back to life and swam her home to the monastery.

'This history comes from the *Christian* era, be it known, during times the monasteries were called on to defend themselves whenever the example of the Son of God was not followed as it should have been.'

John Lynch listened impatiently, finally interjecting, 'Old stories like that have long disappeared from the Christian era of Europe, under the classical influences of Rome and the educated, modern incredulity of learned humanist people. Our defence must go to the Europe of today seeing as we are charged by the Supreme Council to refute the heretical stealing of our Irish saints and the denying that the ancient Scoti were the Irish people.

'People abroad would laugh at us if we wrote about fantastical tales like those I am reading about in the old unreliable sources. They would dismiss us out of hand!'

'And to refute their theft of our Scottish saints, you have no choice but to go back to the pre-Christian eras, immerse yourself in the learned vernacular of the writings and understand the connections between Éire and Alba in all its intertwining of territory and kinship, rivalries and wars, kings, queens and abbots, laymen and churchmen. And to understand the jurisdiction of the dioceses, you must examine the same connections I've just discussed with you, John.'

'Well, either we hold up our end in the Scotian controversy or we sink despairingly in the depths, taking in water so fast that we're baling to no use! Anyway, I've a question for you Dubhaltach, that's putting White out considerably. How are you getting on transcribing that old source of the ancient Scots you have in hand this exceedingly long time? Have you revised its errors of chronology? We'd hoped to have progress on that well before now.'

Dubhaltach faced him wrathfully, 'In faith! Let me put it to you like this. I cannot do what's been asked of me! Yes, master, let me finish! It's unseemly for Clan Firbisigh to alter the books in any way or to omit part of the history, earliest or latest. The laws decree at considerable length the most exacting way history must be handed down. Exactly how instruction must be conducted and in precisely what way the books must be preserved. That's how history has always been studied among the learned classes of the Irish. The truth must be guarded from all impurities even the faintest taint. The laws of Fithil include dire penalties against those who defy them.

'I can show you the documents describing these laws. Actually, they may be in those law tracts I gave you a few years ago, weren't they? I'll make transcripts of them for you.'

'What penalties can anyone fear who undertake the Lord's work?' John cut in when Dubhaltach paused in thought.

'Anyway, see here, the old books only present the history of the Milesian families who came to dominate this island through invasion and war. Those sources haven't sufficiently incorporated the descendants of earlier or later invasions, as I have told you before, though these populations are woven into the fabric of this island's society too.'

'Yes, they have, John. It's not just the history of the sons of Niall they contain, although they dominate it as they became the rulers of the country. We have recorded in addition the descendants of the Fir Bholg and other peoples who were here before the Milesians. The descendants of the Tuatha de Danaan are known to us. We know about their tribes, their learning and their burial monuments.

'John, I've entered chambers under the ground myself, built from stone and lime, discovered near Lecan Mhic Fhirbhisigh, considered to be from that era we are discussing. I was able to stand up in this stone-lined, skilfully crafted chamber under the ground and examine it with my own eyes the work of hands from long eras. It was constructed millennia before ever the sons of Míl's invasion into the country. The new English scholars declare every stone fort and burial place to be the work of the Northmen, claiming that nothing was constructed by the ancient inhabitants of this island. Such is their ignorance!

'We had the pre-Milesian alphabet too, kept in our library in Lecan, in which letters were named after trees and we are able to interpret its meanings. This script was the work of earlier inhabitants here before the age of writing on vellum, as used by the Irish or the Romans, this is clear because it was written on the bark of trees. Perhaps the papyrus of the east is of similar technique. In addition, we interpret ogham writing on stone, which is also from times before the sons of Míl invaded and took over this country.

'Moreover, I say to you John, that in the course of time we did incorporate into our indigenous alphabet the letters for the saints of Christianity and the church, as well as the Scandinavians and Norse.

The interpretation of all these oghams was for long centuries the duty of our family.'

'What about the lineage of those families of the later invasions as well?' exclaimed John. 'Those of the Northmen, the Normans and the English? Your books of genealogy have omitted their descendants. Your books are an incomplete record of all the peoples in the island of Hibernia.'

'Yes, I know we omitted them from our genealogy because they brought us war, dispossession, a changed way of life. They displaced us by force of arms and pushed us from the arable land into bogs and forests and mountains, out to the very seashore. Thus, my own family were displaced from Loch Conn and the Moy by the Normans and Welshmen who took the land and fortified it, forcing us to flee to Lecan on the strand.

'I sorrowfully and truly acknowledge the Milesians in their day inflicted much similar wrongs and injustices on the earlier peoples, dispossessing and enslaving them,' admitted the ollamh. 'Now the sins of the fathers are being visited on the heads of their sons! We acknowledge that same dispossession was wrongly inflicted by our ancestors on the earlier inhabitants of Ireland. We know we wrongfully seized and enslaved Patrick and attacked his people abroad. The slave who in his goodness and sanctity came back to us in the end to lead us to salvation.

'But listen, our genealogists however, despite what you say, have been recording marriages between daughters of Norman families and the chieftains of the Irish for a hundred years. I tell you it's for the people of those invasions to make their own books now alongside ours, John. That is not our responsibility that was laid on us by law long ago.'

'Maybe,' John mused, 'records of the newer heretic invaders will replace yours, just like your books replaced those of the Fir Bholg and the ancient peoples who wrote on bark and stone?'

'Yes, maybe, that is true. But it is not true that we replaced their books. We maintained them in our own keeping, in the alphabets, grammar, genealogy and history and we continued to hand down their interpretation among the learned classes of the pagans. When Patrick brought us the gift of Christianity, old vellum books which were for long ages held by the poets of the pagan kings were brought into the libraries of the monasteries. They were kept there alongside newly written chronicles of the Christian era until the Northmen invasions. They are like the early Testament of the church from before the time of Christ. Just as you defend the true faith against the heretics' books, I defend our books of those descended from the Milesians and earlier. This we've always done since the time of Niall of the Nine Hostages and altogether for nearly two thousand years between the pagan scholars, the monks and ourselves. There is no difference between you and me in that, is there?'

'But do you not agree that we're all in crisis together now?' responded John, 'Irish and Old English united before a new great invading power of Puritans from Britain?'

'Yes, in faith I do, although I note you did not answer my question, John. And now I stand before you since our own school in Lecan was closed, our students and people slaughtered or scattered to the world, our library brought away from danger. Everything is changed nowadays.'

'Yet you've been speaking in public among our students here against making the transcript. I don't understand why this should be.'

'You are asking me to desecrate this old book that's come down to us,' Dubhaltach said, 'because you're asking me to transcribe it incompletely. This is a different task from making an extract from it or a recension. I will not do it. I will only make it available in its true original form.

'I'm already transcribing the old literary Irish into simplified language suitable for the understanding of the lay person who can't read the old tongue of the manuscripts. We kept its interpretation obscure, its secrets to be unlocked only by the learned families who laboured seven years in our schools. It was protected from all enemies in this way and could be handed down intact, in answer to accusations of elitism being brought against us. I am prepared to do this because the ollamhs' schools in which the old writings were studied are in difficulty these years and will be until the return of our hereditary patrons.

'You further desired that, in making my abstract, I would omit the early pagan history. This is what I cannot do, because it must never be said that such a crime was committed by Clan Firbisigh in all their days. A disgrace greater than this has never been known, to be truthful.'

126

John was trying to interject, but Dubhaltach rushed on, 'You can implore the heavens John, but it won't get you anywhere. Exact fidelity in the transcribing must be adhered to from beginning to end.'

In the heat of this entertaining debate, the students reclining on the floor were not aware of the warden Walter throwing open the parlour door, until they noticed the guests around the fire rising suddenly to their feet in the gust of cold air. The students followed the guests' example with speed.

'So, John,' Dubhaltach's voice boomed in all its melodic resonance into this sudden silence. 'I've never heard of desecration so terrible as the notion of omitting the early chronicles, as if the laws never brought them down to us through the long ages, as if they'd never even existed.'

'What's this?' called Walter Lynch from the door, pausing before striding into the parlour.

'Are the scholars of this house disputing even on these blessed days of martyrdom? Surely these matters have been long settled by now, Dubhaltach?'

The arguing masters turned towards the door with a start. Dubhaltach placed his cup on the table and nudged John. The two masters rose and bowed.

'I stand by my position in this debate, your Excellency, which I've already placed before yourself and Stephen White, before John here, Geoffrey Browne, Patrick Lynch and all. I will not abbreviate the old book,' Dubhaltach said calmly in reply to the frowning figure at the door.

'That's a serious matter but not however so serious that the residence should be disturbed with it tonight. It's not fitting that this argument should be going on here for so long. You should not be quibbling and squabbling over something like this in light of the threat facing the faith. Let me advise you to reconsider your stance and make that transcript speedily, ollamh. The Primate of Armagh no less has called for our works to be printed without delay. Each of us must answer the call in the same way and obey the orders of the church in its hour of greatest need. Aye, Dubhaltach, we must bend our will when the call comes. We must do our duty and take up the sword.'

Walter's voice rose. 'Let us follow the example of our blessed martyr O'Queely!'

Then quietly, emphatically, Walter added, 'Now let us have an end to this wrangling.'

He approached the men at the fire, 'I have news just come tonight.'

Dubhaltach turned towards the door, but John stood in his way. The ollamh's face was grey and haggard. The priest was like a man in desperation, pleading in a low voice,

'You've heard it now Dubhaltach, from the mouth of your esteemed friend Walter himself.'

'Since when did you ever pay much heed to that particular kinsman of yours, John Lynch?'

'Shh! Quietly! I agree with his arguments! Never mind making faces at me! The writ of heresy issuing from the followers of Camarius and Major and their claims to the glories of the Scotian church must be stemmed! Don't keep shaking your head at me!'

'I can't go against the laws.'

'Even O'Neill since his return in the country is following the laws of the Confederation. Why should *you* be the only exception? You're living in the past, Dubhaltach. You will only do right by making this copy. No blame will ever be attached to you only praise. You know our time of freedom is short before we're overrun by our enemies. Open your heart to the needs of the church and hasten the work of your hand without dissent or delay.'

'Oh God of Graces, what'll become of Clan Firbhisigh if I contravene the laws of our calling?'

'This argument day after day! If you don't do this, then our work of refutation of our enemies will never succeed without the availability of the great records from Ciarán's monastery. Remember the news from Sligo!'

'Ah no! What more can I say? You know I came into town employed to assist the priests' work. But to spend the labour of my days here making a desecrated copy?'

'It's in the interests of following the way of the monasteries and the saints, the object of Louvain, of John Colgan himself. Colgan! We have had delivered the *Acta Sanctorum* finally from Louvain! The first three months of the calendar of our saints! See, I've got it here! Look! Well? Wait! Where are you off to now?'

'I'm going over to the church to pray for a better time for Ireland in the future years when the sins of Clan Firbisigh may be forgiven... I'll talk to you again.'

'Wait, I'll come with you to pray for the living and the dead.'

The two masters went out the door still muttering to each other. They crossed the dark street to the church, filled to the rafters with the all-night vigil for Malachy. The lads beside O'Flaherty whispered unkindly that Mac Fhirbhisigh was really heading to the Franciscans for his whiskey and his spies. Their antics were ended abruptly when they took in what the warden was saying. 'Thirty pounds sterling is the ransom for the archbishop's body, Judas' price for the betrayal of Christ.'

Walter, weeping, began to sink to his knees on the floor and bowed his head. Everyone in the parlour followed suit to kneel in terrified prayer.

And Ruaidhrí, despite all this trauma, was bursting to tell them — I actually have a neighbour at home who proudly claims to this day that he's descended from the Fir Bholg who were driven by the Milesians into West Connacht! — but he managed to keep his opinions to himself and followed the others across to St Nicholas's to pray for the archbishop cruelly slaughtered.

Ruaidhrí never forgot the bells of St Nicholas of Myra's and the other churches within and without, tolling and tolling across town on the days following the news of the archbishop's death. He knelt in the great church packed with frightened praying people, feeling their doom drawing ever closer.

Studies in the schoolroom were soon disturbed by the terrible news from the northern parts. A Parliamentarian army, mustered in strong numbers, was on the move to conquer and destroy the inhabitants of lower Connacht on their own borders. The victorious army overran those parts to the sea, murdering and burning all in their path.

Within days Galway city beheld the refugees, the displaced from the expanding war who had abandoned their homes ahead of the soldiers, carrying all they possessed. In their midst a red-haired young man arrived slowly with the body of a dead soldier draped over the horse he led. The young man stopped at the northern gate in exhaustion as people crowded around him shouting, 'Which lad is that you have there, the Lord protect and guide us?'

The overactive busybody, Francis Fitz Peter Brown, was the one who got to the leather shop first to tell the heartbroken, distraught family the news about Dominic. Francis could not resist adding, 'That young stallion will never do a day's good again after the way he's been ridden.'

Kneeling and weeping in the parlour with relatives and neighbours, their numbers overflowing into the street, Ruaidhrí saw the crowd separate as Dominic was carried on boards, covered in linen, into the parlour. He was rested on two chairs by his weeping father, brothers and uncles and the screaming women were gathering around to bend over the broken body. Sounds of the sawing and hammering of Darcy's men came through from the yard as his coffin was being made, mingling desolately with the wailing as Dominic's wake began.

Imperceptibly the atmosphere had been changing from energetic euphoria, hope and freedom to something darker and heavier that emerged as the years of war lengthened without any definite resolve. The fall of the archbishop of Tuam and the dead from the battle marked the lowest point, a sharp reminder of the vulnerability of all, regardless of what side they were on.

Nothing after this was as it had formerly been, when the coming of the ollamh Mac Fhirbhisigh had initiated a time of joyous labour, interspersed at times with upheaval and strife in Lynches' library and the residence. Abroad, hostile armies marched throughout the Three Kingdoms.

Ruaidhrí's fellow students and friends continued leaving school to work on the fortifications of the walls under orders of the corporation. They drilled and practiced their weapons under a captain on the field well outside the city. Ulick Burke, the Earl of Clanricarde, had succeeded in getting colonel John Burke dismissed as commander of the Connacht Confederate army. This greatly weakened its development for the defence of the province, leaving the population vulnerable as before to the Parliamentarian threat. Local militias of young men were as determined as ever and remained faithful to their local leaders. Other students from distant families departed with their brothers to scattered militias. Many simply ignored what was happening in other parts of Ireland where the campaigns carried on under Rinuccini's command with varying success. Displaced relatives of town families arrived at the gates in greater numbers daily, frightened parents with their children, carrying their possessions on carts and every house sheltered refugees. All they could do was dwell in the moment and pray for peace to return.

Breaking Silence

Since the Nuncio's arrival, Burke's and Sir Valentine's men guarded the entrances to the residence day and night, reinforcing the warden's militia. Outside beyond the city's farms the vigilant Earl Ulick Burke and his lieutenants maintained their armed men in readiness to exercise control whatever way the wind might blow. King Charles Stuart had lost the civil war in England and had surrendered to the Scots. The dreaded Coote raided Connacht as far as Loughrea and Portumna, - Clanricarde's own strongholds - terrorising and killing the population around these garrisons. Coote wished to remind Ulick that he was not the only power in the province. Would Coote and the Scots launch a full-scale invasion soon, people wondered and Connacht with no one to defend it?

Every morning Tadhg, the amanuensis, walked with a heavy heart to the residence. He was alert for incidents of individuals jeering and threatening each other in the street. This was happening even as people went about their daily business, only quelled by the appearance of armed men. The lad went past the armed man at the residence gate and paused to look at the houses across the street. He had managed to locate which house was Peter Fitz Stephen Brown's, however. Soon after his conversation with the *bacach,* Tadhg noticed that cocky fellow, Francis Fitz Peter, bang the front door shut after him and stride whistling down the street with his purposeful gait.

Tadhg stood for a while outside the residence staring at the upstairs windows on the other side of the street. He took an apple out of his pocket which Richard Athy had given him before he left Blake's and began eating it while he thought about Úna Ní hEidhin. The *bacach* had a hidden cache of food stolen for him by an agitated serving woman in the kitchen given to him in exchange for news about her husband. The latter ne'er do well had absconded recently from Blake's boat in France to live with a woman in the port of Lorient.

Tadhg's thoughts were wandering back to the last time he had seen Úna, when a militiaman came over to him to demand roughly, 'What's up with you? What are you looking at over there, you young pup?' snatching the partially eaten apple out of his hand and sinking his teeth into it.

The lad fled up the stairs to the ollamh' room with a beating heart.

When he knocked on the door and entered Dubhaltach's room, the muttered greeting was, 'What's the day like out? Any news?' and the ollamh added a dry little laugh at this new addition, glancing at him out of the side of his eye in amusement.

The question 'any news?' coming from the master was not the same as coming from Richard Athy; it was to be taken seriously. Tadhg related everything he had heard in the new drinking house at the Cross. Dubhaltach always listened and seldom said anything.

Tadhg occasionally saw Ruaidhrí in this new place, inevitably in his cousins' company which included round-cheeked Patrick Bodkin, one of the best of the seminarians and he would report to Dubhaltach afterwards about their doings. The latter was interested in hearing news of O'Flaherty. He once said he was concerned the young man's studies might be left behind in the chaos into which the city was descending. He occasionally asked about rumours going around town and even asked what people were saying about Rinuccini and his sermons in St Nicholas's on Sundays to which the leading families listened.

These homilies were focused on the Pontiff's prayers for Ireland, the need to prosecute the war to a successful end and the anathema of the Irish compromising for temporal gain with Protestants. Tadhg did not know whether Dubhaltach ever dined in the evenings with the Nuncio between Rinuccini's trips to the Supreme Council. According to gossip, the Nuncio complained endlessly about the food put in front of him and he did not seem very friendly with the clergy of the house. The latter were in turmoil, falling out with each other amid terrible rows and shouting. This was followed by confession, penance and retreat under the heavy hand of the warden, their spiritual director.

Dubhaltach was a layman eternally engaged in his writing and research, not involved openly with any clique that Tadhg knew about. Rumour had it from the start that the ollamh was in the Franciscans' party, as these churchmen were his closest associates in the city, although he wouldn't admit to such a thing.

The Nuncio's unwavering message on the pulpit was that the Catholics of the country must not under any circumstances make terms with Ormond or any other Irish Protestant heretic.

'Never, never!' thundered Rinuccini in St Nicholas's. 'We must hold out for religious freedom in an independent state.'

Rinuccini's foreign Latin and outlandish gesticulating left the less well-educated among the congregation uncomprehending.

'What was that foreign fellow going on about in there?' and on being informed were loud in condemnation in the middle of the street after mass.

The Nuncio's visits to the friar houses, the nuns, the holy wells, the hospitals, the jail, St Bridget's church outside and the population in the suburbs, on the other hand, met with large enthusiastic crowds of the dispossessed. The noble archbishop seemed to be the only champion of the poor and the Irish, those owning neither *talamh ná trá*. He was the lone, firm, unwavering supporter of Eoghan Ruaidh. Rinuccini financed O'Neill's army and every other army that was in the field for the faith. The Nuncio was the 'man with the gold,' the delight of the soldiers and the provider of arms. He directed the war on the Supreme Council until it was taken over by the Ormond faction. After that, the clergy met to declare a new oath of confederation and they set up a parallel military command. This splinter Supreme Council moved between different locations during the campaigning in Leinster and Munster. Rinuccini was desperate for them to seize the Munster ports of Cork, Youghal and Kinsale, as a prelude to importing reinforcements for the Confederates. These towns were, however, too strongly defended and stood steadfast against all Confederate attacks.

Tadhg declined to tell Dubhaltach about the tunnel under the walls. The boy was afraid he had actually imagined it within the dimness and frightful shouting of a rancid, sunken room. It was full of a low class of people with whom the ollamh never associated.

He did tell Dubhaltach of rumours circulating about Irish John, as everyone called him, a foreign engineer in charge of the fortifications. One morning, following Dubhaltach's usual greeting, Tadhg remarked there was lately a lot of whispering and winks going the rounds in connection with a spy for O'Neill, said to be conspiring among the inhabitants. The spy was directing apprentices and the militias in a plot to wrest control of the city gates at the first opportune moment, in order to let in the Irish army. Dubhaltach turned over to him sharply on hearing this, even carefully placing his quill in the ink pot. His hands were permanently ink-stained now, the mark of his trade.

'What's that? Who do they say he is?' he asked sharply. *Is it me they're accusing?* went his wordless question.

'The corporation has a foreign engineer employed to oversee the new fortifications, a fellow called Jan Vangrysh. But that's only his nickname from Flanders. He was in the Irish Regiment during the wars with the Spanish army under O'Neill and Preston. He fought at the siege of Breda, a great genius they say in modern bastions, ramparts, reinforcements and big weaponry against siege. And who does he turn out to be really but a *nephew of Eoghan Ruaidh in disguise!* His real name is Shane O'Neill, the son of Brian O'Neill and they call him Irish John, who was born and reared out there and speaks foreign languages. It's claimed the corporation intend to arrest him when the bastions are complete. Though some are making out the story is nonsense.'

There was a long silence from the other side of the table. Dubhaltach was obviously turning this over in his mind. Eventually he said, 'What proof have they that he's a nephew of Eoghan Ruaidh, and not a Flemish engineer?'

Tadhg was ready for this. 'Because, sir, he also speaks Irish! Have you heard of this brother of Eoghan Ruaidh's?'

'But you've just said, *a mhac*, that he was in the Irish Regiment. He would have picked up Irish there living in the army camps season after season with our exiled men. How wonderful is the language of the Gael!'

Dubhaltach held up his hands in a sort of joy, then controlled himself and folded his arms, whispering so quietly to himself Tadhg could hardly hear the words.

'And how terrible is the banishing of our armies to seek pay in foreign wars time after time under English monarchs. We declare loyalty to English kings, yet they permit the robbery of our land by settlers old and new. They do nothing for us when the settlers refuse us English law, ensuring we are reduced to beggary. A careful strategy on their part! Ah well!'

After a pause Dubhaltach whispered,

'That Brian O'Neill, you talk of is head of the Clannaboy O'Neills, to answer your question if you must know.'

After a further pause Dubhaltach continued, 'But you won't be repeating that around the town, will you now? There is obviously no truth in that rumour. You will say foreigners in the Irish Regiment abroad can speak Irish like the natives! Now, what will you say?'

Tadhg repeated it back to Dubhaltach, who nodded slowly.

His disappointment was sharp as Dubhaltach's wisdom poured cold water over his enthusiasm. He continued in a similar whisper, 'I'd have much preferred he really were one of the O'Neills operating in disguise to take the town for the Irish.'

Dubhaltach leant forward, still speaking in so barely audible a whisper that it was difficult to catch what he was saying, even sitting beside him. 'Well, seeing as O'Neill's army was unable to take the Munster ports when they should have had the strength to do so, allied as they were to Preston's army in Leinster and the Munster armies over the last few years, how on earth can they hold the country now, even seizing this port of Galway? Preston failed to take Dublin when he should have. The Scots army has taken Ulster in the greedy grabbing of land and why in the name of God has O'Neill not been able to recover it? Strong Parliamentarian garrisons control the ports that Eoghan Ruaidh needs to allow in reinforcements. Sligo is still garrisoned by Coote. Connacht is vulnerable, seeing as the Old English leaders have kept out O'Neill and have gone against the Nuncio and the foreign military aid he would have brought in.'

Tadhg heard something in the tone of Dubhaltach's voice - not exactly a warning, but he suddenly felt uncomfortable. Could it be that Mac Fhirbhisigh's position of patronage in the residence made it necessary for him to maintain total silence about tensions between Irish and Old English, especially seeing as he was living in the middle of it all, the main location of Irish support? The well-meaning priests, his collaborators in research, had accommodated him here among the warden and the students where unfortunately militancy was centred, making it the most watched house in the city.

Why did Dubhaltach mention the war now? This was the only time he had done so since the time the shock of Rinuccini's arrival spurred him into discussing the situation with Tadhg. He was reminded of the first day Dubhaltach took Tadhg on to assist him. He had warned him then about the need for discretion.

'You are never to talk about the war to me or to anyone in this town.'

That was not an issue for Tadhg who became unwell when he thought of what had happened in his home place and never told anyone.

The next thing Dubhaltach had said that day was even worse.

'If you carry one word out of here about me or the work, I will dismiss you from my employment.'

Tadhg could tell he meant every word.

Yet here he was himself talking about the war even though he was whispering. One never knew who might be listening outside the door or in the next room in this house. Did this mean Dubhaltach had trust in him now? The happy thought struck the lad suddenly and he sat back with a sigh.

Tadhg was aware that because Walter was supporting a war allied to the Irish and the fact that he had armed their own militia for this purpose, he was in open rebellion against the civic authorities. The independent wardenship was free of any outside control, its warden could do what he liked, including raising his own armed force. The corporation of Galway had long built up a similar position of independence in political and military affairs, however, and it was well known the councillors thought little of a man like Walter Lynch, posturing as a better Catholic than the rest of them. Walter had little or no support among his fellow Old English hierarchy and even less among the upper-class elite of city freemen and merchants, except for the maverick Sir Valentine Blake. This was a fellow who was troublesome since the day he was born.

Only the fools and ne'er do wells of the city were following the mad Walter, it was said by the corporation, ignoring the overwhelming support given to the warden by the ordinary religious of all the churches and their poor congregations.

'Rome will look after fellows like Walter, come what may,' was the next thought in the freemen's minds.

'If we don't protect what we have, who will look after us when everything we own is threatened? *We* have to compromise ourselves for our families, even if that self-interested zealot in the collegiate does not.'

Words failed the freemen whenever they saw Walter strutting about the place with his supporters like a messiah. The collegiate priests of St Nicholas's were under the power of the corporation in name only. The dominant influences in the corporation were controlled by the wealthiest Old English freemen under Sir Richard Blake. In the hinterland Ulick Burke, who was nobody's friend, controlled everything with his castles and militia surrounding their own 'county of the town of Galway' from the Corrib to the Shannon. The freemen therefore allied themselves to archbishops like Kirwan in Killala, in seeking a truce with the Parliamentarians under any powerful Protestant Old English leader in the country they could get behind. Their representatives proceeded to seize control of the Supreme Council, outmanoeuvring the clerical party and ultimately splitting the Confederates. The clerical party under Rinuccini was disadvantaged and weakened. Perhaps this is what Dubhaltach's best friend, a small, stout, pock-faced, studious Franciscan, meant when he muttered to the ollamh on a recent holy day after mass outside their church.

'The leading clergy of the Old English are no friends to us, Dubhaltach, negotiating with Ormond and leaving out O'Neill,' he had observed. Dubhaltach had glanced around tensely in case anyone was listening, frowning at the eavesdropping Tadhg trailing closely beside them on the street.

Neither Dubhaltach nor Tadhg said anything for a while in the ollamh's room and they stared unhappily out the window at Lombard Street. Graceful houses lining its other side filled their view, especially the elegant facade of Brown's house. Each knew wordlessly what the other was thinking: the Old English are temporising, compromising as ever. They are even backing the Old English Protestants in the hope this will guarantee their property and privileges.

Everyone knew that the main reason the Old English rebelled with the Irish was the knowledge the Parliament was committed to confiscating a great quantity of Irish land. This was needed to pay the large amount the king had borrowed from investors to finance an army in Ireland. Charles I intended bringing this Irish military force to England to aid him against the Parliamentarians.

No one felt safe the way things were going. Even Rinuccini would be lucky to get out of the place alive, closely allied to the Irish as he was, aware the Old English and Ormond were betraying them. It was on O'Neill's boat the *San Pedro* that he had sailed to Ireland in the first place and this vessel at anchor below in the Pool represented his last escape route back to Italy.

To break the heaviness of the moment, Dubhaltach picked up his pen again, only to sit twisting it in his fingers. Tadhg, struck by a thought, half rose from his seat, leaning on the table to carefully scrutinise the upper windows of Peter Fitz Stephen's Brown's house, muttering to himself. Dubhaltach stared at him in surprise for a while, before asking.

'What are you looking at?'

The lad sat down with a crash. 'I, ah, nothing.'

'It must be something.' Dubhaltach thought for a moment then leaned back in his chair and smiled.

'It wouldn't be the young woman Úna Ní hEidhin, would it? I used to wonder if she was smiling for me or you from the window over there!'

'Which window?'

'The upstairs gable one on the left, you know it!'

'I cannot see it.'

'Here, sit in my chair and look to your left,' Dubhaltach said, standing up smiling. Tadhg moved awkwardly into the other's chair and did as he was told.

There it was, a casement on the jutting gable extension of the house, which happened to be opened to the freshness of the day. It was only visible from the ollamh's chair. There was no one at the window today.

'She hasn't been there for a while now,' remarked Dubhaltach with a small laugh when he was back in his chair. Tadhg glanced at him red-faced and Dubhaltach laughed aloud and thumped the table. He leant over and opened their own window to the sea breezes blowing along the street.

'Well, let us continue our work, in the name of God,' he told Tadhg almost light-heartedly.

Tadhg knelt beside Patrick Bodkin in the oratory and prayed, 'Help me, O Lord, to live an exemplary life, not to lead lads like him astray from your calling by showing bad example. Give me strength to avoid controversy among these churchmen. Forgive me my sins.'

The tension he felt was palpable to Patrick whenever he glanced at him. They walked in the courtyard after their prayers.

'Why are you downcast, our Paper 'n' Ink?' Bodkin asked him teasingly with a smile.

He shrugged, muttering, 'For my sins. I'll never be a priest like you will one day. I want to lead a good life. I don't want the Parliamentarians to come.'

'You have too many concerns, my poor friend. One day you'll join an order in your tranquil native countryside where there are no loud bells, you'll see. You lead a worthy life serving the ollamh Mac Fhirbhisigh's work with the clergy of this town, to their eternal gratitude and to the greater glory of the church. And yes, we don't want the heretics to come but they'll take Munster and once they capture Limerick, they'll cross the Shannon to attack Galway, with the devil Coote ready on our other flank. Everything will certainly change for us after that.'

Tadhg was chilled to the bone and could not stop himself shaking, which he hoped Bodkin would not notice.

'Don't say things like that, Patrick.'

The seminarian slipped his hand through his arm, showing that he had indeed noticed. They strolled together into the busy street, turning from the Cross at the markets, the scene of too much of their recent activities and instead headed away from the crowds out the western gate to lean on the bridge. The noise of the rushing, gurgling river calmed Tadhg somewhat, the wind from the sea in his face and hair. He sighed, feeling the smooth wood of the drawbridge beneath his folded arms as he stared over the edge.

Patrick patted his hand gently as they leaned side by side, asking him was his disturbance over.

'It is,' he said.

'Do you like boys, Paper 'n' Ink?'

Bodkin's question came without warning, casually, as if it were of no importance. It was a question that came up in the friars' house, too. It flashed through Tadhg's mind when he felt a growing attraction of his guardian angel towards him during their prayers. This practice was first brought in by English soldiers, his grandfather said.

'Not really, I have a woman I like very much,' he said slowly, wondering would Patrick spread this information, the certain end of his shaky intentions for the church still nurtured deep within him despite everything.

Only the *bacach* knew about the affair, who was responsible for Tadhg's secret meetings with Úna. Richard surreptitiously set these up for them out beyond the holy well of St Augustine and on special feast days when people gathered for prayer and benediction. Tadhg felt he was in paradise in Una's company. Their encounters were brief, self-conscious, stolen moments during which little was said as he was tongue-tied, and she too spoke little. Afterwards he could not recall their conversation while he processed the memories of Úna in her cloak and neat skirts, her hair shining under her maid's headdress, the pounding of his heart in his head drowning everything. Richard would inevitably relate the news, half in disbelief and half envious, that Úna was in love with him and Tadhg spent days afterwards in a fever of emotion. He wanted to ask her to marry him, he was sure of this. There were married priests in his part of the country after all. He knew the idea was anathema in the town and never to be mentioned.

'Hmm.' Patrick thought for a while and then said. 'I see that now but you know, I was unsure about you. You're so different to most fellows, I have to say. What a pity! Who is this fortunate young lady, may I ask?'
'Oh, I'm not in a position to reveal that for her protection, I'm afraid.'
'Do you intend to marry her?'
'Well, I don't know. Nothing is certain these times.'
'I see. That's true, our future is less clear by the day.'
'And you, Patrick, will you be a priest?'
There was a pause and Bodkin said, 'Yes, I suppose so, but you know how all certainties have been shaken in our day, with the wars and the Puritan threat. We would all be compelled to continue our priestly lives abroad if religious toleration were denied to us when this war is over.'
Something Bodkin said struck Tadhg.

'I've never known any certainty in my whole life, anyway,' he said, an unbearable weight taking shape inside him.

'Neither have I, indeed. That is why I thought you were one of us, the sodomites condemned to secrecy and despair. But it's more than the sound of the bells that troubles you, *a stóir*. The troubles of the world weigh you down, a true pilgrim on the road to Calvary, burdened like Atlas holding up the sky! What's the load you are carrying on your back, if not that of the sodomite?'

'I'm foolish and different from everyone else, that's my great misfortune in this life on earth.'

He simply did not understand people as Richard Athy told him more than once.

How could Patrick Fitz Nicholas, son of Nicholas Fitz Walter Bodkin with his fine mansion, boats, land and a houseful of beautiful sisters with whom everyone was in love, his well-off student friends and sound connections in church and council, his rosy cheeks, fair curling hair and lovely smile, how could *he* ever know uncertainty?

Words failed him in attempting to explain the way he himself was locked into his own world, his head full of evil pictures and terrible voices. Tadhg Mac Seáin saw over and over again his grim journey escaping south through the mountains with his family from the Scots soldiers. They followed the lake by night, hunting rabbits and fishing carp for the pot, which was his younger brother Eoghan's responsibility to carry. They huddled in hollows and ditches by day, the crying of the baby finally silenced when she lay cold in his distraught mother's arms. They were shunned in townlands already stripped bare by the desperate, foraging Ulster soldiers of Eoghan Ruaidh's *creachts*. Tadhg and his sister were sent among the houses by his father to ask for bread. Ragged, starving people screeched and threw stones after them, but they were safe in Irish-held territory, though far from home.

Tadhg was conscious as well of a feeling of strange assurance in talking to someone who was admitting to the sin of sodomy, as Patrick Bodkin called it. That made them alike in secret troubles. The lad knew this practice was condemned and abhorred among the town clergy.

There were married priests and bishops in many places and not a word said against them until the town bishops started to promote the Counter Reformation out to country areas. They banished married priests to half-starved churches on the western coast. They must not have realised this other abomination existed, as he never heard of them going after anyone for that.

The church in town was authoritarian and rigid unlike Patrick and Brigid's church in the countryside.

'You're honest and dedicated in your duties to the ollamh. The warden and the masters are well satisfied with your diligence, my friend. And Mac Fhirbhisigh collaborated with John Lynch since White's time in the school — the '*Polyhistor*' of the foreign universities,' Patrick said.

Patrick Bodkin in his gentle way made Tadhg feel a little less alone in a hostile world. He proved to be the priest, John Lynch's, most special gift of all to him.

'Now,' said Dubhaltach, 'while the day is still in it, take these pages where we stopped last night before the supper. Read out from this line here.'

'Yes, master.' He did as he was told and they recommenced their work, himself reading out the lines, Dubhaltach taking time to work out the modern equivalents, then getting Tadhg to point out again the beginning, followed by silence while Dubhaltach dipped his pen and wrote with great care on his folio. They were near the foot of the ollamh's page when the words came out, as if with a life of their own as Tadhg blurted out unthinkingly.

'Master? What did John Lynch want those transcriptions for? I wondered as you told me you transcribed for him a few years ago.'

'Ah! what! I did I suppose?'

Dubhaltach, startled out of his concentration, blotted his folio with the distraction.

'Sorry, I am sorry.'

Tadhg leapt up to seize the small cloth, which Dubhaltach whipped from him and began minute dabbing to remove as much of the blot as possible.

The boy knew better than to say anything and slouched with hands folded.

'I'll tell you,' Dubhaltach said levelly, 'and maybe tomorrow we can have an end to questions of this nature, or I'll hire a reticent old scribe from below in Peregrine Ó Cléirigh's in Mayo to help me and you can sweep the courtyard alongside our friend Benildus.'

Dubhaltach sighed and told Tadhg the story of the efforts made by Galway clergy in refuting heretical history. They needed records of the *fenechas*, the laws of Ireland, to prove their arguments. John Lynch required additional resources for ecclesiastical historical research on the reign of kings, on the important Synod of Uisneach which established the dioceses, bishoprics, monasteries and abbots. He himself had provided the priests with such sources over the years, Dubhaltach added.

Dubhaltach sat back, drew his breath, rubbed his eyes, and looked at Tadhg sideways, wondering no doubt would he have further questions, but the lad was staring at him open-mouthed.

'You're catching flies,' said Dubhaltach, waiting for what might come next.

Tadhg fingered his playing cards in his pocket for comfort, pondering how words could describe the image of the old, grey-haired scribe, his grandfather, who had taught him how to read old manuscripts in his native Roscommon.

Whenever he listened to Dubhaltach it was Tadhg Mhóir his grandfather he saw, despite whatever effort he made to keep his thoughts in the present and on track. Dubhaltach somehow became a living connection to something wordless and undefined in the lad's mind, uncontrollable and nameless. He saw his grandfather lying dead outside the door of the burning house. Two troopers with muskets were bending over him, shouting to another who was stripping bodies lying on the street of the houses. They turned over the old man's body to search his clothes. The still, small shape of Máiréad his sister was revealed in the folds of the grandfather's coat. Fitful rain blew in smoke-laden silence across Loch Allen while his mother held her hand on the baby's mouth. The huddled family crouched at the bottom of the ditch in the haggard under dripping sally trees and wailed silently. In the dead of night, the rest of the family crept from the place and began the long walk south to safety. His traumatised mind took him back to where he closed his eyes, shuddering as he dropped down under the bank. He had retched into the pools of cold water covering their feet, vomit and muck swirling among watercress and nettles.

Dubhaltach, observing him, picked up his pen and shook his head, He understood the visions seen by survivors of such things and put his own nightmares determinedly to the back of his mind that he might continue his task until it was done. But Tadhg left down the manuscript Dubhaltach had handed him and began to shake.

'Things happened down my way during the war,' the lad muttered, 'Terrible things.'

'I know.' Dubhaltach put down his pen again quietly and waited, glancing at the huddled figure beside him.

The silence lengthened in the room. Tadhg gasped for air, his mouth opening and closing. He looked at the nodding figure of the older man.

'The same happened in so many people's place during that time,' Dubhaltach said.

Tadhg sat up in his chair with an effort, rubbed his face with his hands and slowly took up the manuscript he had just left down.

'I suppose so,' he replied and waited for Mac Fhirbhisigh to pick up his pen.

Chroniclers in the Time of War

On the day John Lynch arranged with Ruaidhrí to accompany him to the college residence, Ruaidhrí left Darcy's house soon after dawn to meet the priest in front of St Nicholas's. Ruaidhrí, his wardship years behind him, had become his own man. Lynch was going to formally introduce him to Walter and the scribes in the collegiate, in order to bring Ruaidhrí into the milieu of research and writing. Religion and politics intermingled in an increasing vacuum where schooling and commerce had once been. The schoolrooms had gradually descended into dust and silence, the boys because of the changed priorities of their families in town and county were taking up arms.

The day came when the Lynches wept and prayed while locking their school, a day they had seen coming for a few years with the general deterioration of ordinary life. It was one of the hardest blows of all.

Thick snowflakes were swirling over the roofs, settling in the chilly lanes. The morning light was obscured by low cloud as the pair walked towards the residence, white under its covering of snow.

'Only prayer is left to us,' John told Ruaidhrí. 'Everyone is on their knees in the churches or at council meetings in the Tholsel, going from one to the other.'

John had summoned him back from Moycullen in early spring and arranged with his former host John Fitz Richard Darcy to accommodate him once again in Cross Street.

The aged and silent relative who greeted him in the parlour was a shock to Ruaidhrí. John Fitz Richard looked like a man much older than his years. His wife Bridget sat knitting wordlessly beside the fire after she kissed him, a shadow of the vigorous woman she had once been.

'You were always a good boy,' Cousin John said when they shook hands.

'How are you keeping in these terrible times, cousin?' he asked, staring from his shrunken frame to the gaunt mistress of the house. John was no longer the lively, laughing relative who took them rowing on fine summer Sundays upriver from Woodquay, nor the man who could once shift huge piles of baled hides single-handed onto carts.

'Ah, the physicians don't know what's up with me,' John replied. 'Some class of bile in the stomach they're making out.'

Cousin John brought Ruaidhrí up to Dominic's room without another word, indicating he was to share with Ambrose and Robert. The war came to every family in one way or another and maybe that had been the beginning of the end for Cousin John. In Ruaidhrí's imagination, he seemed to embody their awful times every time he sat at table with him and the family in the silent gloom of evening.

The days were tense and unreal, spent brooding inwardly on the fearful expectation of the Parliament's armies arriving at the gates sooner or later. It seemed as if they had never known anything else. The excitement and happiness experienced in the years after the liberation of Galway slipped away almost unnoticed as the Puritans overran their opponents in England and in key parts of Ireland.

Wealthy families started leaving quietly to go abroad, well-dressed women and children climbed in silent desolation aboard boats of passage moored on the quays while their menfolk prepared to fight. Strange families lodged in Quay Street while they organised and paid for passage to France down on the Strand. The militia's ranks swelled, drilling unceasingly. Refugees with family connections amongst the townspeople were still arriving. The Nuncio continued to preach resistance every Sunday and holy day in Saint Nicholas of Myra's, when he was not away with the Confederates directing the military campaigns. People got on with daily life as best they could, shivering in the coldest days ever experienced, doing the banal ordinary things, while old certainties shifted under them, rip tides pulling their keels out on open sea.

'You will all go out to your uncle Andrew in Tuam like you did before, when the time comes,' John announced at supper one evening. No one said anything or asked anything only continued eating in silence, eyes downcast. The Darcy lads bore the loss of Dominic with mixed feelings of pain and guilt that they had neither gone with him nor been able to stop him. They changed into silent young men under their burden, friendly with Ruaidhrí in a new way since he returned.

On visits to his family to see his stepfather and his sisters in Moycullen, a mere six miles out the western gate, Ruaidhrí saw how fear of the Puritans overshadowed them too. For the first time

Ruaidhrí began to understand the belligerence driving young men everywhere, who saw the coming confrontation. He said little about the war to his stepfather, John Bermingham, who was allied with Ulick Burke in the assembly in Kilkenny. In his family, as in the city, people were divided.

Ruaidhrí's friends in town had changed too. They spent their time in meetings at the Cross and marching with the militia. They travelled in and out the port in their fathers' boats on business. Trade was reduced mainly to dealing in provisions, passenger transport to France, army transports, guns, powder and shot and carrying military information up and down the coast. Even some of the steadiest of his relatives began considering taking up arms, changing their outlook over the months as news of the Puritans' sweeping victories devastated them.

All the while the mayor and council advocated cessation and terms as their strategy in dealing with the Parliamentary Protestants, contradicting Rinuccini point blank.

Ruaidhrí never wavered from his resolution to engage in historical research. He had chosen the pen over the sword. He realised from childhood he was no Éamonn Mac Morogh na Maor, no soldier, no colonel, no family hero leading his troopers and infantry. He was following the road his grandfather had taken in the ways of reading, growing up in a milieu of learning richer and more intense than had existed in the city for centuries.

The residence had turned into an infamous place once the Nuncio Rinuccini used it as his base. He offered mass on Sundays when he was in the city but his work took him away often once the Ormond peace was published. This peace did not include the previous concessions made to the Catholics, insisting the army of Ireland would be Protestant, thus debarring both Eoghan Ruaidh and Preston. The Confederates responded to the treaty by splitting along class lines, the richer members accepting, it regardless of their religion, and the poorer rejecting it, supported strongly by Rinuccini.

The place was fortunately quiet the morning John and Ruaidhrí trudged through the snow-filled courtyard, the trees bare and stark. Shaking snow off their cloaks in the deserted hallway, they crossed the polished wooden floors. John paused outside a door on the ground floor, putting his finger to his lips. He bent down with his ear to the door, his starched black clerical robes rustling. He peeped in through the keyhole.

'Dominus Vitus is within addressing the seminarians and students. Thank God he still has the strength left to do that! The warden is with them. I can't see whether Dominus Firbissius is in there or not.'

John straightened up with a sigh.

'We might as well go in and join them if Walter doesn't throw me out on my head. Anyone connected with Tuam is now anathema to Walter since poor Malachy's successor is an Ormond man,' he whispered quietly.

'This place has been engaged in evil dissent for years and if you want to study in this house, you'll have to avoid all factions, Ruaidhrí. If his Excellency tries to manoeuvre you into the militia or the party of Valentine Blake, inform me straight away. Only my duties in choir and pressing affairs with Dubhaltach bring me here nowadays.'

John knocked on the door and they were told to enter. The clergy and students were seated at tables in a huddle before the lectern, listening to Stephen White in silence and taking notes. A pile of texts and papers lay in front of the old man. The warden, Walter, was sitting on his right, hands folded in the depths of his large, ornate robes, vicars and priests beside him. There was no sign of the ollamh. John and Ruaidhrí stood together silently at the rear of the room looking around them, finding themselves immediately under the stony glare of the warden, hearing the clear, tired voice issuing from the lectern.

The elderly Jesuit's lectures were increasingly rare due to his infirmity and age. The great event in Irish hagiography he was lecturing on was the publication of Colgan's book. The priest John Colgan had been a lifelong friend and collaborator of Stephen White's in Louvain. The arrival in Galway some time earlier of this publication on the saints Patrick, Bridget and Columcille, cornerstones of the Irish church, opened up those eras, rallying and bringing a new life to the scholars of Ireland. Leaving his sick bed after a long illness, White stood once more before the clergy and scholars of St Nicholas's on this important anniversary to celebrate the native antiquities which this book had authenticated and vindicated.

John closed the door softly behind them as they caught the thread of White's concluding words.

'None of us remain indifferent to the assaults on our foundations, shaken by cunning twisted arguments, declaring proven eras to be falsifications. These false witnesses advance great heresies against us through confusion, ignorance and the fabrication of gross, persuasive errors against our native church and its early saints. Their authority is given credence, indeed acclaim, in the eyes of the learned in Europe. All in the cold and calculated misrepresentation of our beloved country abroad!

'Central to this argument is the ignorance of European scholars regarding the ancient inhabitants of Scotland. How many of them know the original Scoti were really people from Ireland?

'I tell you they do not know this. They have absorbed into their mainstream learning Dempster's errors on the life of Columcille, as well as those of Camarius on the early Irish church. John Colgan in Louvain has given us the glorious, true life of Columcille and the other saints: a grounded authority we may use in our battles to counter the erroneous authors. You must leave no effort undone until the lustre of truth is restored to our antiquities. The love, devotion and confidence of our suffering Irish faithful deserves no less.'

White paused to gaze at the silent students, still and black garbed in their scholastic cloth; pens and inkpots left aside on the table in front of them. Walter's fidgeting was stilled as he leaned back to investigate the old professor's face.

'The books which guide us through the dark ways of this controversy are held in libraries in this town, works of authority and renown, illuminating the glories of the monastic centres of the Scotias. When you preach the lives of our beloved native saints, those shining examples, our suffering faithful, will draw courage and consolation from them in their persecution. And with these works we will be vindicated! I stand before you, my dear young friends of Galway, to exhort you to venerate the names of our native saints Patrick, Bridget and Columcille. Venerate Ciarán and Kevin, Ursula and Attracta, our own Enda and Macdara and many more from our blessed island. Go forth for Christ in their names!'

The old man bowed and clambered down awkwardly from the lectern, holding the side of it shakily, to stand among the students. A vicar jumped up to place a hand hastily under his thin arm as the silence was broken with prolonged applause, John Lynch and Ruaidhrí joining in at the back.

'Old *Polyhistor*'s able to hold sway yet,' John whispered, his eyes shining with happiness. Ruaidhrí marvelled at the frail old man, catalyst of the scholarship that flowered in Galway during their glory days.

Following the slow, painful departure of White, Walter approached the door with his vicars and Ruaidhrí moved to one side as John bowed to Walter in greeting, speaking briefly in Latin. He heard John murmur his name in quiet tones to the warden and Walter's burning face turned fully upon him, raking him with bold arrogant eyes.

'So, you are Rodericus from Moycullen the young protégé of John's,' he said loudly. 'Welcome among the scholars of the house! I know your face well around here. I know who you are. I've been hearing for a long time how you are versed in your learning far beyond your fellows, beyond any we have had come before us. I hope John here hasn't been over-encouraging you in the ways of compromise and circumspection ... We heard lately he has preached that politics and the church are separate.'

Walter emitted a sharp, bark-like laugh. John attempted to speak but the warden stopped him with raised hand. 'We agreed to differ since his Lordship Rinuccini spoke to us!' Walter glanced warningly in the direction of the guest rooms and John subsided with a shrug.

'We warmly welcome the young man and any of them who have benefitted from your tutelage. Long may you produce such pupils skilled in the ways of Cicero, Plato and the saints while others of us are holding back the heretics from the gates with men in the field, with sword and fortification! However, be that as it may!'

Ruaidhrí shrank from the hateful venom in Walter's voice, his mouth twisted in scorn. John watched him with narrowed eyes, seeing the naked hostility Walter made no effort to hide anymore.

Later John explained how the elevation of John de Burgo, the Ormond champion, as the new archbishop of Tuam in succession to archbishop Malachy O'Queely had come as a great set-back to the warden's faction. This had followed the elevation of John's relative Francis Kirwan as bishop of Kilalla, that most ardent Ormond supporter. The tide in Connacht had been decisively turned in favour of the pro-treaty faction and against the belligerents in the wardenship of St Nicholas and the diocese of Tuam. This mirrored the rise of the pro-treaty side throughout the country and the split on the Supreme Council. That morning he recognised the enmity that had irrevocably arisen between them, two kinsmen, as the country fell apart in civil opposition under the trauma of Parliamentarian aggression, invasion and occupation.

'However, be that as it may,' the warden repeated in an insulting tone and after a pause enquired, 'Have you come to confer with Dominus Dualdus Ferbissius? I believe he's up in the library. Come with me… and I hope you are respectful towards him. We need his services so I want you to be good-natured to him, even if he is a bit peculiar,' added Walter bitingly while glaring at John.

Walter nodded towards the priests standing behind him and all followed him down the passageway towards the stairs. Behind his back John raised his eyes to heaven in annoyance. As they walked the warden started questioning Ruaidhrí over his shoulder about the latter's newly fulfilled expectations: his property, proposed nuptials and family affairs, although Walter seemed to know these in fine detail already. Ruaidhrí felt the pent-up agitation, the nervous energy of the warden in every step he took on the stairs, his black, well-soled, leather shoes silent as he ascended, robes held in his hand. Midway up the stairs the warden halted suddenly, forcing the rest behind him to pause in a close crush on the narrow steps, clutching the rail for support. Without warning Walter changed the subject, swinging around to look back at Ruaidhrí and demand, 'Tell me my dear young Rodericus, what do you think of Dominus Vitus?'

'His arguments indeed inspire the listener on the controversy of the native church and the saints, Your Excellency,' Ruaidhrí replied, looking up at him warily.

'Weren't you lit up by the fires of indignation against the evils of our enemies?'

'Yes, master, yes, in truth I was!' he said, looking from the warden to John behind him.

'Blessings have been bestowed on us since the day Vitus first came here,' and with that Walter continued to climb the stairs, all following behind him as he relapsed into silence. John said very quietly behind Ruaidhrí on the stairs, 'When the Chancellor in Dublin suppressed the secret classical school maintained by the Jesuits; White went on the run to Waterford and afterwards went into hiding here. He brought with him the texts circulating abroad of the erroneous writers attacking our country. He also brought his own works in manuscript and from that time onwards he has directed our work of refutation.

'Stephen is a master of the antiquities, of the Hebrew tongue, the history of the Jews and the ancients of the east, known to his contemporaries abroad as *Polyhistor*. He travelled from the west to the east of Europe on his continental mission, lecturing in the great seats of learning of the Jesuits at Ingolstadt, Dillingen, Metz and Schaffhausen. A strange thing happened while Stephen was the professor of theology at Dillingen. He was put in touch with Archbishop James Ussher, the Protestant primate of Armagh, with whom he has since collaborated - a little-known fact. White went on to become a leading light among his colleagues in St Anthony's College in Louvain. He began his studies of our own antiquities under the Franciscans who have the native sources collected there and the printing presses.'

'The Supreme Council have been encouraging the Franciscans for years to return home with the printing presses,' Walter interrupted him loudly over his shoulder, 'in order that they might continue their work at home.'

John continued without comment on this interruption.

'Stephen came across the life of St Coleman, patron saint of Austria, in the Benedictine library in Keysersheym in Switzerland and he sent it to Ward in Louvain. When the manuscript of Adamnan's life of Columcille was brought to him from the monastery of Reichenau, he sent copies to both Colgan in Louvain and Ussher in Ireland. White's searches led him to the life of St Erhard at the monastery of St Magnus of Ratisbon and materials on the life of St Bridget, copies of which he sent to Ussher. Another copy he sent to Colgan was the life of St Patrick reposing at Biburg in Bavaria.

'The Franciscan College in Louvain is a repository for manuscripts gathered from monasteries all over Europe, Ruaidhrí, priceless records of the piety and scholarship from the foundations established in Europe by the Scoti in earlier centuries. So magnificent was their contribution to Christendom, so equally great is the disgrace that much of their history is still to this day scattered undiscovered, moth-eaten in remote vaults of far-flung libraries, in the places where their schools and monasteries had once flourished.

'Tragically the world is ignorant of those unique saints who rescued the continent from darkness, those early Scoti.

'Stephen followed up the attack on these Scottish historians in his own great work of refutation and vindication, completed during his years with us but as yet unpublished. The fact is, the Jesuit Superior in the end vetoed the publication of his work out of consideration for the hurt it would inflict on the grievously suffering faithful in Scotland because of their great veneration of our Columcille. Regrettable of course but understandable.'

On the upper floor Ruaidhrí found himself on a small, dark, wood-panelled landing, statues placed on windowsills from where the town could be seen spread out below. Here the library was situated. He proceeded along a corridor with the two Lynches and ventured to say,

'You refer to the continental world during the dark ages following the fall of Rome?'

'Exactly,' said John. 'The onslaughts of Goths and Vandals brought down the darkness upon Christianity wherever they conquered the former countries of the Empire.

'But it's clear that the ancient Irish or Scoti were wandering pilgrim souls. We now have an emerging picture of them travelling far and wide across Europe amid the ruins of the church, striving to revive embers smouldering beneath the ashes.

'Ireland, the blessed island, was untouched by the barbarians, who like the Romans did not cross the sea to occupy our shores. Our monks and nuns went out from here to found seats of worship and learning in places which proceeded to become great centres of the faith. We know of their pilgrimages across Britain, France, Germany, Italy and beyond. They brought their relics and sacred books with them, performing miracles, converting souls, spreading the message of the gospel, founding churches, schools, hospitals, great monasteries to which the people flocked.

'Stephen White has spent a lifetime on the continent in search of those ancient Irish, unearthing their glory wherever he could, burning with a passionate fire to vindicate them.'

Ruaidhrí could sense Walter's brazen impatience to get a word in, who finally got to declare loudly, 'They weren't afraid to traverse stormy seas, to climb treacherous mountain passes, make their way through dark forests, to bring the light of the Word to those in darkness. Yes, even as we are marching into the chaos and murkiness of war, resisting dangerous negotiations with modern barbarians who bring a new darkness on Ireland. Remember that my dear young man!'

By now Walter was shaking Ruaidhrí's arm vigorously while watching John Lynch. Ruaidhrí stole a glance at John and noticed the fury in his face when he was distracted by Walter's hoarse cry.

'We know well you preached against Rinuccini's campaign, John Lynch!'

They were at the library door.

'Well, Ruaidhrí, let us go in,' John said, stiff with anger, his hand on the handle, turning his back on Walter whose rage could no longer be contained.

'And I know every precise detail of the latest plotting of the renegade de Burgo in Tuam.' The roars petrified them as they stood at the door. Priests came into the corridor, hesitating in doorways.

'De Burgo will prevent the Supreme Council from conducting a just and lawful war, will he? He will have us compromising ourselves with enemies, will he? Aided and abetted by that connection of yours, Francis Kirwan, your patron Richard Blake and Clanricarde himself. Kirwan plotting with our enemies instead of looking to protect the affairs in his suffering diocese, occupied and terrorised by the marauding Coote. And you scheming with them all in Tuam, yes, you, John Lynch! You!'

Disturbed by this crescendo, a crowd gathered from the lower reaches of the house shouting, 'What's going on!'

John faced Walter with clenched fists, shouting, 'Such seditious, scandalous untruths! The scheming in these parts is occurring in this jurisdiction within these very walls, where you yourself are organising the rabble-rousers of the place. Instead, it is plainly our beholden duty to preach settlement and negotiation to lead our flocks to safety.'

John's clenched fists were raised to Walter's face. The latter's towering rage propelled him forward to strike John, who deflected the blow with his arm. In the rush Ruaidhrí was knocked aside against a statue of Our Lady near the door.

Clerics and seminarians were crowding excitedly onto the corridor shouting 'Are we being attacked?' jostling to see the protagonists.

'Ah, so you admit to your scheming with them! My spies have informed me well!'

'Not so! Not true! I do not scheme with any churchmen! Your head is turned so badly you cannot see the truth, Walter Lynch, or admit the depths of the Nuncio's misinformation and misguidance on the Irish situation! Never mind his awful inability to conduct negotiations. He is a terrible misfortune in our midst who is only leading us to our doom, even if his heart is genuinely filled with loving concern for us.'

Walter and his clergy were flapping their arms frantically, agitated black crows, jumping up and down to quieten John Lynch. They were glancing anxiously in the direction of the guest rooms situated on an adjacent corridor. They turned back hissing in horrified fury at John in case he had more to say, glancing again at the shut door of their illustrious visitor with its draught-excluding carpet blocking the threshold. It would be a miracle if Rinuccini didn't emerge to make a bad story worse.

Pushing and cursing erupted with the sound of blows being struck on the stairs behind them. A man wrestled through the crowd on the corridor, struggling and shouting for John Lynch. It was the bloodied, agitated Brother Matthew, John's assistant, his arms pinned to his sides by stern men of the warden's militia.

Seeing Brother Matthew in this state John Lynch called in dismay, 'It's done, let there be an end to this.'

The warden managed to regain self-control. He ordered them all back and walked away from John, beckoning his community ahead of him without a backward glance at his adversary standing shaken and white-faced at the library door, now wide open with anxious faces staring out.

John backed away from the door looking around him in sudden confusion. 'Where are you Ruaidhrí?' he called.

'I'm here master,' Ruaidhrí replied from his refuge inside the library.

John walked towards him and, noticing how the young man's eyes were fixed beyond him, he turned to follow his gaze.

He saw the figure of Mac Fhirbhisigh in a shadowy recess peering out at them, partially shielded by a large sepia coloured globe of the heavens and earth on an ornate wooden table. The alarmed librarian and his open-mouthed scribes hesitated beside him, looking as if they were ready to flee their shattered sanctuary; one of them already poised at the top of the narrow back stairs at the far end of the library.

Statues of the saints graced alcoves in shelves laden to the ceiling with volumes and papers. Tables and chairs filled the spaces between the books. The frigid air, heavy with its old cloying odour, was gradually settling back into silence. The northern ramparts of the town spread out beyond the far windows, grey under driving snow blowing in steadily from the east. Stony-eyed scribes returned warily to their table in the corner of the room after the commotion died down, hissed at by the stern, bald-headed librarian who marched heavily back to his seat trying to regain order once again in his sanctum. The scribes sat before their abandoned tasks trembling, pale in their dark scholar's coats. Only the sound of John Lynch walking back and forth on old creaking floorboards broke the silence. Dubhaltach finally seated himself too. Everyone wordlessly watched the unnerved, pacing figure of Lynch.

'That the hand of God may guide us now,' John was panting.

He finally stood beside Ruaidhrí who leaned against the wall with folded arms and racing heart.

John gazed at Dubhaltach.

'I run the gamut these days to come into town to see you, Dubhaltach, as you can see,' he said to the ollamh who sat at a table, leaning back in his chair staring at him.

'I came in to see you with good news.'

Dubhaltach only nodded and glanced significantly at Ruaidhrí. John corrected himself at this hint to make a formal introduction.

'I have brought the student Rodericus to assist in our work, Dubhaltach, Ruaidhrí Ó Flaherty.

He broke off in surprise as Dubhaltach rose to his feet and bowed politely to Ruaidhrí to the amazement of the youthful scribes craning their necks like agitated turkeys from their corner.

'I am pleased to have such a diligent student, Ruaidhrí and honoured to be of service to the Uí Briuin of Maigh Seola of the line of Eochaidh Muighmheadhoin as is handed down by O'Duibhgennáin.' He bowed again so gracefully the lads were out of their seats now to get a better view.

'O'Duibhgennáin's poem!' cried John so loudly they all jumped. 'Strange indeed you should bring up that name! That is the very book I wished to discuss with you today! Good God in heaven!'

John, still shaken, sat down beside Dubhaltach, and folded his arms on the table.

'I intend to translate this particular work for the treatise,' John continued after a pause, turning towards Dubhaltach. 'I hope the Latinizing will not lose the beauty of the poetry, do you think? My question to you today is whether this is a work of sound repute? How does it acquit itself against the genealogical records of your own family? What is the respected learned opinion of its authority?'

'That poem is of prime importance in thoroughness and content, indispensable to the learning of descent in its place and order,' replied Dubhaltach at once, turning his eyes away from Ruaidhrí finally and giving John his full attention.

'The compilations of Giolla Íosa Mór Mac Fhirbhisigh derive from the same origins, Giolla Coeman's poem, Giolla Modud's and the other poems, the true unassailable sources drawn on by all the ollamhs. Let me see, I have extracts of it somewhere made by Tadhg an tSléibhte, may he rest in peace.'

Dubhaltach stood up again and went over thoughtfully to examine papers on the shelves, snapping his fingers at an attendant, sending the lad to search on his knees at a lower shelf.

'An irrefutable authority,' Dubhaltach added emphatically in Lynch's direction. Then he noticed John drawing a large bulky document from his bag with both hands and reaching over wordlessly to put it down at the ollamh's place.

'What have you there, John?' he asked curiously.

John sat back with his eyes closed and arms folded in quiet, satisfying drama. This was a moment worth waiting for.

'This, my dearest Dubhaltach, is that very compilation which I obtained a few days ago from Clanricarde's library, with all its poems and other miscellaneous pieces!'

With that John opened his eyes to regard Dubhaltach, a small smile of triumph on his face. He was gratified by the disbelief in the ollamh's voice as the latter stared transfixed at him still bent over the shelves.

'*You* have that compilation, the Leabhair Uí Mhaine? And what's the condition of the book? Where does Ulick Burke keep it?' Dubhaltach slowly straightened up, never taking his eyes off the manuscript John had placed on the table.

The note in the ollamh's voice caused the scribes to listen in curiosity. Dubhaltach faced John excitedly.

'Yes. The parchment is in good condition, Dubhaltach. After all you've said of the antiquity and authority of the book of Uí Maine and all its parts, I made it my business to look it up,' John said, indicating to Dubhaltach to come over and sit down in his chair.

'This is the Leabhair Uí Mhaine itself! Yes! Come over and look! We have been given the loan of it.'

Dubhaltach stood speechless, leaning on the shelves, staring mesmerized at the manuscript on the table, his thoughts racing.

After a pause John continued, 'And I declare to God, it's landed me in dreadful trouble since I managed to gain access to Clanricarde's people, helped by my new archbishop John de Burgo, on whom Walter has set spies. Sir Richard Blake was the friend who pulled those strings for us, of course. Word went around like a whirlwind that I had met with Clanricarde. I was spied upon every time I visited the earl's library. I run the gamut coming in here after that, as I said, with that mad scoundrel Walter able now to accuse me of being in the earl's pocket! I'm being spied on every minute since I came back home with the book, all my comings and goings are watched. And I have to guard it with my life until we are done with it.

'So, you can see for yourself I've been busy all this time since I last saw you.'

'His Excellency our warden seems to think so at any rate,' replied Dubhaltach weakly, coming slowly over to take the celebrated book in his hands, his eyes wide, savouring the first moment, feeling its weight and overcome with emotion.

Finally, he put down the book carefully, sat down laughing and half crying and clapped John on the back who laughed too.

'And what other news have you from your travels?' Dubhaltach asked to give himself time to take it all in. 'You never breathed a word about this, faith!'

'Is that not enough news for you in one day?'

They were talking together about this triumph, examining the manuscript together in excited, muttered tones too low to be heard. They had forgotten all about Ruaidhrí and everything else in the world.

The scribes had not. They watched for their chance when the librarian finally dozed off once there was no further interesting eavesdropping to be done, his snores competing with the masters' chatter.

They beckoned Ruaidhrí over excitedly.

'Have you come to assist us?'

A sleepy faced, round-shouldered youth introduced the group to him, whispering, smirking, looking him up and down. One of them jumped up dramatically to bow in admirable imitation of Dubhaltach.

'The ollamh seems to have a right high regard for you anyway, my young lord'.

They glanced cautiously at the masters over at their table and whispered from the corner of their mouths. 'Maybe he won't boot your behind when he comes in mad roaring drunk. His terrible rages drive us under the table, you know.'

They rolled their eyes in fake fright.

'He might not threaten to slit your throat with the *scian* hidden in his belt!'

The boys were drawing their fingers across their throats, making rattling sounds, hunched up in suppressed laughter.

'He's a spy for O'Neill lodged here by the warden! Shhh!'

They held warning fingers to their lips. They were lifting the corners of Ruaidhrí's cloak, feeling the cloth critically in their hands and asking,

'Where's your knife, young gentleman? Hidden in your belt too?'

'Is it here? Or here?'

160

They seized Ruaidhrí, feeling in his pockets and inside his shirt. One was even under the table fingering the inside of his boots while they wheezed and gasped with stifled laughter.

'The warden appears a fitting match for the ollamh,' Ruaidhrí said when he could get a word in, standing up and trying to brush them off. 'I heard Walter whips malefactors himself.'

A chorus of whispers replied, 'Sit down! You don't know the half of the things we've seen here, the fighting and plotting and conspiring! The swearing of oaths! It would make a lad's hair stand on his head!'

The scribes pulled Ruaidhrí's hair and his ears. They finally whispered that he was a promising lad who would have good times with them, good times as he had never seen before! Their giggles out of control, they woke the librarian, drawing his wrathful, reddened eyes towards them. They pushed Ruaidhrí into the chair, threw a paper in front of him, thrust a pen in his hand and took up their work before the librarian arose to walk over in their direction.

Ruaidhrí could hear the masters now the lads were silent.

John and Dubhaltach seemed to be engaged in a debate about Ó Duibhgennáin, the long dead ancestor of an ollamh who still visited Moycullen by the lake. Old memories came back to Ruaidhrí while, taking his cue from his new companions, he pretended to be busy. He was picturing himself as a child coming down into the room and seeing that old man beside the fire drying himself from the rain of the roads, surrounded by old people of the family. 'Good health to you!', as they drank his health all night, while he talked of their family's illustrious, long dead ancestors. Everyone knew Ó Duibhgennáin, carousing wanderer of the roads, famous ollamh of the *seanchas*.

Raised voices from the masters haranguing each other in intricate, Jesuitical debate over the ethics of transcribing, roused Ruaidhrí from his reveries,

'They never leave off this quarrelling,' the scribe beside Ruaidhrí whispered in delight nudging him, winking at him, pulling comical faces at the masters' backs and making him nearly laugh out loud.

They heard Dubhaltach pounding on the table.

'Whist!' whispered the scribes, cocking their ears, eyes shining.

161

'I will proceed in the task laid on me under the precepts of the law. I will engage in no further debate in this town.'

John's voice rose too. 'Your duty is to complete the chronicle of the Scots. Will you give over burying your head in the sand?'

They awaited the reply with bated breath. The silence lengthened. Ruaidhrí took a quick glance in the direction of the masters. He saw Dubhaltach rising to his full height, the great arc of his arm throwing his cloak around him. John, in a rage, was putting the old manuscript back in his bag with speed, throwing papers on top of it, marginally ahead of Dubhaltach in the rush for the door. Papers and books scattered in their wake to the horror of the old librarian. The latter hurried awkwardly to gather the papers up and run after the departing figures, the door slamming loudly after him.

Left unsupervised, the scribes erupted in delight. A holiday atmosphere took over as they ran yelling down the back stairs, Ruaidhrí following them on their gambols, like released puppies. Out on the street they hurried around to the Cross to hear the news from the loiterers sheltering from the weather in open doorways. They listened to boasts about the wonders of drinking and gambling in outlawed dens. They did not feel the east wind gusting through the cold and slush of the streets.

Ruaidhrí passed his days subsequently in the cold, musty library scribing for the priests. He saw little of either John Lynch or Dubhaltach, the former being out in Tuam engaged in his work and the latter coming and going on his own business.

Ormond temporarily abandoned the country and the Supreme Council sought terms with a new, even less likely champion, Morogh O'Brien, Lord Inchiquin. The notorious, bloody champion of the Parliamentarians had earned a hated reputation for himself in the course of the war. Nevertheless, he now prolonged hope for the pro-truce party.

News of O'Neill's outstanding victory at Benburb in his home base in Ulster, renewed hope in Rinuccini's pro-war advocates. They lit candles in windows, made bonfires in the suburbs and praise for the Nuncio was on everyone's lips in the churches and religious houses. Apprentices and students toasted the Nuncio and the

Confederate Catholics along with the marginalised and the disaffected in the pothouses until cockcrow.

Their antagonists among the freemen shook their heads, declaring the Confederates were failing to hold the liberated zones under their control. They said, before they shut their doors against such shocking celebrations, that the very idea of the Irish in the field with Eoghan Ruaidh and Preston ever winning back the cities and ports was utter nonsense.

Lombard Street: Love

na, bring up the po to mistress Margaret, she's been calling for you this past half hour, can you not hear her! Where've you been?'

'Here, mistress, I'm washing the baby.'

'Well, would you ever see to the old lady before she falls out of the bed thanks to your idleness.'

'Yes, mistress.'

Una placed the child in his cradle, seized the chamber pot and headed for the back stairs to avoid mistress Anne, who was still shouting from the front stairs, holding her stomach. Francis Fitz Peter, the oldest son of the house, was coming down with a slow, dramatic swagger. Francis had no business whatsoever on the back stairs. An aura of menace preceded him as he paused on the second last step, blocking her way, his malevolent, inquisitive eyes boring through her.

'The toll to be paid today is an embrace, my sweet,' Francis said under his breath.

Úna turned and fled for the front stairs, where her mistress was in the entrance passage, still holding her stomach, groaning and listening to the old lady, bedridden for years up in her room.

'Have you not seen to mistress Margaret yet?'

Mistress Anne was more and more agitated as her time was near, more contrary than ever since this confinement.

Her head reeling, Úna ran up the stairs towards the querulous weak calls of the matriarch of the house, mother of Peter Fitz Stephen Brown. She rushed into the old lady's bedroom.

Mistress Margaret was sprawled on the floor, confused and cursing her to eternal damnation.

Mistress Anne demanded that the old lady's linen be aired out the window each morning after she lifted her out of bed onto her po. While busily doing this, Úna noticed a serious, handsome man across the street at his upstairs window looking up every time the billows of white linen dancing in the sea breeze caught his eye. He smiled at her as she leant out shaking the sheets gleaming in the morning air and she smiled at him. Everyone knew he was the ollamh Mac Fhirbhisigh lodging with the priests but not a priest himself. He was a chronicler from Sligo working on antiquities in the collegiate.

Glimpses of the ollamh coming and going on the street were noted by his neighbours and soon the talk revolved around his fine appearance. Everyone heard something different about him, this mystery was filled in by rumours and conjecture. The men were prepared to think he was a spy or a clandestine recruiting officer for the Irish army. The women decided he was a lord of some distant house who had taken a vow to serve God in atonement for his sins and wondered was he married. Úna said nothing about his discreet smile and hoped nothing was noticed by anyone on the street.

One day Úna went up to the old lady's room at dawn, found her cold and rigid in her bed and ran screaming for mistress Anne.

She no longer shook sheets out the window at dawn but spent her mornings washing the soiled clothes of the new baby as well as those of the older children.

Her brothers Mícheál and Éamonn and their wives informed her at the Corpus Christi procession that a stranger from the schoolmaster's beside the wall had taken up employment with the ollamh. This former monk, Tadhg Mac Seáin, known as *Dubh 'gus Páipéar,* happened to be lodging with Richard Athy, their cousin, at the chandler's and they heard about him regularly from the loquacious gossip Richard. They repeated to her with glee stories Richard had related about the ollamh's man, who in Richard's opinion was so harmless he would not have the ability to spy on two old women relieving themselves in the street. Tadhg believed everything he was told, Richard reported, and everything upset him, loud noises, sudden movements, noises from the shambles, large crowds and above all the Angelus bells. The thing about him was, he was not the worst you could meet as he would not hurt a fly, but he was still capable of driving the fellows in the lodging mad with his undeniably *seafóideach* ways. Once Tadhg nearly drowned by leaning against a boat in the docks, if you could believe such a thing! Úna was washing the step of mistress Anne's house when she first saw the lad coming out the side door of the residence and set off, head down, towards the quays. She knew at once he was the ollamh's man from the uncertain, awkward way he walked and the respectable but ill-fitting coat he wore which looked like it had been cut and sown for someone else. As he passed Brown's, he glanced at her and quickly lowered his head without speaking. Úna saw the expression in his deep, blue eyes and it was as if that extraordinary moment filled her entire existence. He was like someone from another world, like the face of Christ and the saints in the church. Behind the open front door, she sensed the watching figure of Francis Fitz Peter lingering in the shadows, watching her so he could fumble with her clothes on the way to the kitchen. Loneliness swept in through the ornate entrance as she squeezed the cloth, the muddy water bleeding through her fingers into the heavy bucket.

The resourcefulness of the *bacach* manifested itself in arranging a meeting between Úna and Tadhg.

'Here, I don't suppose you've any interest in seeing Gregory Philib Mhóir stretched next week?' Richard whispered to Tadhg one night. 'I bet you won't be in the front of the crowd placing your wager on how long it will take him to stop kicking!'

'No, I will not,' Tadhg whispered back with a shudder, looking away in the darkness. 'I don't care what he's done. Will you be there?'

The sentence of death passed on Gregory Philib Mhóir by the Tholsel was the talk of the place for weeks, especially as the execution date drew near.

'I will of course, and he's done plenty. He stabbed his neighbour out in the suburbs who caught him red-handed trying to steal his pig in the middle of the night. He was seen leaving the poor man dying outside the door and running away. They're making an example of him now because of all the robbing that's going on.

'It's a chance not to be missed for yourself and Úna. She wants me to escort her to the road through the bushes beyond the swamp as soon as the Browns allow the servants out for the hanging. She'll give them the slip in the crowd. You can make your way there earlier, keeping well down, so I can be back in good time before it starts. The whole town will be at the gibbet and afterwards one of her brothers will bring her home. You stay out of sight and if anyone asks afterwards where you were, say you were praying for Gregory's soul out at the sea. They'll believe you, never fear.'

On a special holy day in summer Richard Athy arranged with significant solemnity to bring Tadhg out to the home place in the Claddagh. Everyone knew mistress Anne had no option but to release the servants to visit the holy well of St Augustine after mass. Úna Ní hEidhin left the prayers and devotions at the well when her mistress's household were all kneeling and joined her brother Mícheál's family in their usual spot on the strand side of the crowd. When the Browns' people lose interest and their eyes turn away, she quietly slipped unnoticed from the crowd. Her sister-in-law, Bríd, at this signal knelt in her vacated place with her shawl covering her face and Úna crossed the bridge over the river to her family waiting to see her.

This year Úna hurried more eagerly than ever before. The *bacach* had appeared at the back entrance of Peter Fitz Stephen Brown's a week before, under cover of the clattering and shouting in the busy wheelwright's yard nearby, whispering his plans excitedly through the gate.

She knew Tadhg would be at her father's house on the holy day.

The house was full, an expectant hum of conversation carrying out into the street when she arrived, flushed and breathless after her furtive run from the holy well. Tadhg was in the place of honour beside her father at the fire, talking awkwardly about his own father down the country. He fell silent, looking at her with eyes as blue and as open as the sky. Úna looked down in embarrassment and her father continued the talk, asking him about his life in town. Her ears were pounding and she did not hear his replies. When the meal was finished Richard, uncharacteristically quiet in the corner, suggested she would be nimbler than himself showing their guest the sea and the boats.

Úna led him down the street of the houses, every door opened, men and women seated outside in the sun enjoying the holy day. They both looked back to see that Richard was standing in the door of his maternal house, hat on his head, waving the stick happily at them. She took Tadhg's hand and they ran along the stony *cladach* the village was called after. Úna's sisters told her afterwards Richard, on seeing them holding hands, hobbled back to the fire in great satisfaction, announcing to them all the business was done, reaching out for the *poitín* her father was already pouring.

Tadhg looked at coloured stones and seashells, examining bits of seaweed so closely that it brought to her mind what the *bacach* had said about his friend, 'That's a fellow who never set eyes on the sea until he came here.'

167

Tadhg, with his odd gait and awkward movements, moved in wonder to examine each object. His voice so sonorous and cultured she could listen to him forever - a voice soft and wounded. He found a stone and showed Úna the shape of a shellfish hardened into it from long eras past, a true wonder. She brought him to the *currachs* pulled up on land, idle for the day. She gestured towards *púcans*, *gleoiteogs*, various *báid mhóra* moving at anchor in the gently moving waves, sails furled. She named the master of each boat, indicating the one which was her father's.

'We went on board the day the Puritans started fires in the town,' Úna said pointing to her father's boat. 'The whole crowd of us went out to sea and all of them went too,' she indicated the other vessels. 'We came ashore below in Clare and went to old Mártán Mháire's cousin's house - my grandmother's people, and we stayed with them for a good while. We returned when word came it was safe.'

Úna continued her story saying that on returning to the village the people had to bury the dead and rebuild the roofs. Tadhg's head swirled under the pressure of his own thoughts, reflecting with wonder that some people can speak of these things and that the telling lightens the load - for a while. Úna Ní hEidhin told it all with a extraordinary naturalness and quietness. She could talk about events that created a swirling, nameless madness in his head. A peace settled on him as she talked. He prayed wordlessly that it would last forever.

They sat together on an upturned *currach*, feeling its warm, lightness beneath them. She pointed towards Aran, indicating where the fleet went out when herring and mackerel shoals run and the best times to go after salmon and trout. An unusual light in Tadhg's face arrested her. He was smiling, even laughing with joy as he looked around at the shimmering sea, lapping and splashing over the multi-coloured stones. He inhaled the seaweed scented wind, feeling imagined waves through the stretched hide of the *currach.*

The cruel turbulence of their times was mercifully being washed from his mind on the ebb tide of love carrying him away. Úna noticing a brightness in his eyes, took his hand again to embrace him. She led him to the garden of sean Bairtle Mháire's roofless house, derelict since he was killed and with no one to take it over.

They lay in each other's arms, sweet smelling sea grass their haven, seabirds calling overhead.

'Will you marry me?' he asked and she says she would, knowing a peace she too had never felt before.

She made her vows silently to live in the shelter of his goodness forever.

Lacuna: The Last Pagan King of Ireland

tarvation ravaged the poor in stinking back lanes and suburbs of Galway. Fear showed on faces one met in the streets, trade in the shops went quiet. Anything that could be stolen disappeared in an unprecedented rise of crime among the formerly settled, law-abiding citizens, despite the example made of Gregory Philib Mhóir. Filth piled up in running drains. It became treacherous to be out alone once darkness set in. Landed gentry avoided their relatives in town and suburbs and set armed guards on their stock at night.

Quietness settled within the precincts of the library with its view on one side over Lombard Street and Bóthar Cam, and St Nicholas's Church on the other. Controversy continued to rage behind doors among clergy and politicians.

John Lynch was keeping to himself in his residence in Tuam.

Dubhaltach Mac Fhirbhisigh appeared one day after a lengthy absence and ordered the scribes and attendants to undertake a great transcription. The remaining seminarians of the Lynchs, few in number, were engaged exclusively in theology and philosophy in the chapter house, busy attending sermons and lectures in preparation for their vocation to the church. A future exile in the universities of France and Spain lay ahead of these young men as the country gradually fell to the Puritans. Without warning, some of the lads left their books forever after a night of vigil in the oratory, solemnly bade the others goodbye and walked out the door to take up arms for the Nuncio. Rinuccini's preaching had convinced them to fight for faith and country.

The swiftly turning tide was heralded with news of the defeat of Thomas Preston, leader of the Leinster army for Rinuccini, at a place up the country known as Dungan's Hill.

A different storm arose in September with a ferocity Ruaidhrí never thought possible. Strong winds lashed the convulsed land so powerful that the waters of the river Corrib flowing from the lake to the sea at the city walls were blown clean off the riverbed. People strong enough to brave the gales walked up and down the exposed banks of the dried river, coats and hoods tied around them with ropes, bent double in the howling storm. They stumbled over the slime-covered stones to gather a pocketful of the fish dying in wind-whipped fields. No one had ever seen the river dried by wind, sucked up by the elements, an unprecedented ill omen.

Another wind blew through the city the day Ulick Burke, Earl of Clanricarde, now elevated as Marquess of Clanricarde, arrived in state wearing a blue velvet cloak, silken shirt and satin trousers with a fur-trimmed, feathered hat. Ulick, riding on a magnificent horse followed by his large retinue, entered in through the main gate from Bóthar Mór, proceeded down Mainguard Street to dismount at St Nicholas of Myra's. He was to be reconciled with the town, both civil and ecclesiastical. The canny, fence sitting Ulick had got himself elevated to the position of Catholic Viceroy of Ireland, the pinnacle of a career carefully nurtured and manoeuvred through thickets of the hysteria and chaos of the war. The earl knelt alongside archbishop Rinuccini before the great altar of St Nicholas's in solemn ceremony. He promised to negotiate with the Parliament for the Catholics of the country. English-born Ulick, an unlikely saviour, was what is known as 'a man unto himself,' so went the skulking thought pushed at the back of people's minds as they grasped at this straw like drowning people.

Amid these gales, the freemen and women shook out their own silks and satins and for a little while relived their happier former days of quieter, more genteel peace and prosperity. When they could, they organised masses, entertainments of all sorts, outings held in honour of these events, culminating in a ball at Sir Richard Blake's out at Ardfry. The students and attendants of the library followed these great events from their vantage points of the residence windows and their favoured spot at the Cross - the doorway of a shoemaker's shop. This premises doubled as a drinking house which was concealed at the back. Jugs and tankards were tucked discreetly behind lasts, awls and strong-smelling piles of leather worked by the tradesman and his apprentices. From the bakery next door, the aroma of freshly baked bread mingled deliciously with the leather and the ale, making it an irresistible retreat that satisfied the senses.

A great change occurred in St Nicholas's at this time. Walter Lynch was elevated bishop to the See of Clonfert with sacred pomp and ceremony as part of the Nuncio's flurry of elevations of his supporters. Walter quit the residence in a mighty burst of activity and

Patrick Lynch, the scholarly vicar, was elevated to the wardenship in succession to fiery Walter.

An uneasy peace settled in and about St Nicholas's. January brought ice lying thicker on the lake and river than anyone could remember.

When they placed candles in the windows for the new year dust covered the tools and work benches in John Fitz Richard Darcy's once-bustling leather shop in Cross Street. The men were occupied in endless meetings with the corporation and the militia. Mistress Bridget, the woman of the house, supervised the girls and servants in frenzied sewing and knitting in between prayer and visiting the church. The Darcy lads turned overnight into men. Business was all but a thing of the past, replaced by running weapons, carrying passengers fleeing abroad and provisioning armies in the field.

Ruaidhrí was reading the church fathers of north Africa, Clemens, Tertullius, Lactantius and towering above them all, St Augustine's *City of God*. He listened as the seminarians debated the authors of the native antiquities, Keating, Wadding, Ussher, Ware and their own White, an unquestioned authority. They discussed and expanded John Colgan's *Lives of the Saints* endlessly, the cause of controversy with Mac Fhirbhisigh when he brought the annals to bear in the interpretation of that masterpiece. The ollamh accepted no early history could be omitted. When Mac Fhirbhisigh spoke he held them spellbound, the living personification of the *seanchas*. The students were transported back to the far-off origins of the native church with such passion and breath of learning that they left him inspired anew in their study and work.

A lecture White once gave on the Hebrew tribes at the dawn of their origins came back to mind and sent Ruaidhrí looking for Josephus's *The Antiquity of the Jews*. While the snow, hail and storm battered the town, he saw caravans of dark-eyed patriarchs marching in historic migrations across hot sands of storied realms. They were founding dynasties that flourished for centuries afterwards, bringing God, knowledge, language and learning to new places. Ringed and jewelled hands wrote on papyrus with sharpened reeds, chronicling the descendants of kings who rose and fell.

The peace of the collegiate library was shattered once again, in unison with the tension and strife widespread everywhere. A hurricane blew through its shelves, not one born of the Inchiquin negotiations but unleashed by the ancient writer called Eusebius.

'Who was Eusebius?' Ruaidhrí wondered.

A battle raged about the place while Bridget shook her skirts bringing the storms of spring. Later John Lynch entered with the air fresh on his clerical garments, calling a breathless greeting to Ruaidhrí and his companions at their table. He gathered them all around him to deliver a stirring, intricate speech on the subject of chronology. He proclaimed that the counting of years, omissions and inaccuracies in Irish annals made the writing of history harder than pulling hens' teeth. John, without drawing breath, evoked the genius of the bedridden White, the research of Helvetius, the Septuagint, the mysterious Eusebius and the errors of long-dead scribes.

Priests arrived and listened while the seminarians and scribes, some of them drink-sickened and world-weary feigning boredom, nodded vigorously in uncomprehending agreement whenever Lynch's eye fell on them.

'We have to move in the present age of the world, Ruaidhrí,' John said, when he finally sank exhausted into a chair beside the boy.

'The old-fashioned ways will not defend us against our enemies. They just won't do.'

Mac Fhirbhisigh from the reaches of the house heard of Lynch's appearance in public and came rushing in next. Dubhaltach occupied the centre of the floor in front of John's chair to berate all unlettered, misguided fools, clergymen who know nothing about chronology, and heretics.

The scribes brightened at the prospect of such controversy and drew near in expectation. They shrank back again as the door was flung open, noisily heralding the entrance of the new warden Patrick Lynch, reinforced by his vicars. Patrick requested John to remove himself from the library for causing uproar among the students. If he came in again, he was to avoid causing disturbance. Everyone was aware it was the war, not manuscripts that Patrick was shouting about, as John Lynch got up, bowing to him as he swept past him straight-backed and tight-lipped out the door.

Dubhaltach sat down wearily on the chair vacated by John to recover his breath. The lads expected him to take up the subject of chronology, asking him about it, but he only waved his hand in dismissal.

'No, I'd like to talk to you today about how the Scoti defended their allies in Europe and north Africa against the occupation of the Roman empire, in the early eras before Patrick brought Christianity to Ireland. You will then be able to place in proper context our blessed saint's arrival in this island,' he said.

'And you will also understand how the sins of our ancestors in their greed for the spoils of war, slaves and gold, is being visited on our heads in these terrible times in which we live.'

The history of the Roman empire was undoubtedly a favourite topic among the young men, but they had never heard the Irish were involved in fighting against its might. No one had ever presented such an idea to them before. Excited by this strange information they sent a scribe rushing out to tell lads who were absent that the ollamh was lecturing on Rome in the library.

Dubhaltach began speaking while the floor filled with listeners sitting cross-legged around him and the vivid, detailed scenes he was unfolding slowly transfixed them. He discussed how the Romans over time conquered and oppressed tribes across England, Gaul, Spain and the Atlas during the Celtic and Punic wars. The western coastal tribes of Europe were kindred peoples to the Irish in origin, language and customs. Ancient sources of the ollamhs described how these tribes resisted to the end the imperial might and power pushing relentlessly across the Mediterranean and Europe, he explained.

He explained that he wanted to talk about how the Irish were allied to these tribes. Fearless travellers over land and sea, the Irish maintained close contact with their suffering friends in Europe and north Africa who were unfortunately being attacked and conquered by Rome.

Mac Fhirbhisigh went on to explain that the annals of Clan Firbhisigh describe how in the reign of the king in Ulster Hugo Mac Aonghusa, a force was sent from Ireland to fight for Carthage in north Africa and Spain. The indigenous people of the Atlas, called the Berbers in the classical world, had rallied behind their kings and queens to attack the Roman colonies established on their coasts.

Dubhaltach explained how in the fifth century, Niall of the Nine Hostages, grandson of the high king Cormac Mac Airt, and his nephew Daithí conducted raids against the Romans of Britain and Gaul in alliance with local western tribes. He pointed out that both kings were married to daughters of British Gaelic kings whose language they spoke. They were granted lands and established settlements in England, Scotland, Wales, Normandy and Brittany in renumeration for their military alliances.

He further pointed out that both these kings were killed in action overseas. Niall, who brought Patrick the apostle of the Irish to us, fell leading an attack on the Isle of Wight against a fortified Roman settlement established. His body was taken home for burial in Tara, 'facing the rising sun and the lands of my enemies.'

In the year 428, Daithí, the last pagan king of Ireland, grandson of Niall, was killed by lightening at the foot of the Alps. Dubhaltach reminded his audience that he had told them the story how the king's death came about after he killed a holy man of that place.

To emphasise the significance and extent of the Irish assaults on the Romans and their neighbours, he pointed out how Irish attacked them continuously, carrying off spoil, slaves and hostages; motivated, as they were, by greed and the prevailing chaos of war. However, Dubhaltach also pointed out that he felt that now, after fifteen hundred years, the sins of their fathers were being visited on the heads of their descendants through the war.

Dubhaltach went on to explain that the annals describe how king Daithí had a son Amhlaidh, his right hand in battle. Amhlaidh brought his body home over land and sea, through battles and forced marches and laid him to rest in the graveyard of the kings at Rathcroghan. He pointed out that one could still see the tall, red stone marking his grave, Daithí's Stone.

Dubhaltach concluded with an account of Clan Firbisigh, which was descended from Amhlaidh, son of Daithí, or from Amhlaidh son of Fiachra Ealgach, son of Daithí or indeed from both. The clan had spread across the entire division of Connacht. *Tír Amhlaidh* was, he claimed, his original place, the area of Maigh Bróin between Loch Conn and the waters of Moy, the division of the two Bacs and Gleann Néifinn, and that after Daithí's death the new faith of the Romans spread throughout the island.

With this Dubhaltach, sat back in his chair and viewed his silent audience which broke into applause.

Leaving the library quietly, the lads discussed the lecture returning to their rooms, hardly knowing what to make of it, asking each other where they could look up the history the ollamh had just taught them and what books contained it.

Afterwards Ruaidhrí searched the shelves for Eusebius. The prince of ancient chronologists, Lynch, had called him during his brief visit before warden Patrick demanded he leave.

'What are you looking for now, my lord bookworm?' one of the scribes whispered to him, one eye on the dozing librarian sleeping off the night's drinking, irreverent as ever.

'Eusebius,' Ruaidhrí told them. 'Come and help me search for him, layabouts!'

The scribes searched half-heartedly, languid from their confinement under the priests, distracted by their illicit carousing at night and excited by hidden meetings with their relatives in the militia.

Ruaidhrí eventually walked over to the Jesuit house to search their library, tiptoeing among the silent, keen-eyed men who had the ear of the highest in the land, and where the old *Polyhistor* slowly breathed his last. The search proved fruitless and the librarian in charge concluded the masters of the residence must have the texts he sought as they were not on their shelves.

The arguments over the Septuagint, the Seventy Interpreters who set the calendars in their deliberations long ago remained as much a mystery as ever. The ordering of time fixed by God, interpreted by those fathers so that men might understand, was at the heart of the masters' latest dispute.

Why had the masters argued about confused chronology in the Irish sources? the lad asked himself as he wandered through cold, neglected streets full of idlers. Hard-faced constables of the watch manned the gates and armed men were on the walls everywhere. Worshippers kept vigil in the Carmelite and Augustinians churches. The Franciscans prayed beside the walls. A large group of impoverished, ill-dressed women and their children knelt outside the Poor Clares' house while the nuns appeared silently at their hatch to hear petitions, blessing them and withdrew to their hidden chapel. The town was a frightened, mournful place. He entered the residence to seek the comfort of the scribes and take refuge in their scheming and gossiping, but the library was unoccupied except for an elderly priest, and he was alone.

Fragmentation

St Nicholas's affairs declined steadily. Business was left aside in town except preparation for the coming conflict. O'Neill kept the Irish army campaigning mainly in Leinster and Munster. The Protestant Old English and Parliamentarian armies held the ports of those provinces except Limerick. Catholic Old English armies allied at times with O'Neill under Rinuccini's direction in ever-shifting alliances and routed Parliamentarian inland garrisons in endless skirmishes. The Parliamentarian army of Coote occupied north Connacht while the Scots and new settlers' armies held Ulster.

The Connacht Confederates invited Eoghan Ruaidh O'Neill to attack Sligo. He once again brought his army to Roscommon, only to have his siege artillery bogged down in the Curlew Mountains. He then retreated, leaving Connacht vulnerable as ever before the Parliamentarians.

The Confederates on the breakaway Supreme Council under the Nuncio experienced their next convulsion when the Ormondists accepted the Inchiquin treaty. Rinuccini, in his strongest reaction so far, issued an excommunication order on anyone who accepted the Inchiquin settlement. He experienced his greatest set-back in Ireland when he saw the country's fate given into the hands of a cruel, bloodied turncoat - Morogh O'Brien, Baron of Inchiquin.

The town people lived in a whirlwind of prayer, fasting, rumours and omens. The scribes remained in their rooms until they too disappeared finally into the militia.

Ruaidhrí, in his solitude, found a new author whom he discovered by chance in his searches - the Venerable Bede, held in great respect by the masters. The eighth century Briton had recorded the early church of the Angles, Saxons and Gaels of the two Scotias.

He discovered for himself why the masters discussed these chronicles so often because of the picture which emerged from the author's witness of the monastic settlements in the northern regions. A deep satisfaction settled on Ruaidhrí as Irish affairs were being attested to by a foreign witness such as Bede, an outsider view from an authoritative pen. Early eras recorded by Gilla Coeman and the monastic writers as interpreted by Mac Fhirbhisigh, came to be viewed in a special way when they were presented from a foreign perspective.

'You must understand that these writers are to be counter-positioned against Camarius and his ilk,' John Lynch had told him long before, and now he understood the significance of what he meant.

Mac Fhirbhisigh in Galway was defending the annals and records that came down through the ollamh families of the Milesians. These he helped become the foundation of the study of Irish antiquities because, most crucially, they incorporated earlier peoples in Ireland. Ruaidhrí had known of these chronicles since he was a child. The ollamhs of the *seanchas* were the keepers of the history and the family genealogy of the descendants of the sons of Míl, the ruling class in the country. O'Duibhgennáin, in coming to Ruaidhrí's house in Moycullen, as the keeper of his own family's history, was fulfilling a two-thousand-year-old function. Seeing this clearly in his maturity, Ruaidhrí remembered how old people, seldom seen out in their infirmity, left their fire and emerged to line the road in silence when the ollamh was departing after his sojourn in the big house. The ollamhs, in knowing their descent, intertwined with that of the aristocracy, represented who they were and the *tuatha* from which they were descended.

There were also the Old English who became one with the Irish over centuries through intermarriage and custom. This happened despite the ethos of exclusivity adhered to by the wealthier, worldlier, more ambitious Galway town families who married into the Anglo-Normans, supplied the fort for centuries and controlled the city and its trade.

In this terrible war, different factions collaborated for the glories of the early holy men and women of the island, so that, united at last in adversity, they became one in the Irish faith, their nexus in Galway. Without the Old English familiarity with the new ways, without their scholars and libraries, would the *seanchas* of Mac Fhirbhisigh have any future if there were none to succeeded them? This thought implanted itself in Ruaidhrí's head during these days.

'The Milesians were strong,' the ollamh said, 'because they incorporated the Fir Bholg and Formorians as slaves and through intermarriage. They made the buildings, customs and stories of the

Tuatha De Danann and the Fir Bholg their own, as well as marrying into them. They became the one people.'

Lynch claimed that Keating wrote that the blending of *SeanGhaill agus Gael* into one race gave birth to the name '*Éirinnigh*,' referring to all the people born and living in Ireland. 'We're all the *Éirinnigh* of Ireland,' Keating had written.

Dubhaltach fiercely defended the chronicles which had come down through the ollamh families. He explained how the history both pagan and Christian came from the abbots and monks of the monasteries after the Northmen invasions, to families such as his own and many more.

'The body of history came down to us,' he said, 'until our patrons are deprived of their land and position, the schools closed, the authenticity of the native annals denied. Do we have to change and embrace printed books to continue our lawful duty until the times settle?'

'The native annals must be subject to rigorous and methodical assessment,' said John, 'before they may be presented to the light of European debate, especially the earliest books which are not accepted by historians.'

The mere suggestion of this drove the ollamh into a defence of the sources, falling into a desperation of anxiety and frustration.

How do you arrive at the truth? This was the thought occupying Ruaidhrí's mind as he glimpsed the monastic town of Iona through Bede's witness. This was the world of a Scotian colony which Clan Firbisigh chronicled; a vanished world.

Dubhaltach also had another concern. He thundered against English claims that the Irish had built no stone edifices before the era of the Northmen. 'Let those who wish examine the numerous stone churches, graves and forts built by a very ancient people all over this island,' Mac Fhirbhisigh argued.

For Dubhaltach the history the chronicles recorded was from the earliest beginnings. It had descended pure and unassailable through the lawful, professional, hereditary ollamhs. It passed from father to son generation after generation, from the tenth century after the destruction of the monasteries and the dispersal of the monks. Monasticism was beloved by the Irish and spread from centres like Clonmacnoise and Clonfert to Iona and Northumberland, and from there across all Europe. The holy men and women of Ireland crossed water and land to travel the roads of Europe bringing God's word, Dubhaltach emphasised. This was a story they knew well in Galway from Stephen White's life's work.

Some of them, returning to Ireland with knowledge of the Irish manuscripts collected in Europe, came to stand before the ollamh at the end of their days. Or was it the ollamh who came to stand before them? Ruaidhrí placed his head in his hands as he wandered over to the dark windows beside his seat, overwhelmed by all his questioning and reading, all these images and voices of the town.

Again and again, Ruaidhrí pictured with a heightened clarity the day in his childhood when the old *mantach,* accompanied by his companion on horseback, arrived at their door to be received with great welcome and display. The old man's name was well known, his people esteemed. With his awkward gait and intense, mobile face, he received warm hospitality wherever he travelled. A guest bed was made for him, food and drink put down for him by his aunt. Relatives entered the house to sit with the old man in conversation. The people brought the guest the gifts they always brought to the ollamh, butter, bags of eggs, leather for his shoes, skeins of wool, oats for his horse. The crowd in the house by night fell silent to hear him speak, a crush of bodies that spilled out the door. Ruaidhrí was the small boy who sat in the corner beside the chimney, struggling for air while the old man recited.

'Why did he come to the house?' His aunt was putting them to bed, the motherless children half asleep later that night.

'His people have always been coming here, they're the ollamhs', she replied. 'They visit the houses hearing the news, seeing the changes, recording the marriages, births and deaths. Those men know everything of the present day and the past. He told us tonight the history of Iar Connacht. He is O'Duibhgennáin chronicler of Uí Mhaine.'

Ruaidhrí left the window, put Bede aside and returned to the task Lynch set him when they had last discussed their work. This was the comparison of extracts from the *Veterum Epistolarium Hibernicarum Sylloge,* Ussher's respected and well-known work on the native church, side by side with extracts from Ó Cléirigh's annals on the same subject.

A terrible summer, overcast, heavy and ill-omened, saw the mayor and council, urged by those two foremost Connacht prelates, archbishop John de Burgo of Tuam and bishop Francis Kirwan of Killala, publish acceptance of the Inchiquin treaty. The conflict of opinion on how the war should be conducted was coming to its frightful climax.

Rinuccini declared immediate excommunication for any Catholic, cleric or lay, who accepted or promoted this treaty with Protestants. The approach of the outsider Nuncio lacked the subtlety required to bring all sides with him and was clear in this ultimate step he took. All it did was to lay bare divisions, age-old and recent, within church and people in their hour of darkness. Rinuccini would argue later he had no choice, as he clearly saw the king and Ormond were attempting to use the Irish Catholics for their own ends. He could only encourage those Old English who did give him support.

Dubhaltach was making progress with his book, staying indoors to work through the daylight hours, dining in the silence of the refectory while a priest or seminarian read aloud.

The ollamh sent Tadhg off on his errands to the merchants when he needed paper, ink or writing implements. Brother Benildus shuffled in and out to clean his room, asking him did he need his horse. Benildus had started bringing Dubhaltach the local news, whispering in horrified tones that the world was coming to an end fulfilling the prophesies. Normal life seemed a distant memory, something only dreamed of, which mothers talked about to the children, trying to shelter them from the upheaval through which they were growing up. Dubhaltach was too busy with his work to do more than shake his head and whispered quietly to Tadhg, 'It appears the Old English are tearing each another apart, divided on how to deal with the threat of the Irish army as well as the new Puritan English. Where does that leave the rest of us?'

'There's been a lot of falling out in families,' Tadhg concurred, ready to ask questions but Dubhaltach held up a hand and kept writing.

Clanricarde's men surrounded the city to enforce the Inchiquin peace by blocking the war party from moving in or out. These soldiers watched every move of the new warden, Patrick Lynch, and Sir Valentine Blake of the anti-treaty faction.

Then the landed gentleman archbishop, John de Burgo, O'Queely's successor, arrived from Tuam with his followers to make a clear point of what he personally thought of Rinuccini's decree of excommunication on himself for accepting the treaty with the Protestants.

De Burgo offered mass - forbidden now under his excommunication - in the Carmelite church to a packed, sweating congregation. The archbishop surpassed this defiance on the following Sunday when he turned his sights on St Nicholas's itself.

Every door was locked by the warden Patrick Lynch, locks that had been reinforced in better days by Walter. This did not deter a man like John de Burgo. His men appeared early in the church yard, causing consternation in the residence. The warden Patrick and his priests realised too late that a man had succeeded in breaking in through the roof and, along with those outside, broke down the doors despite their supposedly impregnable locks. De Burgo had previously alerted his supporters to defy the Nuncio and these had arrived out of nowhere to occupy every seat in the church.

De Burgo, along with his ally, the bishop of Kilalla Francis Kirwan, offered mass publicly on the high altar of St Nicholas's before a packed congregation. The intrepid archbishop then returned to Tuam, well satisfied with this ultimate gesture of defiance against the warden Patrick Lynch, who could see all this from the main door of the residence. For De Burgo, it was a most satisfying way of showing his disregard for the excommunication brought down by Rome on all, including himself, who had accepted the Inchiquin treaty.

News came in January 1649 that froze the heart of the listeners and brought the clergy to their knees and caused families to lock their doors, praying together that night in terror. The Parliamentarians had publicly executed the king, Charles the First.

On a cold, draughty day in the following month St Nicholas's was filled again with a crowd, shivering and weeping, assembled there to hear Rinuccini's last farewell sermon. He had returned to Galway, having finally recognised his mission to save Ireland was over, despite the petitions of Eoghan Ruaidh O'Neill. The Nuncio's boat awaited him at the docks, the frigate *San Pedro*. O'Neill had taken it in the early stages of the war as a prize in the North Sea from a Parliamentarian fleet trying to prevent the Earl of Tyrone's return to Ireland.

The Nuncio bade his last farewells to warden Patrick, the clergy, the mayor and corporation and the distraught population awaiting their doom. The extent of the crowd seeing him off on the quays at the end of his failed mission greatly consoled him. Their grief was visible as he blessed them from the deck before slowly going below, while every bell in the city pealed goodbye.

The news was heard back in the course of time when he was safely home on his native soil what Rinuccini's final word on his stay in Galway had been, 'I can say in truth that the one called de Burgo of Tuam had been the most defiant of them all.'

By august of 1649 Ormond had lost Dublin to Michael Jones, the Parliamentarian commander, in a great defeat at Rathmines. The new king Charles II rejected the Inchiquin treaty in return for support from the Scots. People could feel the tide turning against the Irish who had risen with such hope all those years ago in 1641.

Dubhaltach was writing his book in his room, doing his best to ignore all this by remaining indoors. He was thankful for his patrons who allowed him this refuge and the remuneration for his tutoring and assistance while the entire country fell apart.

Mac Fhirbhisigh was studying the descent of Clan O'Drisceoil back from the current chief of his name, Finghín O'Drisceoil. While he was scribing Finghín's name slowly and painstakingly Tadhg waved the old manuscript from which they were copying, to ask impulsively, 'How do you know he's the right one to succeed this chieftain, master?' The lad indicated the name on the old manuscript. 'And that the father died in that year and was succeeded by this fellow. I mean, sir, how do you know about all the new names I see you often writing into your book?'

Dubhaltach looked at him silently. Belatedly, Tadhg remembered he should not speak like this to the master. The other carefully placed his pen in his ink pot, folded his arms, sighed and replied, 'Everybody knows old O'Drisceoil died in that year and that this son Finghín succeeded him as head of his name.'

'Everybody knows?'

'Yes. I could ride out of this city to any royal house in Connacht and every one of them would've heard it. Some of them with family married into the O'Drisceoils might even have been at the funeral in Cork. The news would have been carried by word of mouth or by letter to anyone connected to him, spreading swiftly to other houses. I am only updating old news this evening by adding that son's name in the genealogy.'

'Well, I have never seen grand families such as those,' Tadhg said, staring down at the genealogy and sitting forward in dismay while Dubhaltach frowned and resumed his writing.

Days had lengthened into another summer of rain, hail and storm, when Dubhaltach, looking out his window, noticed Brother Benildus rushing as fast as he could into the courtyard at dawn, robes tied up into his belt. The brother was panting and shouting 'Plague! Plague! Plague!' The ollamh opened his window and leaned out in shock. People came running out to hear his terrible news.

'The news beyond at the water source is that a boat home from Spain is in quarantine in the Pool!' cried Benildus.

'There's plague in Sir Richard's Blake's house! And a woman died last night in the suburbs covered in black boils, the Lord between us and all harm! The physicians went in the darkness out to her house to affirm it was plague that killed her. They were seen coming back a few minutes ago!'

Within minutes the news was all over town. 'Plague! Plague!'

Mothers snatched up their babies and called the children off the street. Merchants shut their shops. Churches emptied of worshippers, and the priests locked the doors. The nuns and friars streamed out, running into the crowds. The town's population evacuated their houses, pouring out the city gates, led by priests holding crosses high.

'The hand of God has come down on us for opposing the Nuncio from Rome!'

'*Retribution for Rinuccini*!' became the new catch cry. Opponents of the Nuncio beat their breasts praying for forgiveness.

Tadhg searched for Dubhaltach all morning in the chaos, panic rising in him, but could not find him. Returning to the residence after looking in the streets he found every door locked, the place deserted. Confused and troubled, tears in his eyes, he too joined in the exodus, taking the bridge across the river, and walking out to the fishing village. Úna, already home from Brown's, saw him coming from the door and wordlessly brought him in to the family around the fire.

After a while Tadhg asked them, 'Where's Richard Athy? I couldn't see him anywhere either.'

'We think the Athys have gone out together to relatives of the father towards Athenry,' Úna's mother told him.

'Will you all go?'

'No, we will stay here unless someone in the village contracts the sickness. Then we'll get away by sea out the coast and stay with our relatives until it has passed. And we will not be able to sell in town until the plague passes.'

'You will stay with us, Tadhg,' her father added. 'Úna is back home now the Browns are gone out the country. This has happened before, and it will happen again. You both can go before the priest the next time he comes out to the mass house, God willing.'

Michaelmas came and the freemen and officials elected a new mayor and corporation as they always did at this time. The Tholsel was abandoned like every other building in town, plague by now killing thousands. The Parliamentarians, triumphant in England, were moving to defeat all Royalist support in Ireland. The freemen assembled in the parlour of a county residence located in its woods and pastures. They prayed for the dead and dying from the plague and for the Almighty to strengthen them against their enemies.

The new mayor elected was Oliver Óg French and the Sheriffs elected were James Fitz Edmond French and Peter Fitz Anthony Lynch. Oliver Óg, James and Peter duly elected, they gave over the proceedings to the observers who had intelligence and reports from throughout the country. Blood ran cold as they sat in the crowded, lavish parlour, hearing from these men how the Parliament's new army was greatly reinforced. They could scarcely believe what they were hearing.

'The Puritan commander himself is in the field in Ireland, with England crushed beneath his ruthless heel. He is leading them from the front in every battle, yes. He is close to crossing the Shannon.'

'Twenty thousand strong. Was that reckoning exact?'

'It is exact, yes, it's been verified by other reports since. He gives no quarter to the Confederation towns taken while holding out against him. He massacres them all, the garrison, priests, men, women and children. Yes, it's true.'

'We all know his name, this Lord Protector.'

'Oliver Cromwell, yes. Let it be written into the records of this city.'

Every eye rested on the stricken face of Oliver Óg French, whose hand now steered their helm through tempests stronger than winds on the feared French coast.

'Oliver Óg, what will we do before the wrath of that other Oliver who spares no one before him?'

The new mayor rose slowly to his feet, looking around at them.

'This Oliver will be ready for him, or any other Oliver the Parliament sends! Let Coote and his cohorts come up through Connacht too! Let every Puritan regicide come to our walls! We'll defend ourselves with cannon and fire! We'll defend faith and town as we have always done! So, help us God!'

Later, Oliver Óg declared the city free of plague and directed the watch to open the gates. The inhabitants slowly returned to their abandoned houses and masses of thanksgiving were celebrated in the churches.

Word spread now in the town that Eoghan Ruaidh O'Neill had died of an illness in their hour of greatest need. He was never to wear the crown of gold. The command of the Irish army passed to his only son, Henry.

Lovers in Early Summer

áire welcomed Ruaidhrí in Aughnanure when the warmth of May began to creep into the air, ice melting on sheltered banks and streams. The graveyard was full of newly made graves after the coldest winter in living memory. Joy had left the fields and stone-walled gardens.

The days of his schooling and wardship over, Ruaidhrí was now the chieftain of West Connacht between Loch Corrib and the sea. His father's lawman in Moycullen was drawing up the marriage papers with Morogh na dTuagh's man since the weather had improved. It had been an unforgettably hard winter. Red deer appeared near the lake to drink at evening since hunting declined with the lack of young men around the place. Sections of the lake had frozen over. Máire heard wolves howling at night for the first time in her life. They were crossing the ice to take sheep on the distant shore, driven by hunger. People rejoiced in their unbidden return, and they became the talk of the place, the sacred, revered *mac tíre* was with them again, an omen God was going among them in their days of suffering.

Two friars, travelling in late autumn, had told them the roads were empty, not a herdsman between the lake and Caol Sáile Ruadh, not a pedlar or pilgrim was abroad. Gloom cloaked the village street with its neglected tillage land and men, newly mustered for the campaigns, departed with her father.

Máire and Ruaidhrí passed the time in Aughnanure sitting at the warm hearth of the grand, well-furnished castle house overlooking the lake. Between her family and his existed a wealth of old, intricate connections that made them feel comfortable in each other's company. They strolled together in the vegetable garden where women were opening clay-covered pits which preserved their dwindling produce over the winter. They wandered along the road to the boats' landing place to see who was coming and going in the village. She brought him out to look at black cattle grazing as far as the eye could see in the green, fresh-smelling fields where wildflowers were slowly appearing.

'Here's the cattle of my marriage portion,' she said excitedly, showing him the beasts, cows, calves, heifers and bulls, watched by the herd and his children sitting on the wall.

'You've more wealth than many a fine merchant's daughter in town,' he laughed.

'Ah, but town women are beautiful and stylish. Aren't they always seen in the latest fashions?' she joked.

'They're nothing beside you, *a rún*. I have always desired you and no other,' he said simply, taking her hand and together they set off on their favourite outing, climbing up the higher ground behind her family land until the sea and mountains could be seen below.

Sitting side by side in the heather, Máire named every townland for him from the lake to the sea - small, homely details that life in the town had a way of being pushed to the back of the mind. Ruaidhrí remembered her words for the rest of his life. She brought alive an ancient rural world about which town people knew little: places of turf banks, sea rod beds, wreckage rights, shore rights, flax pools, holy wells visible at low tide on the shore, rights of way, haunts of the good people, the drinking places of cattle and sheep, rents and shares, summer booleys, sweat houses, parentage of children, divisions of land, houses of the wise ones and which cures they had.

Ruaidhrí told her in turn his father's place, Moycullen, was called Uillin's Field, the grandson of Nuad of the Silver Hand, king of Ireland one thousand two hundred years before Christ was born. The field or cleared plain was the battleground where Uillin killed Orbsen Mac Alloid, the Mankish man who had traded throughout the Brittanic islands on the western Atlantic. Loch Corrib was originally called Loch Orbsen after him. He believed a certain stone, six miles from the town, marked the actual battle site.

She marvelled at the extent of the old knowledge he had and how his learning had not changed him from the child she had known, He was still the soft lad she remembered, except his voice and language had grown peerless in its perfection – educated, as he had been, among the elite of the west.

The Stricken City: 1651

In the last years of the Eleven Year's War which had begun with the Rising of 1641, Dubhaltach sent for Ruaidhrí.

'Where is the master?' Ruaidhrí asked Brother Michael who brought him the message. 'I haven't laid eyes on him since we came back but I heard he has been seen in town, fit and healthy, thank God. Is he keeping well?'

'The master is well and above in his room as always, sir. Contrary as ever but still engaged in the writing.'

Ruaidhrí accompanied the man to the residence and up the stairs. Dubhaltach was sitting with the amanuensis, Tadhg, at his table writing in a cramped, dark room.

The amanuensis, his old friend *Dubh 'gus Páipéar,* greeted him seriously and began rubbing his eyes and scratching his head. Manuscripts were scattered everywhere, on the table, rising in piles upon the floor, heaped in corners.

Dubhaltach arose and embraced him silently. The ollamh was still the shining, well-dressed man, but more serious, gaunt and grim-faced. The lay brother who had escorted him up bowed at the door.

'Do you require anything, sir?'

'I require nothing, Michael, thank you. Except maybe, send word to the Franciscans I will be at their church for mass this Sunday.'

The brother nodded his head and glanced frowning at Ruaidhrí as if to say, 'Didn't I tell you he was troublesome these days! Now he's ignoring our own church while living in the residence not two steps from its door!'

'We've been discussing the future here before you came in, Ruaidhrí,' Dubhaltach said after Brother Michael left. He nodded towards *Dubh 'gus Páipéar* and patted his arm. Tadhg appeared to be terribly upset.

'I want to give you this,' Dubhaltach had just been saying, 'and take your wife Úna Ní hEidhin with you back to your own illustrious people in Roscommon while you still have the chance. My time may be short here, so I want you to understand this and take steps accordingly.'

Tadhg looked at the money Dubhaltach was holding out to him, frozen by his words, unable to move. Dubhaltach lifted his hand and placed the money into it and held his hand in his two hands. Tadhg was too troubled to say anything except look at the ink-stained hands holding his own.

Dubhaltach sat back and continued.

'Present yourself at the house of Mac Donchadha, the lawman in Tirerril. Tell him you worked for me. He's not far from your place. You have heard of him, haven't you? I have written a letter recommending you for scribing and tutoring.'

Dubhaltach took a rolled and bound document from his table and slipped it with a flourish into Tadhg's coat pocket.

'And may God and Patrick bless you both always, *a Thaidhg*,' the ollamh concluded before adding casually, 'Oh, and take this with you also, which the Franciscans sourced for me with their usual admirable discretion.'

Dubhaltach took a pistol from under his jacket and stretched it out across the table to Tadhg, who gave a shout of alarm, 'No, I cannot take that!' and folded his arms tightly across his chest.

'Very well,' Dubhaltach said sharply, raising his voice. 'I'm sending Brother Michael across the road to the front door to request your good lady herself come over to see me.'

He glanced at Tadhg out of the corner of his eye.

'A direct descendant of Guire king of Connacht will not be slow to take precautions ahead of a journey down the country in times like these,' Dubhaltach added.

Dubhaltach nodded with satisfaction at the dumbstricken lad and reached purposefully for his pen.

The other sat back suddenly and stretched out his right hand. Dubhaltach put down the pen to pass him the pistol and watched while Tadhg fumbled in his pockets with his left hand before gingerly slipping the weapon into his belt. Then the lad sat hunched over the table with his head in his hands staring in confusion across the street.

'It is loaded,' Dubhaltach said as an afterthought as he stared frowning at his pages.

'We don't have Benildus to torment us anymore. He was taken by the plague,' *Dubh 'gus Páipéar* cried to Ruaidhrí the minute he saw him, speaking in too loudly a voice for the small room, his eyes staring and haunted.

But it was his best friend the *bacach* of whom Tadhg was really thinking. He and his family never returned after the plague to resume their employment with the chandler. When Tadhg asked the Blakes where exactly they were buried, no one knew except to tell him a mass burial had taken place of plague victims somewhere near Athenry. Tadhg found himself unable to mention Richard Athy after that, in the same way he was unable to speak of his grandfather's and his siblings' deaths. The nearest the lad had come to it was to ask Dubhaltach where near Athenry was archbishop O'Queely buried, wondering would that cast light on where his friend lay.

'Oh, dear God in heaven, how would I know the answer to that, seeing as no one knows the last resting place of that martyred prelate, except the person who dug his grave in the middle of the night?'

Dubhaltach glanced at him in annoyance, continued his writing and sometime later leant back in his chair to demand suddenly, 'Why in the name of Patrick did you ask *where near Athenry* is the archbishop of Tuam buried? What makes you think his grave is there, as opposed to anywhere throughout his widespread and afflicted diocese?'

'Well, ah, because I heard John Lynch tell Ruaidhrí O'Flaherty in the library that, what he said was, "No one knows the place, that's the truth. The mangled body of our pastor was consigned to a secret grave in darkness. No one knows except Lady Bridget Athenry and the close friend she trusted to bury him. You can take it from me that Malachy's grave, like the grave of Moses, will remain unknown until the end of time," was what John Lynch said.

'I thought the archbishop must be buried near Athenry from that, you see. And that maybe *you* might have heard where he was buried, master.'

'A misunderstanding maybe, on your part, *a mhac,*' was how Dubhaltach finished up that conversation.

Soon the ollamh and himself would no longer be working together on *The Great Book of Irish Genealogies* in Dubhaltach's room, the only refuge he had in the world since his lodgings were bereft of his friend's company. He would make a new life with Úna below in Connacht where they could be happy. She had promised him this.

'Shh shh, now, now, *a fhearín,*' Dubhaltach blessed himself on the mention of a plague death, and when Tadhg referred to the late, unfortunate brother Benildus. Ruaidhí blessed himself as well.

Tadhg without warning, threw down his pen, excused himself, bowing, half stumbling and rushed out. After the door banged behind him, Dubhaltach and Ruaidhrí quietly murmured the prayer for repose of souls and protection from plague.

Ruaidhrí sat at the window in Tadhg's chair with a sigh and soon beheld Brother Michael below sweeping grime in the courtyard. Dirt covered the streets, making this an uphill task as rubbish piled outside the walls where it had been thrown during the sickness. A moment later the bent, shambling figure of the amanuensis emerged with the walk of a much older man, heading for the courtyard gate onto the street.

'Poor fellow, he looks unbelievably bad now,' Ruaidhrí thought to himself. 'It is all too much for him.'

At the gate Ruaidhrí noticed Tadhg pause and look back at the house until his eye rested on a ground floor window. He came slowly back and Ruaidhrí could see him tapping on the window situated directly under Dubhaltach's. The window below was thrown open and Ruaidhrí saw Patrick Bodkin leaning out, his fair curls emerging from his cap. Tadhg was slowly taking Patrick's hand, the dark clerical cloth of the seminarian's sleeve moving in silent farewell.

Dubhaltach was saying something about an extract, fumbling through the pile on his table. Ruaidhrí turned his attention to the ollamh 'The evening is nearly upon us. I can't see the words in front of me. Would you be so good as to take the candle from the windowsill there beside you and ring the bell outside the door for Brother Michael? When he comes ask him to bring a light for us. I don't want to leave this task until tomorrow, scarcity of candles or not.'

When the brother placed the lit candle on the table between them and went out, Dubhaltach found the document he wanted. As the light illuminated the room it lit up the bulky collection of pages wrapped in a smooth sheet of leather and tied with a thong which lay on the right-hand corner of the table at the window.

193

'When will your book be completed, Dubhaltach?' Ruaidhrí asked when the candlelight gleamed on the large, leather-bound bundle.

'What? I have no idea. That's the only answer I can give!' Dubhaltach paused turning the pages of the manuscript he had open in front of him and glanced at Ruaidhrí. 'There's still a sight of materials – some I have here, and others need to be copied at source – to be written into my book. I'll have to continue my work elsewhere as I'll be leaving before the enemy is at these walls, despite what John Lynch says!'

'You are certain you won't leave for France with John if the worst comes to the worst?'

'No, that is not what I meant! Yes, I will be staying in Ireland, where else would I want to live?

'No, I'm referring to John's latest preposterous claim that the descendants of the Milesians are in the minority in Ireland now due to the prevalence of peoples on the island from the earlier and the later invasions! By the time I'm done adding all the genealogies and histories of the descendants of Míl, not to mention putting in the genealogies of the non-Milesians that I'm accused of leaving out, and that of the saints, abbots, coarbs and bishops, that book will be twice the size it is now,' Mac Fhirbhisigh declared with feeling, nodding towards his leather-wrapped compilation.

'There are times I don't want to see sight nor light of our John and this is one of them after him coming out with that!

'Anyway, where was I? Yes, this work here. I would be grateful if you would compile a compendium and return the annotations to me as quickly as possible, Ruaidhrí,' he continued.

'Maybe by noon tomorrow? It would be a great help to me. There's no one who really understands our work since Stephen White died, may he rest in peace. And Walter Lynch and Patrick Lynch have left Galway so only scholars like John Lynch and Geoffrey Brown can interpret and critique my work here now, Ruaidhrí, and I theirs.

'I am lucky to have John, even if he is contrary at times, I suppose.'

Dubhaltach fell silent, sighing and shaking his head sadly. Then he said, 'Have you heard the news that John will work with the council to draw up good terms for the town people? Negotiations will surely follow the siege the Puritans will throw on the walls when they arrive, John told me. He has been elected one of the representatives who will go out to parley with the Cromwellians. I hear he's openly involved with the treaty party now, Ruaidhrí, due to all this going on. Everything changed for him when he was elevated to the wardenship, compelled to return to live in town and leave off his writing.

'But most of the clergy are still strongly in favour of fighting to the death for faith and king you know. The divide is as great as ever between Irish and Old English.'

'Where will you go, master?'

'I don't know. I will not be fleeing into exile on that boat which is preparing at the docks to take the clergy to France when it comes to that. I will die in Ireland. The promise of Patrick is, though darkness descends on the Irish, the light will shine upon them again. I informed the priests lately that I will not be boarding with them. They're below at the sea praying and weeping beside that boat every Sunday now!

'Maybe I'll go up to O'Shaughnessy in Gort. In the end I know I will go home to my family in Sligo. Meanwhile, to return to our business here, will you assist me in some pressing tasks until you seek refuge at home in Moycullen with your wife-to-be before the enemy arrives?'

Ruaidhrí made his way down the dark, narrow, side stairs to the entrance onto the street. He glanced up at Dubhaltach's window as an armed corporation man pulled the gate shut behind him. The curse under the soldier's breath was meant to be heard. The light of Dubhaltach's candle outlined the small, upper window in the darkness. Ruaidhrí could just about make out its faint glimmer when he glanced back at the corner of the building. Anxious because he had not meant to stay with the ollamh so long, he thrust the new work inside his jacket.

He caught sounds of whispering and drinking in the blackness of a filthy lane nearby, men and women gathered there, and he moved uneasily in the gloom. He made out the bulk of a man before him on the street, peering at him. From his clothes, the man seemed to be one of the risen apprentices, no doubt concealing wanted men or surveying premises for robbing. He was obviously a lookout, watching warily for the corporation's soldiers who apprehended anyone on the streets at night. Everyone on the darkened streets was suspected of being Greeks ready to open the gates of Troy - and this was true in most cases.

Irish John, the will o' the wisp flittering over swamps before he vanishes, was the subject of ever-growing rumours that he had been seen here and seen there, but never in the open since he had started rallying his secret militia. His weapons and boats were hidden up the coast, according to one of the many stories that could never be proved. Irish John was getting ready to throw off his disguise and emerge from hiding to lead his daring attack when the Parliamentarians would be at the walls.

Ruaidhrí all but ran in panic down Cross Street to his lodging. He was relieved when one of the Darcys heard the whistle under their window, stuck out a thumb and let him in through the downstairs back window which Dominic had sabotaged in more promising days. Its lock had never since worked properly.

Soon after dawn Ruaidhrí started on the appointed task. His last collaboration in the city had begun.

It was approaching midday when he returned to the ollamh's room with the completed work. 'God bless you,' Dubhaltach said when he looked at the notes Ruaidhrí had compiled.

Dubhaltach then took up a manuscript wrapped in linen and gave it to Ruaidhrí. 'I want you to take this book and keep it safe. You will need it for your own work in the times to come.

They began making their arrangements to leave the city soon after this, their final summer together in the city.

Ruaidhrí O'Flaherty's Story

'What did Mac Fhirbhisigh say when he gave you that book you have there, Ruaidhrí?' the journeyman, master Seán O Cadhain, asked, pointing to a shelf on the wall where books were heaped. He was among a number of visitors, neighbouring women and men, who sat around the fire.

Ruaidhrí looked into the fire and held out his hands to the heat.

'Ah, that was a long time ago now, Seán a *stór*. Many years ago.'

'Go on with you!' Máire cried, winking at him. 'You remember that better than what happened yesterday.'

They all laughed, including the man of the house.

Ruaidhrí did indeed remember the day well, as if it were yesterday. How could he ever forget those early times when youth blossomed as if it would last forever?

'As the woman of the house says, I do recall when the ollamh gave me that book,' he said with a smile. Seán O Cadhain rubbed his hands gleefully while his feet danced a few steps under his stool. Everyone looked at their host expectantly.

'As he handed me the book all Dubhaltach said to me was I was to look after this book and remember the promise of Patrick.' Ruaidhrí began.

He continued after he had fallen silent for a bit, telling them Mac Fhirbhisigh told him the title of the work was the *Annals of Clonmacnoise*, a chronicle from Ciarán's monastery recording the history of the Irish from the time of Adam to the twelfth century. It covered the *pagan* history of Ireland among other things. He went on to say that Mac Fhirbhisigh believed that the early annals were deemed unworthy in the eyes of modern scholarship. However, his assertion in the face of this accusation was, and always had been, that long before the truth of Christianity stirred in our island, the darkness of paganism stretching back to the creation had been lit by knowledge. Paganism was illuminated by learning, though a learning not of the true faith, yet still a learning, most ancient, precious and profound.

Looking up at his attentive audience, Ruaidhrí explained, 'And that was the reason why, in time, I wrote my own book, in which I defended our antiquity before the world.' Here he paused in thought

197

while the others turned this around in their heads, watching the bright flames of the fire.

Ruaidhrí continued, 'And then the ollamh returned to the vexed question of the dating of the annals, which were in such disarray that they had become a cause of confusion. This had been another issue that stirred controversy among our group of researchers in Galway.

'Dubhaltach said he didn't mind stating to me privately that there *was* truth in this accusation. He wanted me to work on coordinating the dating of our annals into a comprehensive system. Exactitude and coordination of dates in my endeavours thenceforth was to be considered essential, he told me.'

Seán O' Cadhain nodded his head as he listened carefully to his scholarly old neighbour's story and added a further question, 'And what became of the priest of Galway, John Lynch, your teacher of the classics?'

'After the fall of the city and the negotiations for the terms of surrender, John sailed with the clergy for Brittany,' Ruaidhrí replied, a heavy note in his voice. He lapsed into silence again as everyone waited for what he would say next. The silence lengthened. Was he going to tell more of the story? they wondered.

Finally, Máire broke the silence.

'Tell them what John Lynch said to you before he left, Ruaidhrí' she prompted.

'Ah, sure everyone knows that!' Ruaidhrí cried. 'John asked me to write out the genealogy of the Stuart kings. The old records of Clan Firbhisigh, among others, show the Stuarts are descendants of Irish kings. They are the rightful monarchs of Ireland, owed our allegiance and thus would restore our land and freedoms.

'And so, I wrote that book too …'

Nobody spoke as the silence in the house lengthened. They hoped for more from Ruaidhrí.

'And we're still here waiting for a Stuart king. How much longer will we have to wait?' thought Máire. 'Will God ever send us the likes again?'

She could see the others were thinking the same thoughts at the mention of the Stuarts. She called on Ruaidhrí to tell them more, but he replied that listening to the talk suited him better, as he sat with his eyes half-closed.

He was in the past again, where he always lost himself, whether in his youth or in his old age. They would get no more out of him.

Máire stood up to take out the pitcher of *poitín* from the press and started pouring the drink. She called on Cáit Taimín Sheamus for a song as she handed around the cups. The low song filled the house and the drink lulled them in the glow of the fire.

Ruaidhrí's thoughts went back to Galway during the last days before the city fell to Ireton and Coote, a place affected by plague deaths and overcrowded with refugees. Every day news of Cromwell's marches and victories petrified them. Colonel Thomas Preston had fallen back on Galway with his men retreating before of the Cromwellians, bringing more frightening news of the ruthlessness and strength of the Parliamentarians. The corporation appointed the brave and gallant veteran, Preston, commander of the city defences and he stayed with them until the end.

Ruaidhrí clearly remembered the day outside the residence of St Nicholas after mass on his last Sunday before he left town. He met up with John and Dubhaltach on the Bóthar Cam. It was after Tadhg had returned to Roscommon with Úna. Ruaidhrí had asked Dubhaltach did he need any help now his amanuensis had left. The ollamh thanked him and replied he had all he wanted and that he was making his own preparations for leaving.

Ruaidhrí's memories had been stirred. He recalled how Dubhaltach turned to John Lynch to ask him when the devil Coote would be at the walls and John replied that it would be soon. He still remembered the shock of being informed that their spy, who had infiltrated Coote's command, had ridden from Sligo the night before bringing key information. In Limerick, messengers had delivered letters to Ireton from Coote outlining the Parliamentary army's plans to attack Galway. The Sligo army had started mustering. Ruaidhrí recalled then that John knew their time was over.

Changing the subject, Ruaidhrí told of how John had asked Dubhaltach, with a little smile, if he had satisfied himself fully with all the ramifications of the genealogy of King Charles's son. This was a matter on which John knew the ollamh would have a strong opinion. Dubhaltach had replied emphatically the ollamhs had always been satisfied with that genealogy from the seed of Fergus down through the high kings. It was given in the books formerly held in Lecan and its antiquity was sacred and unassailable, Dubhaltach had added for emphasis.

Ruaidhrí went on to say that John believed Ussher's library was still out of the country, maintained in safe hands loyal to the king, thus letting the ollamh know that this great primary source had not fallen into Cromwell's hands. He added that, despite Dubhaltach's doubts, the Jesuit, Stephen White, who had gone to his eternal reward, had realised as soon as his learned, authoritative eye fell on the Book of Lecan, that it was the brightest jewel in Ussher's crown. Ruaidhrí then went on to add that, tactfully and graciously, John had acknowledged that the ollamh was the jewel's setting, more precious beyond any words because he had their meaning.

In conclusion Ruaidhrí added that he and John had parted to go their separate ways, jostled at every corner by shouting men in the insignia of town and county who were beginning to occupy the streets. Yet privately he reflected on how the three of them were ordained by God to be washed like pebbles on the *dúirling*, pounded by the overwhelming power of the tides.

The song died away in the dim house. The company praised Cáit Taimín Sheamus. The woman of the house poured more drink. She offered Ruaidhí a cup.

'Tell them about the other books now, Ruaidhrí,' Máire prompted him back to the present.

Ruaidhrí sat up in his seat beside the fire and told them how John Lynch had eventually published his famous refutation of Gerald de Barry in France and had kindly sent a copy of this magnificent work to himself.

'In return, I sent him a copy of my own book *Ogygia* on publication,' he continued. 'We wrote to each other over many years until he went to his final reward.'

The listeners nodded their heads, staring at the old man, waiting for the ending of his story which was not a happy one.

Eventually Ruaidhrí said, 'You have heard before what happened to the ollamh. When the news came of his cruel death in Sligo, his friends were left heartbroken and the antiquities of Ireland bereft.'

After a moment he spoke again to enliven the company.

'Now Seán O' Cadhain, you give us the story about the old man married to the young woman, who was fooled by her lover. It's a while since we heard that one.' Everyone laughed as Seán began.

The Ollamh's Murder: 1671

Slow footsteps entered the open door of an inn near Dunflin, the tapping of a stick carrying on the still air. The serving girl looked up from her seat beside the table as a slender, elderly man walked into the room, his eyes adjusting to the dimness of the low-roofed interior after the winter brightness of the road outside. His carriage, dignified and self-contained, was noticeable. The girl noticed his neat beard and long, grey hair when he turned in the light of the door. A rough wooden plank supported on two stools stretched on the right of the door near the hearth where two lit sods smouldered, filling the room with smoke in the calmness of the day.

The girl rose from her seat beside the table where she kept tankards and jugs.

'God save all here,' said the old man.

'God save you kindly, *a Dhubhaltach*,' she replied recognising him.

'A small drop if you please.'

He began making his way into the outshot, a private space annexed beside the fire. The girl poured the whiskey for him, enjoying the sweetness and clarity of his speech, unexpected from a man of his years; the only one thereabouts she ever met who asked for his drink with gallantry. The aura of gentility was obvious in the confidence of his carriage as he opened the outshot door, bending gracefully to enter the small space. She brought the tankard to where he was seated, wondering would money be forthcoming and was relieved to see him fumble for a coin in his pocket.

Back at the table, the serving girl's ailing mother called from the adjoining room.

'Who have you there?'

'I have only Mac Fhirbhisigh, mother,' she shouted back.

After nightfall the fire illuminated the drinkers who wandered in, nodding in greeting to the occupant of the outshot who was then humming quietly to himself.

'Has the old ollamh been in long?' a man asked the girl as she served him.

'Since before the mail for Sligo passed,' she replied.

Later, the muted talk was silenced when young Crofton walked in and, passing the people on the bench, called loudly for whiskey. Ignoring the occupants, he sat at the fire on the hob which was suddenly cleared of drinkers.

Dubhaltach could be heard in the sudden silence requesting service. Crofton became aware of the other's presence in the outshot, half rising from the hob to peer in through the door at the old man and laughed aloud. They heard Dubhaltach's voice rise in a chant like the priest at high mass. He was reciting genealogy, which he was well known to do on occasions when anyone got on the wrong side of him. Such a person was likely to hear their seed and breed handed to them whether they wanted to hear it or not. The men near the front door stiffened and eyed each other in alarm, wondering could something be up now that Crofton was on the drink. Putting their cups on the table they said goodbye to the girl and left, soon to be followed by the two men from the hearth.

The fire died down. Crofton was sitting above the sods stored under the hob and so no one wanted to disturb him to bank the fire. He craned his neck in the direction of the ollamh, rubbed his hands together and laughed. A low, lengthy retort issued from within.

Darkness filled the house when the mother heard the girl screaming from the main room. The girl's mother got up painfully from bed, calling out to her daughter as she rushed and fumbled to rake the coals from their mound of ashes. She attempted to feed the tiny flames with twigs and hard, dry clods.

The mother felt the girl clinging to her dress as she bent to blow the fire. Scuffling noises could be heard from beyond the room. The flames took off and the women turned to see the light shining on Crofton backing into the room and then it gleamed on the knife in his hand. The figure of Dubhaltach was stretched half out of the outshot lying on his side on the floor, a dark stain seeping over the rushes beneath him. Crofton faced the women where they were huddled weeping in the corner, wiped the knife on the ollamh's jacket and walked out the door into the night.

Epilogue: The Booley House

The following is part of an account written by Ruaidhrí for the celebrated Welsh antiquarian, Edward Lluyd, who visited him in Park some years previously. It was never sent however and was discovered among his books by Ruaidhrí's family sometime after his death.

Seaweeds petrify slowly at this time of year arrayed on airy walls above the shore. Their mineral properties nourish the soil for spring sowing. Today men and women on trá were labouring on the sea harvest, low water exposing the beds for a few hours. I sat outside on the stone wall above the sea thinking and praying all day until the sun sank beyond Aran. I am living in my old age at Park in our booley house beside the sea, dispossessed within sight of my ancient inheritance, I dwell in the margins of my own land. It was confiscated after the Eleven Years War although I had never risen out in arms. I obtained repossession on the Restoration of the Stuart king and honeybees returned to swarm in the warmth and fragrance of our plant-entwined old gables and fertile lakeshore meadows. May 'Fuil an Rí,' the relic dipped in the anointed blood of our executed king, protect us in the days of our persecution.

A nobody from the town, the devious turncoat, soon dishonestly got his hands on my father's entire estate at the end of the recent War of the Two Kings. This man traversed the country brandishing his possession order and letters for monies owed, seizing my forefathers' house and land in the aftermath of the tragedy at Aughrim.

Máire declares that one of us must speak of important things going on in the world, suggesting her view that the man of the house is only interested in his books from the past. Those old books on my shelf will one day pass into other hands coming after me, providing authoritative sources of our country's records for those who will seek them.

I am Roderic O'Flaherty on the coast of Galway this night of the Lord 1710.

Bibliography

Bedell Stanford, William. (1976) *Ireland and the Classical Tradition.* GJAHS.

O'Sullivan, M D. (1931-1933) *The lay school at Galway in the sixteenth and seventeenth centuries.* (VOL XV, I AND 2, JGAHS.

Berresford Ellis, Peter. (1988) *Hell or Connaught! The Cromwellian Colonisation of Ireland 1652 – 1660*, Dufour Editions.

Berry, JF. (1912), *The Story of St Nicholas' Collegiate Church, Galway,* JGAHS.

Boyle, Patric. *De Praesulibus Hiberniae, A D 1672, (*Sept 1902) MS of John Lynch. Irish Eccles. Record.

Canny, Nicholas. (2001), *Making Ireland British 1580 – 1650*, Oxford University Press.

Coen, Martin. (1984) *The wardenship of Galway,* Galway KG.

Corcoran, Timothy, (1916) *State Policy in Irish Education AD 1536-1816.* Fallon.

Costello, Thomas B, (1940) *The Ancient Law School of Park, near Galway,* XIX JGAHS.

D'Ambrieres, René. Ó Ciosán Éamon. *John Lynch of Galway (C1599 – 1677) : His Career, Exile and Writing,* Vol 55 2003. Ps 50-63, JGAHS.

De Buck, RPV. (1869) L'Archéologie Irlandaise. 1641 Depositions Galway. www.tcd.ie

Donovan O'Sullivan, Prof Mary. (1942) *Old Galway. The History of a Norman Colony in Ireland*.

Evans, D W & Roberts. B F, (2007) *Edward Lhuyd, Archaeologia Brittanica, 1707*, Celtic Studies Publications-Cymru.

Gwynn, Aubrey. (1945) *John Lynch's De Praesulibus Hiberniae* VOL XXXIV, Studies.

Gwynn, Stephen. (1909) *A Holiday in Connemara*, Metheun & Company.

Hardiman, James. (2020) *The History of the Town and County of the Town of Galway*, Clachan Publishing.

Healy, John. (1886) *A Family of Famous Celtic Scholars*, Vol 1, No 152, Feb 1886, pp 59-69, The Irish Monthly.

Hogan, Edmund. (1910) *Chronological List of the Irish Members of the Society of Jesus, 1550-1814*, Dublin Four Courts Press.

Kenney, James. (1929) *Sources for the Early History of Ireland*, Columbia University Press.

Lenihan, Padraig. (2001) *Confederate Catholics at War 1641-49*, Studies in Irish History.

Lynam, E W. (1914) *The O'Flaherty Country*, Vol III, No 10, June Studies.

Lynam, Shevawn. (1989) *Humanity Dick*, The Lilliput Press.

Lynch, John. (1848 -1852) *Cambrensis Eversus*, by Gratianus Lucius (John Lynch) Matthew Kelly. (ed. trans, notes) Dublin Celtic Society.

Lynch, John. (1848) *The Portrait of a Pious Bishop, The Life and Death of the Most Rev Francis Kirwan, Bishop of Killala*, by, C P Meehan (ed trans intro) Leopold Classic Library.

Mac Fhirbhisigh, Dubhaltach. *Leabhar na nGenealach, The Great Book of Irish Genealogies*, (ed & pub) Nollaig Ó Muraíle, (2004), Dublin, De Burca Books.

Chronicum Scotorum, William M Hennessy (ed trans 1866).

Two poems on Ó Seachneasaigh of Gort, 1667, (MS N 12, page 173) Proceedings RIA.

Of the Registry of Clonmacnoise. (1857) Kilkenny Archaeological Society.

An Account of Extinct Irish Bishops. British Museum, Clarendon 68. Ughdai na h-Erend. Bodleian Library (Rawlinson 480).

Of Certain Bishops in Ireland. D H Kelly (1869) Proceedings of the Royal Irish Academy.

Mac Lysaght, Edward. (1969) *Irish Life in the Seventeenth Century,* Irish University Press.

Mac Swiny, Valentine. (1928) *Notes on the history of the Book of Lecan.* Proceedings of the RIA. XXXVIII.

Madison, P L. (Dec 1922) *A Scholar Chieftain of the West*. Vol L Irish Monthly.

Moody, T. W, Martin, F X, Byrne, F J, (2009), *A New History of Ireland 111. Early Modern Ireland 1534 – 1691,* Oxford.

Moran, Gerard & Gillespie, Raymond. (1996) (Ed), *Galway History and Society, Essays,* Geography Publications.

Nicholson, William. (1724) *The Irish Historical Library*.

Ní Dhonnchadha, Máirín. Eagarthóir, (1996) *Nua-Léamha.*
Gnéithe de Chultúr, Stair agus Polaitíocht na hÉireann c.
1600 – c. 1900, 'Aimsir an Chogaigh Chreidmhigh'- An
Dubhaltach Mac Fhirbhisigh, a lucht aitheantais agus
polaitíocht an seachtú haois déag.' Nollaig Ó Muraíle.

Ó Cahán, T. S. *Owen Roe O'Neill,* (1968) T Joseph Keane & Co.

Ó Concheannainn, Tomás. *Scoláirí Gaeilge I nGaillimh sa*
Seachtú Céad Déag. Galway Town and Gown, 1484 – 1984,
Ed. Ó Cearbhuill. (1984) Gill & Macmillan.

O'Curry, Eugene. *Craobha coibhneasa agas geuga geneluigh*
gacha gabhala dar ghabh Ere. Dubhaltach Mac Firbisigh.
UCD MS Collection and copy (1836),Library Proceedings
RIA.

Lectures on the Manuscript Materials of Ancient Irish History.
(1873) Library Proceedings RIA.

O'Donovan, John. *Tribes and Customs of Hy Fiachrach.* (1844)
and *Three Fragments,* (1860) Irish Archaeological Society.

O'Flaherty, Roderic. *Chorographical Description of West or H-*
Iar Connacht James Hardiman (ed) (1979) Galway: Kenny's
Bookshops.

Ogygia or a Chronological Account of Irish Events, London, 1685
(ed. Trans.) James Healy (1793) Dublin.

The Ogygia Vindicated: Against the Objections of Sir George
MacKenzie, (ed) Charles O'Conor of Belanagare (1775)
Dublin.

Letter to Edward Lhuyd Oxford, from Roderic O'Flaherty.
Gilbert's Facsimiles of Irish Mss. (Part IV, 2. Page XCV)
(2013) Catalogue of Manuscripts. Proceedings R I A, VOL
III, 1847, Proceedings R I A.

A letter from Roderic O'Flaherty to William Molyneux, 27 Jan. 1697, Micheál O'Duigeannáin, (ed), Vol 18 (1938-9) GJAHS.

Letter book of Samuel Molyneux 1707 – 1709. (N, 2680. P1586) Corporation of Southampton.

Ó Muraíle, Nollaig. (2002) *The Celebrated Antiquary Dubhaltach Mac Fhirbhisigh (c.1600-1671) His Lineage, Life and Learning,* An Sagart, Maynooth.

Dubhaltach Mac Fhirbhisigh and County Galway, (1997) JGAHS. Vol 49 pp 22-35.

Ó Siochru, Mícheál. & Ohlmeyer, Jane. (2013), *Ireland 1641 Contexts and Reactions* , Manchester University Press.

O'Riordan, S. *Rinuccini in Galway 1647 – 1649,* (1946-7), JGAHS XXII.

Herity, Micheal. (2009) *John O'Donovan, Ordnance Survey Letters-Galway,* Fourmasters Press.

O'Lochlainn, Colm. (1947) (ed) *Irish Men of Learning:* Studies by Paul Walsh, Dublin. Sign of the Three Candles.

O'Madden, Patrick L. *The Last of our Classic Historians, Roderic O'Flaherty, 1629-1716* (Vol 35, Feb 1930), Irish Ecclesiastical Records.

Ó Neachtáin, Eoghan. (1902) *Dubhaltach Mac Firbisigh*, Leabhairíní Gaeilge IX.

Petrie, George. (1837) *Remarks on the Book of Mac Firbis*, (trans. XVIII), Proceedings RIA.

Quane, Michael. *Galway's Classical School,* (VOL XXXI,1964-5), GJAHS.

Rabbitte, J, *Historical Account of the wardens of Galway*, (1936) GJAHS XVI, 1&2.

Alexander Lynch, Schoolmaster, (1936) (VOL XVII, nos I and II), GJAHS.

Reeves, (1921-8) *Memoir of Stephen White*, July Collection 1861, Proceedings RIA.

Walsh, Paul. (1992) *An Account of the Town of Galway*, Vol 44, pp 47-118, JGAHS.

White, Stephen. (2010) *Apologia Pro Hibernia Adversus Cambri Calumnias.* Stephano Vito, Mathew Kelly, Kessinger Publishing.

Other antiquarian Irish classics reformatted and produced by Clachan Publishing

Hardiman's History of Galway by James Hardiman

The West of Ireland: Its Existing Condition and Prospects
by Henry Coulter

Highways and Byways in Donegal and Antrim by Stephen Gwynn

A Statistical and Agricultural Survey of the County of Galway
by Hely Dutton Dutton

The History of Sligo: Town and County - Volume. I
by Terrence O'Rorke

Captain Cuellar's Adventures in Connaught and Ulster
by Francisco de Cuellar

The Cromwellian Settlement of Ireland by John P. Prendergast

clachanpublishing.com